Springheads

A Novel

Mary Jo Dyre

REDHAWK
PUBLICATIONS

Redhawk Publications
The Catawba Valley Community College Press
2550 US Hwy 70 SE
Hickory NC 28602

ISBN: 978-1-952485-91-6

Library of Congress Number: 2022950679

Printed in the United States of America

redhawkpublications.com

Praise for Springheads…

Mary Jo Dyre's *Springheads* travels through Time. Springs erupt, scattering narrator Sarah and characters – Colin, Miss Sadie, the baby William, his mom Savannah, on and on – in and out of Time. Bodies breathe demonstrably, enlightening each moment. Stories rest and rally, settling contact in "the deep dark pools" of every character's eyes. This novel renders what it means to be a human being lost in Time to be found in someone else's presence. Sarah, the "I," tells all for characters like Savannah, the Native American whose life and region is displaced and taken over by mostly white settlers. Seeking a freedom of place may be the main theme of *Springheads*. Time warps the need to want to know. The effect is to not know, as Sarah ponders feelings of Love for Colin. She literally falls for Colin Stewart, professor in the English Department at UNC-Asheville. And then the news: Colin goes missing, officially. The singular reality of every moment becomes fact and dream together. Sarah learns that the real treasure springs within herself.

—**Shelby Stephenson** author of *More* and *Shelby's Lady: The Hog Poems* among others and former poet laureate of North Carolina from 2015-2018.

Springheads will take you to another time and still keep you wrapped in your own heart. Mary Jo Dyre is a master of story who weaves truth and tweaks it with what might be, ingrained with vibrant characters set in a world where all returns to two Springheads. Take this book to bed with you, but don't expect to sleep.

- **Mary Ricketson**, author of *I Hear the River Call My Name, Hanging Dog Creek, Shade and Shelter, Mississippi: The Story of Luke and Marian, Keeping in Place,* and *Lira.*

This book is lovingly dedicated
to family.

"The truth is stranger than fiction...and often more incriminating."
—Greg Cox

Chapter 1

"You're right, Colin. I should be thinking about the obvious mess we're in at the moment." I could feel both my body and voice tremble almost in unison. "*If* I can get past the fact, just minutes ago, we stood in a dilapidated building located down the hill from my home on the river property... *If* I can wrap my confused brain around the dream we just discussed as we stood outside my office .... Yes, *if* I can magically leap one more step ahead to an even scarier thought: We have no clue where we are at the moment. I suppose...." I stopped. Exhausted from the effort to say something, anything that made more sense than all that just spilled out, I added. "Yes, I've said the word *if* way too many times."

Overwhelming disorientation moved over me. Some part of my muddled mind picked up on what I thought might be the most brilliant night sky I could ever recall. Tiny stars pierced the dark canopy above my head with a brightness not shared with any nearby city lights. The full moon tugged at me with a gravitational fierceness. The freezing air chilled me to the bone, almost as much as Colin's total silence.

§

Life seemed fairly predictable back in my twenties. As years passed, I'm the first to admit my day-to-day existence falls habitually far beyond the boundary of the white-picket fence dream. However, before the eyeball-deep, insane situation in which Colin and I found ourselves the night described above, life certainly embraced the basics of predictability. Sure, I have a vivid imagination. But until recently, discerning fact from fiction had never been a serious issue even though I indeed prefer fiction.

No explanations come easily with the event that unfolded in the late afternoon of New Year's Eve, 1999. The number 2000, in reference to a calendar year, still, at that time, seemed somewhat strange to my vocabulary. That is about all I can say with any certainty. However, before I go any further, let me say something for the record. To reduce all that happened to mere words proves challenging. I cautiously use *time travel* out loud. I certainly hesitate to put those two words down in black and white. A *trip*, a *journey*, or

an *adventure* seem woefully disrespectful to the reality of what occurred. Just as challenging, my involvement in the saga. Any good
editor would insist that I burrow down deep into layers of fiction to
hide any real connection to the events that unfolded. It is one thing
to be the person trying to reduce this far-fetched tale to mere words
on a page. It is, indeed, another issue to be a character on stage.

   The setting proves equally challenging to hide behind veils
of obscurity. The land itself, the close proximity of two bodies of
old water, ritualistically coupling to produce the legend of a bigger-
than-life leech monster. Both are factors not easily dismissed in the
sense of place. How do I factor in the influence of loosely-connected
generations of innocent childhood play in the cool waters of the
double springheads? Is it safe to assume that another piece of the
puzzle is my long-held fascination with old homesites that stood on
land washed, purged, and certainly made richer by the delta deposits
of yet another ancient source of water, the Mississippi River?

   At this point in my life, I now understand that pockets of
elder Cherokee have long been open to the phenomena of *circular
time*. Most of us non-natives are too busy and out of sync with nature to connect the dots about such profound possibilities within
reality. Our conversations, at best, bat around the word "quantum" to
attach the inexplicable to science. As for "*Why me?*", I suspect it was
much like accidentally falling into the magic rabbit hole of a much-
loved childhood tale. I do realize, however, that not everyone is open
to such an exhilarating tumble.

§

   Back to the details of that day. I shopped for groceries earlier
in the afternoon. My mind strayed from my shopping list at every
turn. I'm not sure I ever nailed what I dreaded most: *the thought
of a New Year's Eve celebration spent alone* or *the television coverage
of the endless predictions of a problematic new millennium*. Even as I
got home, the restlessness did not stop. I fought with my door keys
caught up in the plastic grocery bags straining under over-packed,
dead weight. A cold December wind blew up from the run of the
nearby river as my unruly curls blinded me briefly.

   Did someone just call my name? Turning toward the sound of
the voice, I spotted a man moving just past the mailbox. Even as

he continued to walk toward my office home, the winter hat pulled over his ears prevented me from a clear look at his face. I felt slightly nervous about being caught outside the office with a stranger coming my way. As he got closer, I recognized the smile spread across his face. *Why is Colin Stewart walking up my driveway?*

As I started toward him, I could clearly see the sweep of silver-grey hair streaked with remains of coppery red that stuck out from under his winter gear. I sensed the excitement in his eyes. Before I could ask what was going on, he pulled the wool cap from his head. Instead of asking my question, I laughed softly as I noticed that he looked several weeks past a haircut. *Well, at least you look about as rough as I do since this wind has left both my hair and grocery bags in a tangled mess.* At last, I shifted my amusement enough to ask a question. "Why are you walking? Your car okay? Need me to take you someplace?"

"Everything's fine. I am staying in a bed and breakfast near the post office. I've been on the restless side most of the day." That comment got my attention. "I needed an evening walk."

Again, I noticed the glint of mischief in his deep blue eyes. He pulled something out of his coat pocket. "I was hoping I would find you here. Since my last visit, I came across an elderly man who worked right down there at the old lumber mill joining your property. Lots of interesting information to share. He also happened to have a picture of the place. I thought you might like to see it."

"What do you mean, you thought? Colin, you know, good and well, I am fascinated with the property and its history." The partially spilled groceries, soon forgotten, I hurried over to him. Eager to take the photo from him, I added, "Here, let me see what you have there." I immediately commented on what my eyes were taking in. "Well, that's the old sawmill. Some remains are still down there." With excitement, I asked, "What is this long, white, two-story building with shutters? See, right here on this low ridge of land. I can only assume the area must have been graded down years ago since the building is no longer there. Look, there's even a porch along the front side."

Before my mind could fully define the troublesome detail that was trying to surface, Colin added, "That must be the boarding house old Mr. Neely told me about."

My head felt light. My confused brain began to focus more

accurately on the rectangular building in the picture. It just had to be the very place I saw in my dreams. It sat at the base of the rough trail. As I looked closer, I could remember the lingering details haunting me even when I awoke each time from a night of compelling tales. It still took a bit of time for the specific nagging thought to surface. The picture I held in my hand showed the building as it must have looked in its better days. My dreams captured the place in its decline. Images remained vivid and sharp in the tucked-away recesses of my memory. Only faint traces of white-chipped paint clung to the old boards. I did recall any shutters from my sleep state, just the many boarded windows.

In my dream, I had hoped some crack or opening in the board-covered windows would give me a glimpse of the inside of the place. The longer I looked at the photo in my hand, I remained certain. Even though time had taken its toll on my dream memories, Colin's picture captured the same building. The certainty of my conclusion caused me to mumble out loud, "But how could I have known about this place? How could I have dreamed about something that really existed at one point in time long before I laid eyes on this picture?

§

Now, almost three years later, I know more about the surroundings Colin and I stumbled into the night of 1999 New Year's Eve. Even the circumstances have taken on much-needed clarity. As to how it all happened, at best, the two of us are guessing. There's simply no hard and fast logic to lean on. Any precedent has been cloaked in multiple layers of fiction. Then, of course, there is the need to keep such strange, inexplicable events all tucked safely out of earshot. Some would surely declare me crazy. The press…well nothing short of a field day. NO Trespassing signs would pretty much be useless against the curious.

It helps to look back to earlier experiences. Various doors from those sought-after, treasured, abandoned homesites of my younger years often stood slightly ajar. Maybe I should have figured someday one such passageway would swing open fully on the hinges of time.

Chapter 2

Daddy bent over the hand-cranked machine he set up earlier under the carport. He worked the delicate balance of adding just the right amount of ice and salt. The magic happened every time: perfect ice cream to go with birthday cake. Papa Baker, my grandfather, or PB as we all called him, had the job of trying to contain my excitement until closer to party time. PB always got stuck with the task of keeping me entertained. Mama and Grandma would often say, "Two peas in a pod, for sure." I wished I looked more like my beautiful grandmother Anna Baker. Her flawless olive skin and the soft waves of her shiny black hair often had me longing for a way to exchange my show of freckles and curly, auburn hair for a little bit more of her. Then, I'd remember the stories PB filled my head with every time he had the opportunity.

All it took was the mention of jumping freight trains, heading across the country, finding jobs where he could, and then, of course, the time PB spent with my great grandfather, Grandma Anna's father, Finn Pinkney Campbell, II. Deep down, I treasure the fact that I am a lot like these two men in my family tree. No question, I am drawn to the excitement of their adventures. Besides, I did get Grandma Anna's eyes, brown with streaks of copper. It took years for me to understand why PB often added when I talked about how much I loved my eyes that looked just like Grandma Anna's. "Lots of responsibility comes with those eyes. Don't forget that, young lady."

Daddy, not about to stop his work with the ice cream, called out. "Hey, PB." Knowing my grandfather was a bit on the deaf side, he yelled again, "Hey, Papa Baker. Get Sarah out of the driveway. They're turning in now."

PB didn't need to ask twice. As soon as I saw the familiar blue car, with its side wood panels and upper rack big enough to hold more luggage than my family of three ever hoped to need, I wheeled my red bike to a stop, off in a second. Jumping up and down with excitement, I screamed. "Daddy, PB, my cousins are here." PB greeted them all in his deep drawl. "Well, hello, folks," as he then reached to shake hands with his nephew Laurence who made it out of the big car in record time and headed straight to PB. The ribbing that always took place between the two started immediately. My grandfather PB, Lowery Baker, is the younger brother of Uncle Laurence's dad. Daddy always says it takes a road map to keep up with all the Bakers and Campbells in my list of ancestors. He usually adds that sometimes it's best not to keep up with them.

Uncle Laurence continued. "I see you're letting Anthony do all the work here." He nodded and smiled toward Daddy.

"Now, Laurence, don't come down on me too hard." Pausing to nod in my direction as he rolled his eyes in exasperation. "Looking after that one is a full-time job." The banter came to a halt as the flock of Baker cousins swarmed in multiple directions at once from the massive Ford station wagon. Shouting over the screams of excitement from the younger kids, PB greeted the rest with hugs. "Mildred, girls," he paused as he shooed the early evening gnats away from the intoxicating scent of perfume that engulfed the older cousins and their mother. "Mary Louisa has had Anna working in that kitchen ever since we got here earlier today. I suggest you walk on in through the house in case something needs refrigerating. The month of June has turned up her temperatures mighty early this summer."

The only child of older parents, I always looked forward to Uncle Laurence's passel of kids coming out to the house. The slow southern talk mingled gently into the hot, muggy, Mississippi evening. The summer night unfolded. The menfolk made regular trips behind the old pump house to pour nips of Gilbey's Gin as the womenfolk pulled and tugged at the girdled undergarments, part and parcel to southern ladies in the early 1960s, no matter the occasion. Laughter lingered over the scene. Sweet tea and sweat poured equally. Grilled hamburgers, homemade vanilla ice cream, the best chocolate cake in the South, and mosquitoes a plenty mixed with the shrieks and shrills of childhood play in celebration of my 8th birthday.

Mama brought out the Mason jars with holes punched in the lids. The summer night ritual pulled us in. We kids spent a good hour of darkness catching fireflies. Annie came up with the idea first as we were filling the jars with the magical lights. We all agreed I should ride back to town with them for a sleepover with her and her older sister Terri. Sandwiched by age between my two cousins, stair steps in height, my hair was more auburn than the chocolate brown of my cousins'. We took pride in the obvious similarities of our facial features and the fact we were often called "those Baker girls." Technically, I am a Bryant. Mama says they had just about given up on having children when I surprised everyone. Then on top of that, she figured my Uncle Jake and Aunt Bonnie had no plans to add any little Bakers to the family tree. Mama decided it was up to her to preserve the Baker name with me, Sarah Baker Bryant.

As the night's festivity drew to a close, the three of us, our heads sweaty from the nonstop play in the humid night air, piled eagerly into the back of the station wagon. We wedged our way in and over Terri and Annie's younger brother, now sprawled in sleep across the rear-facing seat. Except for the occasional scratch of a fresh mosquito bite, we contained our excitement to plans whispered back and forth among the three of us. We figured we would sit up till the wee hours of the morning watching the flickering display in our Mason jars now held tightly in each of our grimy hands, still sticky from a night of sweet memories.

The firefly watch and even the giggling and whispered talk under the covers eventually came to an end. We got enough sleep to wake up ready for more play the next morning. I loved spending the night with my cousins. To me, town meant stores and nonstop adventures. It would be years later before I learned to treasure the solitude and the endless outdoor play that defined growing up in rural Mississippi. Little did I realize making mud pies within an imaginary kingdom created under the boughs of pine, elm, and dogwood could hold a candle to life amidst what I then thought of as busy streets.

§

At home, a bicycle ride meant going down a long, gravel drive, connecting to the Moore property, checking out the cotton fields, turning around, and coming home. A ride in town was a different story. In summer shorts, sleeveless tops and flip-flops, my cousins and I left on our adventure. Within ten minutes of peddling in the thick summer heat, my naturally curly hair had formed a tight mat of ringlets around my sweaty forehead.

As we topped the hill, I could hear my cousin's question easily. "Wanna' stop at Marascalco's?" The small grocery was just around the corner at the bottom of a slight hill. As an established tradition, we three birds of a feather always took a vote as to whether we would stop at different places along our route. Teri didn't ask again. Within minutes, all three bikes pulled up in front of the store. Pooling our nickels, dimes, and occasional quarters, we came out with an orange sherbet Push-Up, several Lik-M-Aid straws, and one bottled Coke, all shared on the spot.

On down Mound Street, then under and through the big Highway 8 overhead bridge that provided a brief moment of shade, the glare of the morning sun almost dazed me for a moment. The road eventually connected to the subdivision around the golf course and cross street that led to the football stadium. *How had I ended up at the back of the line?* I slowed down long enough to realize I had never really taken in this section of town on a bike.

Off to the left, an old, abandoned house caught my attention. The old structure sat back in the thick and tangled growth of magnolias and wisteria as hardy as any kudzu my father ever battled. By the time I eased closer and noticed the faint hint of turquoise chipped paint on the arched shutters of decaying dormers peeking timidly through the thick wall of trees, all doubt disappeared. I had to go farther in.

It never crossed my mind to yell to the others. Instead, I got off my bike, crouched into a crawl, and made my way through the maze of undergrowth till I reached the old wrought-iron gate leaning against one post. The crumbled remains of a brick wall ran from each side of the gate. Mounds of purple, pink, and white flowers managed to hold on in the midst of years of untended vines and weeds.

When I look back on my first discovery, I am certain it was the combination of colors, the touches of turquoise peeking through the colorful blooms surrounded by multiple shades of verdant green, that immediately took root in my imagination. The white, distressed paint enabled me to sense, even fleetingly, the years behind this still-inviting place. Thoughts danced in syncopated rhythm across my brain. *Children lived here. The home had welcomed the busy sounds of guests. Summer evenings provided treasured times on the big expanse of the front porch.* Without warning, my cousin's worried voice disrupted my revelry. "Sarah Baker Bryant, what are you up to now?"

I believe to this day, if Annie had not yelled from the other side of the thick growth, I would have gone on inside, ignoring the obvious danger in two stories of rotting wood. For some reason, my eight years could not explain at the time, I did not want to share my find with my cousins. As I made my way back through the undergrowth, I could feel, in a strong way, the once-thriving life still faintly holding on. As I turned to take one last glance at the old place, I fully expected to see a woman looking at me from an upper-story window.

This house, on a road from my childhood, provided the beginning of a fascination, and perhaps, even a connection with the past. The brief revealing shadows filtered through thin cracks of my young, vivid imagination.

§

My introduction to teaching took root in a hole-in-the-road, split-down-the-middle between the haves and have-nots railroad town in the Mississippi Delta. After high school, I decided to take the road less traveled and enrolled in a small teaching college. My mind expanded with big thoughts as I explored the depths of an education rich in literature and art. I did not at the time fully understand the sense of place in which my learning unfolded. Later, I would often wonder if I learned as much from the Delta itself as I did in the college classrooms. Indeed, this area of Mississippi historically provided the perfect mixer of the Blues pouring from backroad dives, mingling with the words of Eudora Welty, Richard Wright, William Faulkner, and Tennessee Williams, all filling my hungry brain. It was not uncommon for my elbows to brush against Pup and Lee, with river clay still on their McCarty hands as they arrived at my art professor's house for one of his regular soirees. My decision to teach in a public school instead of the many, newly sprung, conveniently segregated private schools raised concerned questions from both family and friends.

The seasonal rituals of Delta farming unfolded alongside my school life. Vast acres of farmland ran flat as far as the eye could see. Blankets of white spread for miles along the ribbon of road stretched between the town where the school was located and the even smaller community where I lived. In the thick of cotton-picking season, dinosaur-sized, green machinery kicked up dust from the long-running rows, resulting in endless piles of bales stacked at the local gin. Sections of the drive hosted pecan groves with tree boughs heavy from the growing weight of a near-ready harvest. Sunsets seemed to last for an eternity over the large expanses of rich, fertile soil. A lone AME church, clapboard with peeling paint, stood quietly within the protective shade of the few trees still standing in the many acres given over to the crops. Only on Sundays could the rich sounds of soulful gospel singing be heard over the clapping of many hands.

My after-school jog often found me on one particular loop of street, within a community occupied by approximately one hundred people, many of the older generation. One lone, Chinese-owned business with gas pumps and small grocery items, stood in the middle of town. Directly across the street, the post office, with Mrs. Clairee as its postmistress, typically had more people gathered for mail and gossip than even the single store could attract.

As always, I slowed down from my run enough to at least pop my head through the PO's front door and give a ritualistic hello. I would then quickly pick up my pace and head out on the road that led to the cemetery. The cypress trees, the aged tombstones, along with many new ones reflective of a dying community of elders left behind by the young always seeking the city life, intrigued me. I took in the few family names still easily read on weather-stained granite and marble. The lower section of graves, all tilted slightly toward the banks of the bayou. Without fail, my stride slowed just a bit to match the almost stagnant rhythm of the dark waters filled with cypress knees and all sorts of mysterious wildlife.

I should make it clear to those of you who have never visited this area, much less lived in it, the Delta is a place guaranteed to suck you in one way or the other with a fifty-fifty chance or better to produce creative or crazy, or both. Its black, fertile soil and thick summer heat grow a passion that drives the Blues, the writer, and the insane. Its deep layers of rich history gave me the opportunity time and time again to run upon an old home site. The classroom additionally started an awareness of purpose in me.

Still a student myself in many ways, I learned to navigate the waters of a school with a 92% black population of students and staff. One of four white teachers, I got my first feel for being the one who stands out as different. Fortunately, the lure of my students proved stronger than the color of my skin. As I tapped into the potential of the kids in my classes, I found myself stretching and becoming alongside them. Many of my preconceived ideas continued with the slight seismic shift that first occurred with the forced integration of the high school I attended back in the late sixties. Planning the next set of lessons and traipsing around the countryside filled most of my spare time. As I continued the process of growing into the adult package of responsibilities that faced me every day in the classroom, the remains of a long-neglected garden surrounding, a tumble-down house, still had the power to make me acutely aware of the past lives now becoming one with the rich, fecund, black dirt.

As I spent time in the trenches of the classroom, understanding slowly blossomed in me. The tell-tale signs of a sacred former life and the potential in the old structural bones of a house continued to fascinate me. It seemed then I would forever be drawn to the fixer-upper. I gained the knowledge to look at my students with the same sense of expectation, pouring my attention into those that needed that extra time and effort or an additional bit of mind-stretching. By mid-year of my second year as a teacher, I fell hard into a relationship with one of the math teachers at the high school. Caught up in the long-instilled idea that young women married and lived happily ever after, particularly if a handsome blue-eyed, blonde-haired man was involved, I failed to weigh in the full commitment. I stepped in knee-deep, without so much as asking, "Mother, may I?" In love with the idyllic promise of marriage, I ignored PB's warning that it might not be the right fit for me. Within another year I was ecstatically expecting my first child. As if all of those big commitments were not enough, at my husband's encouragement, I walked away from the school and the small Delta community I had come to love, also the nearness of my relatives only an hour away. The move to North Carolina came with the marriage package.

At least for a while, my fascination with the past continued to reach out to me in the majestic, lush forests of the far west Blue Ridge Mountains. I wish I could say that I found ways to keep the sense of wonder alive. Instead, the find of an old house surrounded by the colors of a once beautiful garden soon gave way to a treadmill of responsibility shared unequally with a husband still caught up in his struggles. In a slow-boil fashion, self-discovery sat unattended on the backburner. My hands plunged deep into the pockets of the heavy coat of my mid-twenties' marriage. Wrapped tightly in the challenges of motherhood, I gave over to the move and became what everyone around me seemed to need.

Chapter 3

Our principal Belinda Naples asked me to keep my eyes open for any property suitable for our small but bursting-at-the-seams school. The move to North Carolina had soon forced us into cramped trailer life. The man who once captured my attention as a teacher soon lost himself in the call to preach. I, on the other hand, pushed hard against religion's promises of salvation. Fortunately, our two, full-of-life children seemed fierce in their determination to turn every day into an adventure despite our limitations as their parents. Somehow the energy of our daughter and our son gave me the strength to hold on to my dream of a real house. Brick and mortar wishes helped push aside the dreadful emptiness that had become my reality. So many details seemed out of my control. Most days, in our early years in North Carolina, I headed outside. Nature provided me the release and respite that my two children and I needed as I made my way back to the classroom.

As much as the trapped-in-a-can feeling of the trailer weighed in on me, the wide-open blue of a fall sky, the endless blooms of spring, tall grass that danced with the music of the wind, and the changes of the seasons left me and the kids in a state of endless discovery. Only the need to cook and the sheer exhaustion that came after a long, full day outdoors caused me to gather my babies under my wing and head inside. Many times, we lingered as moonlight unleashed the vastness of the night sky. Observation taught us the stars and constellations. Children's books and the Narnia Chronicles were our ritualistic reads before bedtime. Nature and the wealth of words took root as the gulf between my husband and me increased at a fast clip.

The time came when I knew my children were ready for more. Somewhere buried deep in me was a no-compromise button when it came to the education of my children. There had to be a school that could keep the love of learning alive in the creative way we learned from the outdoors. I first met the principal when I enrolled my two children in the preschool and Kindergarten programs at her school. It did not take this dedicated educator long to figure out that I loved and missed school.

As we got to know one another better, she shared that within minutes, she spotted my hunger for the classroom. Outspoken

Belinda went on to voice the concern that my personal unhappiness was also obvious. She hoped initially that getting me back into education might help turn my discontent around. She assured me that many young mothers simply needed something more than staying home twenty-four seven. Later, when Taylor and I first separated, she was not surprised. Once she took in the great divide, the interests that had nothing in common, on top of the lack of time spent together, she concluded the damage had run its course some time back. The union of Taylor and Sarah Edwards had not held. Deep down, I suspected I never had been much of an Edwards. The paperwork would be filed at some point. I returned to the classroom in 1983, and I counted myself fortunate. Belinda's vision for education provided the fulfillment that seemed missing in my personal life.

§

Five years later, so much changed in my world. A few details had not. In the years leading up to the divorce in 1985, and even after, I rarely went home. PB's death back in '82, of course, brought me back to Mississippi when nothing else had the power to do so. The endless hours in the car amid the non-stop chatter of Macy and Duncan did little to give my mind a break. *PB, you have to know I tried my best to get back home before you died. My car would not have made it without the extra day it took with the mechanic. Now, you've pulled me smack dab into a Mississippi funeral guaranteed to force me to take note of my high school friends and their perfectly happy marriages. Do you think Mama will forgive me if I choose to stay at the house?* As soon as the thought came out, I could sense this wise man shaking his head in disagreement. *I guess it's time to face my failure.*

§

Belinda's hard work with the small school had paid off. The school's need for a new location had me out around town asking questions to all sorts of people. I really can't remember where I ran into Mr. Locke. I do remember he pulled slightly at his mustache as he spoke in crisp-accented words. You know there is one place, right here in town. You might not even know it exists."

He had my attention. I was fairly certain Belinda and I had traipsed over and ridden through every section of our small town the weekend before. Ours is a small mountain community struggling to hold on to a downtown. Most of our traffic comes in from neighboring areas to shop at Wal-Mart.

"Well, where, James? Don't just stand there and make me guess."

With a faint hint of a northern accent still with him over the years, in between a repetitive humming sound characteristic of his speech, he said. "Just think about standing on the front lawn of our health department. Straight ahead, you'll be looking at the old Casey place. There are several acres, even an old home site. I can see it during the winter months from my place. Who knows, it may be just the place you need?"

I could not, for the life of me, bring to mind a piece of land that fit this description. Surely, I could figure it out by using Junaluska County Health Department as my reference point, as Mr. Locke had suggested. Well, I have never been more wrong. I spent an hour riding around, turning back time and time again, without as much as a glimpse of an old house.

At last, through a small gap in the thick summer growth, I spotted a small portion of a structure. Strangely enough, within the brief time it took me to find a place where I could safely pull over, the glimpse disappeared. I started to wonder if I had been seeing things. Out of the corner of my eye, I noticed an almost totally hidden drive off to the left. As I topped the slight rise just up from the park on Conaheeta Street, I hesitated long enough to almost let two cars pile up on my backside. *May as well head down the street and do a U-turn.* Sure enough, from this perspective, there appeared to be a large portion of thickly-wooded land, rich with undergrowth of tightly growing rhododendrons. It had to be the mysterious property ole man Locke described.

The entrance to the long drive with its surrounding, unkept growth provided the perfect camouflage for the traffic that passed daily along this cut-through street. No wonder I had driven by the graveled entrance many times without a thought that it might lead to any place of interest. Just as I started to sink into the feeling of leaving civilization behind me, I saw the rusty outline of a decrepit single-wide sitting abandoned off to my left. The metal eye-sore stirred buried deep-down, troublesome memories that lost root quickly to a couple of tall hemlocks that swayed above my car as I drove by upper, evergreen limbs brushed the pale blue summer sky. They caught my attention fully. How could I have been riding through town minutes before and now be walled in by old forest growth and unruly vine? The bend of the river had to be on my left below the land on which I now ventured. However, I could not see its waters through the thick green of summer foliage. I looked straight ahead. An entrance created from what was now a wild stand of overgrown privet hedge begged me onward.

The car nosed through the growth. My breath caught just for a moment. A large, two-story house with a green, moss-covered hip roof granting it some sort of God-given right to stand sentinel on this land filled my vision. I had to go farther in.

Something about the scene struck me as odd. Clothes hung on a decrepit, ready-to-fall-at-any-moment line. Obviously, someone lived in what had all the appearance of being an abandoned home site. My eyes took in the circle of an overgrown driveway and the possible remnants of a once-elegant, English-style garden. Rocks still outlined the long-neglected flower beds. I glimpsed faint traces of brick walkways showing through thick carpets of summer growth. The mass of long-neglected wisteria had pulled down the arbor, probably once the passageway into the area. Hardy daylilies grew in abandoned rubber tires of all sizes. Old-fashioned wild roses, white and the palest of pinks, thrived undisturbed in the cluttered side yard. Squirrels ran in abundance. Still hesitant to get out of the car, I rolled down my window. A cacophony of bird sounds filled my head.

The scattered junk amid the profusion of flowers, weeds, and poison ivy all blurred as I took in the tall, massive oaks, positioned guard-like around the house. These elegant trees circled by the native ferns, could easily be a hundred years old. I was certain the location of both the trees and the house had been well thought out. I guessed the place was built near the turn of the 20th century.

As I finally opened the car door and took my first step onto this secreted-away piece of paradise, I immediately realized there was so much more to take in. The red rush of a cardinal flew out of nowhere. The noise of a hard-working woodpecker stimulated my brain. It seemed an eternity before I understood that all my senses were on overload at this point. For a brief moment, I struggled to sort through what underlying sound was vying for my attention. The house, the cluttered yard, the flowers, the remains of a garden, yes, even the beautiful trees were mere preliminaries to the heart of this land, the river itself. The intoxicating sound of water tumbling over rocks washed over my senses.

I made my way around the backside of one of the oaks, then inched through limbs of a near-to-tree-sized privet hedge, grown purposefully, so it seemed to create a thick, green wall. My eye caught the play of the sun on the river below. I backed away quickly. Just beyond the hedge was a sheer drop of rocky cliff, stretching at least 100 feet to the tumbling water. As I think back on the moment, I knew with one glimpse that the Valley River, bending to join the Hiwassee River, flowed like a mighty force around the land, shaping and molding it in ways I still do not pretend to fully understand.

Within moments I became aware of a couple of wide-eyed, shabbily dressed children who were staring at me from the L-shaped front porch stretching the full length of both the front and right sides of the house. I explained I had not realized anyone lived here. Reluctantly, I got back into the car. Disappointment washed over me as I thought about the fact that I would not have easy access to leisurely explore this occupied property.

§

My first day of discovery on this mysterious property left me longing for something that seemed just beyond my grasp. Fascination quickly moved to obsession. The sensory overload created by the river and the royal oaks stayed with me. I recalled vividly the cool current of air rising from the tumbling waters below even in summer. Time and time again, some poor soul in town put up with my questions about the place. Before long, I squirreled away enough bits and pieces of its history, whetting my appetite sufficiently to keep going farther with what soon resembled a treasure trove of knowledge about the layered stories behind this mysterious peninsula of land.

I found myself relieved the owner had no desire to live in the house. Instead, he brought in a family to simply have the place occupied. Why this bit of information should please me made no sense at all. The house was a fixer-upper beyond even my wildest imagination. There was not a remote chance I could talk my husband into taking on the repair of a place that probably would never be more than a rental house. From all I had gleaned from questions around town, the owner had numerous offers and was not in the least bit interested in selling.

§

To this day, I do not know how I got Tim to agree to look at the place. Tall, lanky Tim Novak came into my life in the late '80s. I had replaced blond hair with a sandy brown buzz cut and blue eyes with green. The surname Edwards gave over to Edwards-Novak. Deep down, Grandma Anna's words rang true as she commented on my decision to marry a second time. "Sarah, my dear girl, I understand that you are looking for yourself. I do worry that you think self-awareness comes through someone else. Her wise words quickly took a back seat to the passion awakened by Tim in those early years of our marriage. Even so, occasional misgivings stirred deep in my gut. *Was Baker-Bryant the only name that would ever contain me?* On this particular day, I buried all such concerns. Tim was by my side on this adventure.

Late November, trees without their summer mass of foliage, coupled with the absence of the wild abandon of undergrowth, failed to provide the absolute privacy of my first visit to the property. Still, I had a well-thought-out plan for arriving unobserved by the caretaker family. We needed to come in from an adjoining piece and follow the creek as it curved along one side of the land. No one would have a clue we were there.

Well into the morning, fog lingered and rested heavily as a winter blanket. Memories of my initial mysterious introduction to this place rolled back over me. The verdant growth of summer had produced a similar effect as the foggy dampness now provided. One moment I could see the house. The next minute nowhere to be found, reminding me of Merlin's magical land of mists. As we pushed farther into the morning moisture, I hesitated momentarily in the bewitching whiteness. The heavy air wrapped around me. My hair and clothes clung in wetness. The smell of dank earth filled my lungs. My eyes took in the decaying fallen trees pulled down in the ebb and flow of forest life.

The sound of my husband's voice pulled me from my reverie. "Damn, this air is oppressive. I hope you know where you're going; I can't see my hands in front of my face!"

I pushed ahead. *Tim's reaction to the heavy fog is so different from mine. I can't concentrate on him at the moment. This hardy stand of rhododendrons does deserve my attention.* Once again, I marveled at the land's ability to make me feel like I was in the wilderness. In reality, we were in the middle of town. As we walked farther up the gentle ascent toward the backside of the house, I looked back to realize that even in winter, the sights and sounds of the old lumber mill and neighborhood houses seemed to disappear in the distance.

Occasionally a twig would snap beneath our steps on the thickly layered carpet of leaves, accumulated undisturbed for many a fall season. From a distance, the river water crashed over rocks and mixed with other sounds of nature. What was it about this place that made me feel as if I had stepped into another world? As I took in the many details of the backside of the two-story house, I noticed smoke curling out of two chimneys, one at each end, one small and one large. Remains of two more tall, bricked columns evidenced years of no longer providing heat for the massive home.

Tim's almost too thin, long-legged frame made the climb easily and quickly. He pushed out in front again. As we walked in silence, I found myself hoping he was not fixated on the mammoth task of how a place such as this could possibly be kept warm during the winter. As I reached his side, I could not help but notice the questioning look in his green eyes.

Was I seriously thinking of living here? Had such a thought played in my brain well before this visit? Within minutes of the questions firing in my head, while staring up at the looming backside of the house, Tim stopped, turned to face me with hands in his pockets. As his shoulders squared and a scowl formed on his face, he asked, "Surely you wouldn't want to live here?"

"Well, no. Well, maybe with some fixing up, it might be wonderful."

"Sarah, you are out of your mind. This place is not some fixing-it-up-a-bit house. We could never afford to do the work the old heap would require. You know I need to put money into my two growing businesses, not waste it on this pile of rot. If I am going to spend the kind of money you're talking about, I would say tear it down and build a new one."

I could almost feel the painful plunge of his sharp words into my heart. The very thought of tearing down the old place was more than I could take. Quietly seething over the fact we were always putting more money in the inventory for his used car business, and what he claimed was the beginning of a thriving real estate company, I stomped off in the direction of two small buildings standing to the side of the big house. I yelled back as I determinedly tucked the damp stray curls back behind my ear, "Well, it's not for sale anyway!"

Chapter 4

Almost a year after Tim and I made our initial covert trip onto the property, we found ourselves driving over to meet the owner about the house. The constant flow of money into Tim's business ventures coupled with the almost nonexistent salary of a school teacher added up to slim pickins' when it came to our finances. We figured talk would be about all we had to offer. The ten-minute drive to the owner's house seemed an eternity. I feared the meeting would be fruitless. We had heard the stories. People from Atlanta made offers for far more money than we could ever hope to put into the purchase. Then there was Norm Cameron and his family from Florida, who had the cash in hand. The owner still insisted he had no interest in selling.

The closer we got to Floyd Logan's house, the more certain I became that Tim and I had gone completely mad when we had finally agreed to approach the owner about caretaking the place. Perhaps he would go as far as renting with an option to buy? On top of the wishful thinking, I'm still not sure where I found the hope that something would turn our fortune around enough to be able to purchase. We knew this lark was nothing more than a gamble. Yes, the river property was the obvious high stake in the game. However, a greater bet sat squarely in our laps. The first five years of second marriages for both of us proved to be hard ones with many ups and downs. Thank God the ups held a smattering of wonderful in those years since the downs were getting deeper and harder as time took its toll.

I don't see too many marriages without challenges. However, I often wondered if we had taken on more than we could manage. My two children, his two children, his ex, my ex, his bills, my bills, and very little money to spread around. Together, it made a sizable stack of obstacles to climb over daily. I suspect there was one certainty, one absolute given. Odds like the ones we faced had to be met with both of us contributing a hundred percent to our marriage. As much as I did not want to admit it, I found myself scared of what might happen if either one of us held back or added just the wrong element to our precarious relationship. Our house of cards could easily crumble with the next gust of wind.

Wisdom or insanity, which characteristic drove us to Floyd Lo-

gan's house? As we turned into his driveway, I remained certain that we needed to go after this dream. Not one practical reason to do so ever surfaced to support my gut feeling, but the moment we pulled up in front of the house, I knew there could be no turning back. Tim and I headed toward the front door. *I know that I know. The land holds something special for us. The wind from the river that stirs the massive oaks each time we set foot on the land, has somehow despite Tim's initial negative reaction, blown life into our marriage.* My husband and I nodded in agreement. I knocked on Mr. Logan's door.

§

Three months later, we closed on the property. Leading up to that momentous day and often in the time that followed, Tim and I talked about what had possibly convinced old man Logan that we were the ones who should break his long-held resolve to hold on to the property. Although it hardly seemed reason enough to offer us an owner-financed opportunity to make the place ours, I know the wizened man had a look of sheer delight on his face when I got past being nervous and started telling him of the bike ride with my cousins and the long-ago discovery of the old home site in Mississippi. This first sacred find from childhood came to life that night in Mr. Logan's living room. I realized the river property was connected to all the dormant hope, all the endless vitality that had once filled my every waking moment. I can only conclude that the owner had hoped to pass the land and its history to someone who would treasure such a find as much as he did. What a fairy-tale, happily-ever-after story it would make if I could say that buying the house solved all of our problems.

We did move in, the four of us. I hoped for treasures as we began to tackle the much-needed cleaning. After days of work, I unearthed a collection of whiskey bottles from the house's history with moonshine. For the most part, our finds were the sort that filled the endless pile of black bags headed for the landfill.

The mammoth house entertained the kids as they often roller-skated from one end to the other of the long hallway that ran the full length of the upstairs. Tim's twin boys, on track for some holiday and the much longer summer time with our family, were intrigued with the kids' talk of the best hide and seek place they had ever seen. I'll never forget the day we finally cleared enough junk out to notice the trapdoor leading to what had to be a massive attic under the bones of the hip roof. As we waited for Tim to get a ladder, one thought burned in my brain. *Now I will find my treasures.*

With his body half in the opening, Tim hollered down to me. "You're not going to believe this. The place is empty. Someone beat us to the treasures years ago."

I had to see for myself. As I made my way up the ladder, the questions began. "Tim, is there a floor? Or just rafters?"

"Stick your head up around my legs. See for yourself. There's a floor that leads where the big living room chimney comes up through the ceiling. Kids, you guys need to wait and let me get your mom up here first. This is no place to let you two run loose. One step in the wrong direction, and you will be falling through the ceiling."

I stood in the expanse of attic space. The emptiness brought tears. "Tim, I just knew I'd be up here for months, even years, going through old trunks." Not knowing what else to do, I wandered over to the massive chimney. Its construction fascinated me the moment I walked into the big living room for the first time. The number of river rock alone was a marvel. Building this chimney could not have been an easy task, certainly not in the early 1900s. I pressed my hands into the cool strength of the stone face. Eventually, I stretched one arm outward, almost in an embrace. *I am so thankful to be in this house on this river property. That's treasure enough.*

As the thought completed itself, my fingers felt something higher up, around the left corner of the chimney. The flooring stopped some distance short of allowing me to walk to the edge of the rock work. My hand barely brushed the rock ledge. I could not reach any farther. "Hey, Tim, your arms are longer. Come here. Let me get out of your way. Reach around where I have my left arm at the moment. Run your hand slowly up the wall, and you will feel a small ledge. Strange place for such. Might be nothing more than an odd-sized river rock. Can you feel what I am talking about?"

Within moments of taking my place, Tim turned to me with an object in this hand that I would have never expected to find in an out-of-the-way ledge on the uppermost side of three stories of a chimney. He held the horn carefully in the palms of his hands as he let me examine it. "Hon, it's an animal's horn, no doubt. But, look, at this mouthpiece added to it." I think he could tell I was questioning something.

"Sarah, people have been known to use animal horns in such ways."

"Tim, I get that. I just wonder why it is on a ledge hidden away in what has got to be one of the most remote spots in this house."

I reached for the horn. The cool smoothness filled my hands. *There's got to be a story behind this. Someone purposefully hid this away up here. But not so hidden as to not have easy access to it. I wonder....*

The kids' heads popped up from below. Impatient questions soon took over. "Mom, what is it?"

"It's a horn." I walked near them, making it clear I would hold on to it as they ran their hands over its surface.

Tim interjected. "Macy and Duncan. Back on down the ladder. Let your mom make her way to the floor. Hand me the horn, Sarah. I'll bring it to you."

The kids could not contain themselves. "Mom, can we blow it?"

Let me at least wipe the mouthpiece a bit. You can see it is covered with dust. Let's get it to the kitchen. Then maybe we will all take our turns at blowing this horn."

As we made our way down the stairs, the excited chatter continued from the kids. "Hey, Duncan, remember Prince Caspian?"

"Great thinking, Macy. What if we end up in Narnia when we blow that horn?"

The joy of a permanent house to hopefully call home would not keep us warm as the winter temperature would dip lower and lower. However, as we made our way downstairs, the idea of working on the renovation together, as our kids played life into the house, made me feel we could endure anything for a time.

§

I can never put my finger on any set of circumstances that turned Tim away from the house project before he even got started. It seemed the moment we unloaded the last piece of furniture in the move, he lost all interest in the house we jointly agreed to tackle. Perhaps the grey signs of winter moving in early influenced his mood. Whatever the cause, I watched my husband grow colder and colder to any discussion of even the smallest steps toward renovation.

In hopes I could spark his interest, I made desperate attempts to fix up a couple of rooms but soon despaired. I knew, at best, my efforts were cosmetic. Major repairs and structural replacements demanded attention first. I questioned constantly, *why did you abandon our dream, Tim, so soon after we embraced it?* I reasoned that he was simply overwhelmed. I had not yet learned to interpret the warning signs. Somehow the pattern of tossing a plan to the winds after only taking initial steps toward it had not yet fully registered with me. Instead, I hung on tenaciously to my longing to call this place our home. Then winter rolled up its sleeves and punched us hard.

Curled in a tight ball under several layers of blankets, I reluctantly forced one hand toward the bedside table as I fumbled for my thick socks. *Why? Why? Why?* Working my feet into the woolen warmth, I continued with the question that now haunted me most of my waking moments. *How can I shake Tim from this slump?* In the moments it took me to locate both of my slippers, I could feel the early November wind that forced its way through the nearby windows. The antique, bubbled glass of the French-style casements shook as the winter blasts continued to move up from the river below. These very windows that had been our salvation against the early fall afternoon heat when we had first moved in were now just one of the many challenges in winterizing the old house.

I knew my husband was awake. I could not stop myself. I hammered in my first words of the morning with a vengeance, "You promised back in early October that you would at least cover all of these windows with plastic as a temporary measure for this first winter here. Tim, you have never moved beyond the kitchen with that project."

Before I could try to find some way to resurrect our plan for the house, he chimed in, "Just zip it, Sarah. I have a plan."

The past month left me devoid of the hope that had surfaced that night back at Floyd Logan's place. I grew increasingly frustrated with Tim's attitude. But I plead one more time, "Hon, the kids can't exist in freezing temperatures. Christmas will be here before you know it. Your boys will be here. They are just not prepared for the conditions we are living in. And how do you plan to keep our water pipes from freezing?"

Tim rolled over, pulled the blankets tighter around his neck, making it clear there would be no further talk. Grabbing my heavy robe from the foot of the bed, I stormed off downstairs to the one room that was at least close to warm.

By December, there was no question how difficult it would be to make it through the winter months. The need for insulation and heat failed to motivate Tim. Without discussing any plans with me, the day before the twins were to arrive, he let me know they would not be visiting this year. Then he dropped the bombshell, "I think I have located another place for us to live." Any repercussions from the owner-financed relationship we were in with Mr. Logan were never mentioned. Instead, Tim walked out the kitchen door. I stood at the opening, staring at him as he made his way to his truck. What he said next stopped me like a roadblock. "Moving sure beats the hell out of me blowing my brains out all over that pantry wall you just worked so hard to paint." I retreated into pain and silence as the winter wind sucked the kitchen warmth into the great outdoors.

I tried only once, later that night, to explore those hard words. Tim gave me one of his best grins and said, "You know, Sarah, it was the only way I could get you to end the talk." His words, again, almost shut me down. I could not deny the fault line running under our marriage. Perhaps if we had never experienced springtime on the property, I would have found it easier to cut our losses, let the place go back to the owner, and never, ever look back. Instead, we stayed through the spring and into the summer.

§

An exceptionally perfect morning greeted the April day. My daughter Macy, the older of my two children, apparently awoke with a mission. I concluded several years back that her independent spirit would always cause her to follow wherever her curiosity possibly led. Later in the morning, after following through on her wild-haired idea, she confessed it had been impossible to make her way through the old growth of tangled honeysuckle and ivy that almost totally hid the front side of a stone springhouse sitting on the edge of a wooded area, near the main yard. Instead, she found a way inside through the old stand of rhododendron that wrapped around the back of the structure. I'll never forget the excitement on her face as she ran back into the house from that first morning of springhouse play. Her every move filled with animation as she shared her idea of making a playhouse out of the old building. Excitement showed in her copper-flecked brown eyes. Water dripped from her hair. The front of her blouse was soaked and streaked with dirt.

"Mama, there are two boxes of water in the little house!" she yelled. "The water is so cool. I just had to wash my face and pour it over my head. I've come after my tea set and picnic basket. Please, may I take a couple of slices of Pink Lady Cake too? I'm sure to get hungry cause I have a lot of work to do." She made her way back through the rambling dining room, then bound up the stairs to gather what she needed.

"Stop right there, Macy." I yelled as she continued toward the upstairs. "First of all, I can only hope you didn't drink any of that water. It's no telling what could be in it." Before giving her time to admit her guilt or innocence, I pushed further, "That place is surrounded by growth. You need to be careful." Then adding, as an afterthought, "What do you mean by boxes of water?"

Eyes twinkling with enthusiasm, she used her hands to show me the size, as she explained, "Somebody built a box around each place the water comes out of the ground. One is near the front entrance and one toward the back." I found myself lost in what was quickly shaping into a troubling thought, *why had I not yet explored the vine-covered place Macy was now describing?*

I explained to my curious child that the springheads had probably provided drinking water and a place to store perishables such as milk. I could not stop the adult explanations fast enough for my impatient child. Her animated chatter won. She could not contain her ideas about the springheads. As it turned out, she played there often with her brother Duncan, occasionally with the twins when they visited. Sometimes her only companions were her tea set and extra cookies or cake to keep her imagination company. I think she knew she was not the first child to play in those waters.

Whether it was her exuberance or my motherly protectiveness, or maybe something starting to worry me about myself, I felt a stir of fascination with the old springhouse. I found myself heading out with garden tools in hand, ready to tackle the overgrown path leading to Macy's hideaway. With the first cut of a thick blackberry briar sure to rip someone's clothing, I spotted a small, silver-veined plant reminding me ever so gently to take it easy with the trimming if I had plans of sharing this land with the wealth of native growth at my feet.

I long respected the years of work my mom put into the yard at our homeplace back in Mississippi. Often, I worked alongside her, eager to plant flats of store-bought flowers each spring. But for the first time, as I took in the thick, verdant growth surrounding me on my way to the springheads housed in the old stone structure, my definition of gardening shifted slightly. I realized this piece of property was not waiting for me to strip it and tame it into neat flower beds. I did sense an invitation to tend it, to nurture its native growth alongside any desire to add the plants and flowers that typically defined my spring planting ritual. Unfortunately, I knew Tim would insist we leave before the next winter. I guess you could say once again just because I was leaving the property did not mean the property had given up its hold on me.

Chapter 5

During my growing-up years, I concluded that with a name like Finn Pinkney Campbell, I may as well have a body at odds with itself. Feet too long, angled-out ready to trip over just about anything in my path, left me face down on the ground more times than I like to remember. Gangly arms and big hands stretched well below my knees. Mama told me over and over that I would one day stretch out just right before I was done growing. In 1838, the year I turned sixteen, Mama's words came true. My awkward build finally evened out. Little did I know that taking on the body of a young man did not come close to preparing me for all the complications that came with manhood.

Trees reach tall and full in these mountains. The abundant shade never fails to temper the summer heat. The memory of the trek from Tennessee still plays in my mind. I don't suppose I will ever forget the long, hard journey to North Carolina. Only eight years old at the time, Papa treated me like a young man. Mama reminded me often that I was not yet too big to help her out with my three brothers and baby sister. Against all sorts of odds, we found this place. Now it's our home.

In time, I figured out that Papa and Mama had no real plan when we left on our journey to find a new place to settle. Mama talked many a night, late around the campfire. "Angus, I just know it's time we move on. I can't seem to find my peace staying here any longer. Let's strike out farther into those mountains off in the distance. I'll know it's right when we get there." The journey seemed endless. Sometimes double on horseback, sometimes walking the Indian trails. Impatient and full of wanting to get there, I woke up every day wondering if it would mark the arrival at wherever we rode so hard to find. Early into the afternoon, Mama indicated she needed a break well before supper forced us to stop for the night. Thinking that Papa was getting down to take over Mama's horse, I looked back at him in surprise when he pointed ahead and added. "Mary, kids, see that spot up ahead at the base of a gentle mountain ridge?" My eyes could not get enough of the sight that unfolded. The land spread out like a lady's fan I had once seen back in Nashville. Before I could take in what she was doing, Mama was down on her hands and knees. Her worn hands scooped the cool spring waters that ran nearby. "Angus, this is the place." Her eyes came to life.

We figured she could, at that moment, just about see the cabin of her dreams. Papa first met my mama, Mary Murray, in Pontotoc County, Mississippi. She knew Papa was the man she would marry as soon as she laid eyes on him. Papa often reminded us what he had learned early on. "Once your mama gets an idea in her head, in no time, she'll see something to back it up. Then you may as well forget about disagreeing." But, Papa, too, was satisfied with this small acreage of land, just a short distance out from the start-up of what would soon be a town. The creek flowed into a rushing river within walking distance. Yes, the place would grow crops aplenty, including the corn for Papa's whiskey making.

Like many a Scotch-Irish Highlander, Papa longed for these mountains because they stirred memories of his homeland. He tried to find reasons to stay in Mississippi near Mama's family, but the pull of familiar lush growth of the rocky peaks tugged deep in him. As it turned out, Papa was in for more than gentle reminders of Scotland's countryside. A small settlement of Cherokee lived on the other side of the ridge where we staked our land. Within a few years of our move, we began to hear nonstop rumors of the broken agreements between the government and the Indians. Like many a Scot, we soon figured out it was only a matter of time before the natives were forced from the mountains and valleys they had always known.

Our first days near the river filled to overflowing with efforts to build a much-needed lean-to. The threat of relentless spring rains pushed us hard. When a moment of downtime surfaced, Mama pointed me in the direction of the endless stack of chores that she faced every day. I figured it out quickly. *The harder I work early in the day, the more time I have in the early evening to explore.* Papa and I caught our dinner that first night from the cold waters. From that point on, I could hardly contain the urge to answer the call of the creek and river. Every plant growing around my feet, the abundant signs of wildlife all lured me in. The land fed my need for discovery.

After only a couple of weeks living on this land, the glimpse of a red-tailed fox first set me exploring a new area up toward the ridge. The clever animal disappeared. Then, almost in a game of cat and mouse, the bushy tail caught my attention once again. My feet kept up the merry chase. I had to go farther up. The undergrowth on this section of the climb grew thicker than Mama's molasses. The moist ground cover of the underground spring that fed the creek below sucked at my boots. My feet, heavy and hot from thick leather on the exceptionally warm spring day, needed air. My toes felt the cool, soft, moss-covered soil. *I'll just retrieve these boots on the way back down.* Only one thought filled my mind as the ground became even more moist and slippery under my feel. *I must be coming up on a springhead any minute now.*

A thick stand of rhododendron blocked the view in front of me. I veered to the left and made my way around the stand of growth. Run-off from a spring got my attention. Determined to follow through to the source, I used the strong, tree-like growth to keep from sliding in the wetness. I made my way, still upward. Rhododendron limbs slapped me in the face. My head ducked as I dodged to keep the leaves out of my eyes. The moment I looked up, I stopped in surprise.

The head of shiny, straight, black hair stopped me still. My heart felt like it would pound right out of my chest. *She's just a young Indian girl. I hope I don't scare her.* I watched quietly. She sat cross-legged in front of the very spring whose waters brought me farther up the ridge. Her hands played gently in the gurgling wetness. She must have sensed someone was nearby. Slowly her head turned, and she stared directly at me. Eyes dark as a moonless sky. Not knowing what else to do, I stood still and silent.

Her next moved surprised me. She pointed to yet another springhead only feet away and motioned for me to move forward. Stepping slowly and carefully, I took in how comfortable she seemed. *She can't be more than a few years younger than me.* Her head nodded in a downward motion indicating for me to sit down. *I do hope I will not get into trouble. A drink of that cool spring water sure would be good after the climb through that stand of rhododendrons.* I let the water lead the way. Splashing my face freely, gulping its coldness from my hands, soon had the young Indian girl laughing. She smiled as I looked in her direction. The bond between us could not be denied, although no words were shared. Somewhere, deep in my brain, I kept returning to one thought. *I think it best that I tuck this time at the double springheads far away in a safe place. Papa and Mama don't need to know just yet.*

Over the next few weeks, I found myself at the springheads just about every day as soon as Mama let me out of her sight. More times than not, I spotted the now familiar black hair of my new Cherokee friend as I trekked along the well-forged path through the undergrowth. With her broken English and my boyish inability to remember how to talk when in her presence, the two of us still found a way to share some of the details of our lives. A friendship was forming despite a lack of words. Immediately upon seeing the young girl for the second time, I came up with the idea of patting my chest with both hands and added, "Finn Campbell." Then went on to add, "Finn Pinkney Campbell." She replied with a shy laugh, then patted her chest and said, "Maidena Taylor." Dropping her eyes shyly, she quickly looked back up at me. "Your name is funny." I laughed and nodded my head in agreement. *My name Finn Pinkney Campbell seems strange to most folks. I know Mama had her reasons for naming me after the legendary Irish hero Finn MacCumaill, known for his fairness. No use in trying to explain in this situation that Pinkney was the middle name of my grandfather on my mother's side.* I've learned it's best to let people shake their heads in wonder about my unusual name. No sense in wasting my time with an explanation.

Our visits never lasted long. I could feel the smile spread across my face the afternoon when this young girl spoke softly the moment I came near. "Follow me." I moved quietly behind her as we made our way to the edge of the woods. Just beyond a thick wall of growth, she pointed to a log cabin. I knew it must be her home. She took me no closer. From that spot, I could see the roofs of a few more simple cabins dotting the landscape to the point where the land seemed to suddenly disappear. The next afternoon Maidena steered me in the opposite direction from the day before. We stopped at a spot where the cliff made its deep plunge to what she called the bend in the river. She explained in her broken English the presence of a second bend in the river on past the last house. The offer still did not come to take me near any of the dwellings. In time I would learn more about the Cherokee people and their beliefs. I also learned that the double springheads and double bends in the river are sacred landmarks to her people.

The white waters rushed and crashed wildly below. The sound of water hitting rock filled my head. Where Papa and I fished for our dinner, the river pushed onward in a more gentle way. My mind shifted. A similar thought had forced into my brain several days back at the springheads. *We are being watched.* I turned slowly, allowing my eyes to comb the woods. *No one I can spot.* Maidena may have picked up on my concern. She quickly turned to leave. I followed in silence.

§

Several weeks had passed since the walk that led to the cliff overlooking the bend in the river. Papa and I just called it a day from the hard work of clearing more land. As we neared our makeshift cabin, my Scotch-Irishman instinct kicked in again. *We are being watched.* This time, as I turned to look, an Indian man with a turban on his head stepped quickly from the edge of the woods. As he got closer, I wondered if this was who had been watching Maidena and me at both the springheads and the day at the cliff overlooking the river. Papa whispered, "Look at the pouch slung over his shoulder? Now, see. He is lifting it in our direction."

As it turned out, the man approached their homestead as a friend. He brought two rabbits ready for dressing. This lean, broad-shouldered Cherokee had the same dark, piercing eyes that had caught my attention with my new friend. *I'd be willing to bet this is Maidena's father.* Dressed in the garb of his people from the waist down, the man's shirt looked much like the rough homespun that Papa and the other settlers wore.

With a slight nod the stranger spoke, "Long Axe Taylor."

Meeting the meaningful nod, with an extended hand, his father replied, "Angus Campbell. This here is my boy, Finn."

The penetrating look from the tall Indian bore into me. *No question, he has watched Maidena and me at play more times than not.* The sharpness and clarity of the dark eyes held my attention.

Papa accepted the pouch and offered, "Come on in and meet my wife Mary and my younger children."

I would later think back many times on the gesture of friendship shown that day as Maidena's father stepped out of the woods. Our two families found it easy to live alongside each other, with little thought given to property boundaries. Unfortunately, for many white settlers, particularly those in authority, land ownership with paperwork to back it up was the only rule that carried weight, often making folks blind to the characteristics that bound our two families.

§

Over the next years living as neighbors, Papa learned to grow a plentiful corn crop with his neighbor's assistance. Long Axe allowed Papa to teach him whiskey-making and white men's ways. Both lessons could mean survival. I continued to meet at the springheads with my friend. Our families visited each other's homes. My mama learned to make fry bread as she spent time with Isi Taylor, Maidena's mother. I will never forget my shock when I first met this quiet woman. Her short, rounded body, along with the paler skin, flat face, and blue, moon-shaped eyes, fascinated me, as did the fact that the twin boys, Maidena's youngest siblings, looked exactly like their mother. Although I kept the thought to myself, I was pleased that my new friend had the graceful height and flawless skin of her father instead. Gradually as the relationships between the two families grew, all of my family were included in some of the activities of the larger group of Cherokees living in scattered dwellings along the other side of the river.

§

Maidena's mother sat out on the porch as I made my way toward the Taylor's log cabin. I had begged my parents to let me get a head start. The Cherokee had set aside the afternoon and into the evening for games and cooking over the open fire. "Finn, I see you came early. Head on down to the fire circle. Here, take this basket of butter beans so you young folks can start the game. It seems my daughter forgot it in her excitement." It did not take long to join in the fun. Just as it was my turn to toss the beans into the air, the ball from the nearby stickball game came bounding right into the center of our play, knocking the basket and myself to the ground, causing me to send the beans flying across the circle. The game was spoiled for the younger group. Before I could stop myself, I grabbed the ball and ran straight into the midst of the game with the older boys. *I'm as tall as most of these fellas, and I am still only twelve.* Within moments I merged with the aggressive hustle of the game, never looking back, even for a moment, at Maidena.

§

Now that I am sixteen, there is no question my workdays alongside Papa run from sun-up to sundown. When I do get a chance for fun, there is nothing I enjoy more than perfecting the skills of the Cherokee males. *Shoot, I am a sharp marksman with a bow and arrow. I can make my own knives. I've even helped with the work of burning out logs for canoes. I can hold my own.* Over the past two years, I rarely spend time around Maidena unless our families get together for some occasion. *We've both outgrown afternoons of fun-filled child play.*

Spring tantalizingly tickled the land. The Serviceberry once again heralded the change of season as green buds pushed into fullness. Papa, Mama, and all the young'uns had gone into town. I was left to attend to our sickly calf that needed feeding by hand every few hours. I headed to the barn, my head full of thoughts. *I can get in a little exploring before you need my attention again, little fella. I think you are growing stronger by the hour. I'm gonna' head up the ridge. I saw a hawk take flight just before I came in here. I need to roam a bit myself on this fine afternoon.*

I found myself almost to the springheads. Giant woodpeckers hammered in the distance. The stand of rhododendrons had thickened and grown in height just as I had done during the time that led to these sixteen years. Taking the route around the stand suddenly brought me to the topside of the double springs. Breath caught in my chest. The dark eyes that turned upward in greeting had a new, meaningful depth. Maidena leaned slightly to one side. One hand seemed to stir the waters of the gurgling spring. I no longer saw the young girl I had first met at this very place. Feet glued to the ground, I found myself unable to take my eyes from the gentle curves of her body. My mind raced with unfamiliar thoughts and feelings. At the moment, with no way of processing why, the only thing I could think to do was turn and run without stopping till I made my way back to the barn where the calf still slept soundly. As I made my way down the ridge, one thought won out. *I need to stay away from those springheads.*

Only a week later, Mama sent me to the Taylor's with a mess of early collard greens. The moment I walked through the doorway, I saw Maidena, working alongside her mama. *I won't look at her.* Out of the corner of my eye, I couldn't help but notice as I handed over the basket that she turned back to her work immediately and never once spoke. Stumbling at the door in my hurry to escape, I explained to Maidena's mother the need to get back for evening chores. In the days that followed, I accepted this awkwardness as all that was left of our friendship. Distance seemed to grow at every turn of our daily lives. One thought continued to puzzle me. Maidena's father, along with my parents, seem to have their eyes on my every move any time I'm in the same room with the Taylor's daughter. *I wonder what has brought that on?*

The endless days of homesteading often ended in talk with my parents around the fire. Although I did more listening than talking, it was impossible not to be keenly aware of the quiet unrest in the Taylor home and with many of the other Indians that made up the community of Cherokee that had welcomed my family with open arms. The heavy worry came out in torrents each time Papa spoke of the trouble that had reached fever-pitch levels over the Indians. I agreed with my father. The Cherokee had lived off this land long before us white men. *It's not right that the Taylors and other Indian families should be forced out of their homes and off the very land that is, by all rights, theirs.*

New treatises were written and old promises broken time and time again. As the weeks passed, the talk of moving the Cherokee far to the west appeared to be shaping into more than a rumor. My family and the Taylors remained close in spite of the distance embraced by other white and Indian families.

§

The corn crop, exceptionally good this season, produced whiskey in abundance. A steady flow of liquor, of course, meant support for the two families, one Indian, one white. I heard Papa say more than once that as long as he and Long Axe could supply the growing number of troops with whiskey, the Taylors may stay out of the round-ups that had started with some of the Cherokee.

Late evening moved across the land. Done with fence-mending for the day, I headed up the trail leading to the cabin. Up ahead, I spotted Maidena coming in my direction from the ridge. As we got closer to each other, she explained as kept her eyes looking down toward the ground. "Mama sent me after Papa. I believe he is inside meeting with your father."

I offered immediately, "Do you want me to go in and tell him?" But as the question came out, I continued to stand in the same spot, unable to take my eyes off her downturned face. In an almost sheepish manner, her dark eyes glanced upward and met mine. The evening light lingered just enough for us to see each other. Before thinking of a reason not to act on what was unfolding between us, my head moved down to her lips, kissing shyly. Confidence grew. My hands reached out to touch the thickness of her silky, black hair. At that moment, I heard the cabin door opening. Maidena tensed immediately and stepped back. Both Long Axe and Papa came out onto the porch. We faced our fathers in silence. I worked to hold my head high as I forced myself to look straight ahead at both Papa and Maidena's father.

Silence hung heavy in the air. Papa spoke, "Son, go on in and give your Mama a hand with the fire." I looked at the face that I knew so well, seeking the answer I needed at the moment. Longing and concern filled her dark eyes. She nodded in the direction of our cabin.

Long Axe's deep voice broke the silence as he spoke to his daughter. "Let's get you up to the top of the ridge before it's gone over to darkness. You can make it safely to the house from there. I need to come back down." He then turned to look at Papa and added, "There is now need for more talk, Angus."

The two men stood out under the stars for a long time, conversing in quiet but heavy voices. Although my brothers and sister had all gone to sleep sometime earlier, I lay awake in the loft, tossing and turning. Too many thoughts hammered through my head for sleep. Occasionally the wind blew right and I could hear the two men's voices from the front porch. I knew Mama also stayed awake listening. From time to time, she added a log to the fire in the midst of the non-stop, back and forth movement of her rocking chair. *She won't settle down till Papa's finished and back inside.* The creak of Papa's heavy steps eventually filled the room below. I could not make out my mother's soft whispers. My father's somber reply was clear. "We'll talk more in the morning, Mary. My heart is too heavy for words tonight."

§

By midsummer of 1838, I found myself heading west with my family. Papa talked about going as far as California. I remember Mama saying, as we loaded the last of the supplies in the wagon, "Angus, I just can't seem to set my mind on this journey. Surely, I'll know it when we find another place that will be right for us."

The decision to move weighed on all of us. Not long after the night Papa and Long Axe had walked out to see me kissing Maidena, my parents started talking about relocating somewhere in the west. No excitement showed in Mama about leaving the cabin and the land she readily called home. Papa's whiskey- making met the family's needs. Life was good in these far west mountains. *Why leave this life? No question, I am the reason for the move.*

For once Papa did most of the talking. Both my parents sat down with me soon after the night of my eager first kiss. Papa started, "Son, I have known all my days that I think about life a little differently from many folks. I am proud to hold to this opinion when it comes to all of this talk about Indian land and white land. In my way of thinking, no amount of talking or signing of treaties is going to make one bit of difference with these government folks when it comes down to it. The way I see it, they are smart enough to know if they insist on taking all the Cherokee land, they better be prepared to move every last Indian far enough away to avoid any trouble. Long Axe made it clear that he and his family have no intentions of leaving these mountains. When I shared with your mama the Taylor's plan to hide out in caves, that's when she put her foot down. I knew we had to move on."

Then Mama poured out her heartfelt thoughts. "Son, hiding out in caves, dodging your shadow at every turn, and hoping to survive off of hunting during a cold mountain winter, is no way to live." My mother's next words surprised me even more. "You and Maidena will never survive. Try as you might, a white man married to an Indian woman during such times as we are living in at present, will be next to impossible." I sat silent for some time, taking in the fact that my parents seem to know more about my feelings for Maidena than I can even admit to myself. Then Mama spoke up once again, "Your Papa tried suggesting that we talk to you about just staying away from her. I did not mince with words. I think a mama knows her child."

It was at that point that Papa added, "Your mama made it

clear in no uncertain terms. The way she sees it, Maidena is wrapped deep in the fabric of your heart. There ain't no sense in thinking we can keep you two apart. Maybe we can sidetrack you a bit until all this turmoil settles."

During the short time before I started the journey west with my family, Maidena and I continued to seek each other out at the springheads. We both realized that many white folks in the community would not look kindly on our relationship. Despite all, we talked of a future together, hoping somehow, she and her family could survive the hard times that were already nipping dangerously at their lives. I swore time and time again, "Maidena, I will find my way back to you. Let's give it some time." Somewhere, deep in our beings, I think we both knew we would never see each other again. In those days before the move, we found ways to spend time together by the springheads, many times running our hands through the refreshing water to cool the wanting of each other. We promised to remain faithful to the possibility of a life together.

Hope managed to hold on during those first days of leaving behind the familiarity of home. Anger rushed in with a vengeance when I could no longer see those familiar blue mountains off in the distance.

Chapter 6

I bolted upright in the bed, startled from sleep by what sounded like the death throes of the old refrigerator in the nearby kitchen. Dream remnants that filled my sleep rushed into my now wide-awake mind. Details washed over my consciousness. The vivid night tale soon jump-started the questions. *Where exactly was that setting? Why the nagging feeling I have been there before, even though I cannot nail exactly where "there" is? The place seemed very familiar, but why couldn't I fully recall the location?* Throughout the remainder of the day, I hit my rewind button again and again to jog recognition.

The dream unfolded around a small-town walking tour at the peak of the Christmas season. Just as the group left the historic home, decorated with the finest of greenery and seasonal touches, something caught my attention out of the corner of my eye. The remains of an old trail veered off to the left. Without giving my decision any real thought, I moved away from the others in the direction of this fork. As I lingered back momentarily, the rest of the participants headed back down the long driveway of the home we had just toured. I never questioned my decision to strike off on a road less taken.

Immediately I spotted a house farther down the hill. For obvious reasons, it had not been included on the holiday tour. The large, two-story rectangular structure had a porch that ran across its lower front. The full-length view showed many boarded-up windows on both levels and a porch roof saggy with age. *An old hotel? Possibly a boarding house?* Weathered lumber covered the windows. I made my way around the place, hoping to spot one opening large enough for even the tiniest glimpse inside. Curious, I looked for anything to help pry a board off. My sleep state took me no farther. I awoke with a jolt.

It took only one day after the intriguing night tale for me to dismiss my curiosity. *Hey, it's just a dream,* I concluded. *I have enough real-life questions nagging me presently to keep me busy without spending my waking hours on this fruitless effort.* I spent no time questioning how I could possibly move away so quickly from a mystery that would have hounded me relentlessly years earlier. The discovery of an old house, even if only seen in my sleep, would have filled my every waking moment until the mystery was solved.

At the time of this dream, ten years of my life seemed to have slipped away from me since we left the property alongside the double bends in the river. My heart ached daily for the fulfillment that I had been so certain of when ole man Logan made it possible for us to buy the place. Somehow the years of living elsewhere stacked up as useless as the decaying cord of firewood that sat next to the giant fireplace in the massive living room of the now-empty old house.

The upcoming turn of the century loomed on the horizon as a topic of much speculation. The slightest mention of the year 2000 caused fear for many. Interestingly enough, our financial situation had improved to a small degree. We still held on to the land along the river. Initially, Tim assured me we would start work on the old house once we had a warm place to spend our winter months. His promises fell on deaf ears as our days, then months, in a cramped, no-personality, rental house, soon turned into years with not one bit of the hoped-for work even started. Unfortunately, Tim did have a plan, just not the one that I longed for. I'll always remember the cool, calm way he dropped the news. "I think I've found just the place for us to buy."

My first thought came blurting out. "How can we possibly afford to buy another place? "As soon as the words surfaced, I found myself wishing I could reel the question back in. I feared the worst. *What if Tim is planning to sell the river property?"*

"You know, Sarah, I haven't found time lately to discuss just how much the business is bringing in." I could hardly process the idea that Tim's used car efforts along with his recent real estate adventures, were turning into highly profitable efforts, based on the hit-or-miss way he worked. I did know that he reminded me with every cent spent on the household needs that money does not grow on trees. There seemed to be less and less to live on with each passing month. Before I could tear away from my troublesome thoughts long enough to respond, Tim added, "You certainly should be the first to admit that we need a larger place! Besides, the house that I've got in mind is an apartment complex. We could rent out part of it, eventually sell it, or rent it all out as a steady source of income."

"But what about our plans for the house on the river property?" I pleaded. "You just told me a few weeks back that we are close to having enough extra cash saved to begin the renovations. Now you're telling me that we have enough money to purchase another house and hold on to our original investment?" *Why have I not forced the issue of knowing more about Tim's financial situation with his business endeavors?* The truth hit me hard. I did not want to know. *How could I possibly have accepted life with blinders? How had I caved to the idea of the husband solely managing the family business while I remained clueless?*

"Sarah, think about it. We could get this place and make a killing off of it. If we just put money into the old house, that's all we are doing. We have a better chance of keeping your *dream* house if we have extra dough rolling in. Anyway, I did not say we were selling. My plan for the apartment complex gives us a roof over our heads while we also earn some rental income. We can still eventually live on the river property. No matter which way you look at it, I've found us a good investment."

Something in me believed Tim's ideas made sense. *After all, he did not say we were selling the river property. He even said we will eventually live there. Maybe I should hold off on my criticism of my husband's money management.* For some reason, I still could not quite shake my nagging concern. *Will this feel-good moment last? I want so badly to believe your plan will work.* For the first time, I saw all too clearly a pattern in Tim's business adventures. Great ideas came easily to him. He could even manage to get many projects off the ground. Inevitably, he seemed incapable of bringing anything to completion. I knew his excuse like the back of my hand, "Hey, I've now got a better idea."

§

Within a couple of months, we moved from the cramped house to the apartment complex. I have to admit it felt nice to unpack the boxes of treasured items that had never seen the light of day in the cramped quarters we just left. I remembered when I had moved these keepsakes and heirlooms from the big house on the river property. No, they had never been unpacked there either. Instead, I waited for promised renovations to happen. Then I worried about leaving anything of value in a house that stood on what soon looked like abandoned property. For a short period, I faithfully went over to at least work on the yard. About the same time, Tim started using the site as a dumping ground for old cars that he had picked up for spare parts. The used equipment collected for land development projects only added to the pile-up.

As the clutter grew, I gave up on any landscape dreams. Reluctant at first, I eventually gave over to the tame and unchallenging yard at the new location. Flowerbeds sat ready for the planting in all the usual places. I added flats of annuals, pruned the shrubs into submission, and still found time to paint over the tired, drab, green paint that consumed the upstairs portion of the house. I could well imagine Tim's scowl if I asked to replace the olive-green appliances that screamed constant reminders of at least a decade or two back.

As the house took on the feel of home, the kids invited friends over regularly. Macy excitedly talked about her goals for college. Duncan's afternoons and weekends are filled with sports. The twins came to visit more often. Tim and I occasionally invited people for dinner. Somewhere in the back of my mind, I could not shut down the gnawing concern that the bottom of my husband's bucket of plans could still drop out at any moment. I worked to keep those doubts tucked down deep. I refused to mention the river property to Tim. But the sheer waste of it all refused to give up its hold in my thinking.

Tim did begin some renovations, but not on the old house. Instead, he started work on the downstairs apartments. One of the two areas was finished and rented out, in record time, to a delightful old man who kept to himself, for the most part, never made any noise and even loved my cat. The second apartment, close to being ready for another renter, waited for the word that all was a go. Two rental checks would soon be coming in every month. I had to admit my husband's plan seemed to be putting us on the right track.

§

Spring painted its path across the sky in a perfect blue. A slight breeze stirred the kitchen curtain. *Life seems to be going smoothly. My Macy is starting her first year in college in the fall. Tim came through with a sizable financial contribution for her first year and assured her there would be no need for a second semester student loan.* Deep in thought about the fact that we would have another one in college within a few years, the slam of the front door shook me out of my reverie. "Sarah, where are you? I wanted to let you know that a construction crew is coming by later this afternoon. I have a third renter. Macy is as good as out of here at this point. She can move into the twins' room until she leaves in August. I've already contacted their mom, letting her know we won't be able to have the boys here for their summer visit."

My husband's words forced me away from the feel-good place I had found. *It makes no difference whether it's Macy or the twins. Tim, you have no awareness of what I feel are essentials for the kids. The concept of home, a space of their own, the assurance that some things remain consistent no matter what may be coming down elsewhere, all seemed up for debate with you. And, as if we don't have very different opinions about how our daily lives should unfold, why is it that I always hear about your plans after they are in place?* I could feel the anger rising in me before I spoke, "How dare you shuffle the kids from pillar to post. This past year and a half has been the closest to our family having something that resembles a home that I can recall in a long time. And now, with not so much as a word to me, you call in a construction crew to take away what is my daughter's room and move in a total stranger into the midst of this main floor of our house. Did you even bother to think that Macy may want to come home for a weekend occasionally?"

Ignoring my comment about Macy, Tim explained. "Sarah, you know there is a separate back entrance and a separate kitchen. You'll never have to lay eyes on this man."

"I feel like the walls are closing in around us. We are being reduced to an apartment ourselves. And you certainly have not kept your long string of promises about fixing up the house on the river property."

"Sarah, don't start with me about *that place*. I've got a better idea. Just look at what I have accomplished here. We could turn around and buy again with the idea of fixing up more apartments. I'm think I could really make a go of the rental business. Who knows, along with everything else I am doing, I could make enough money to fix up that old heap you are so crazy about. This might be a good time for you to remember that your pitiful salary only takes the edge off the upcoming financial drain we will be experiencing with college costs. Besides, I have not given up on the river property. Oh! Yes! I can see the surprise on your face at this very moment." He only looked me directly in the eyes briefly before he headed toward the back stairs. He then added quickly, as he called over his shoulder, "I've decided to put the real estate office over there."

Stunned, I felt the tears in my eyes first, then the words spilled out, "What real estate office?" Not even waiting for one more empty explanation, I ran out the front door.

My world seemed to spin off its axis. It mattered very little about any plans that Tim and I had once talked about together. I could hardly remember the closeness we experienced briefly when we had gone after the river property, now, so many years back.

§

At first, I just sat in my car, taking in how the blue sky began to match my mood as it gave over to the dark, heavy clouds that now loomed overhead. I cranked the car. No real idea of where to go. *One thing I know for certain, I need to get out of this driveway.* More thoughts seared my mind as I rode aimlessly up and down various streets in town. *As much as I want to see the house on the river renovated and made beautiful, there is something I want more. I long for a place to call home. Tim, you have just got to understand that I cannot survive too much longer. Moving from place to place, always bogged down in renovations, it's taking a toll on me. Is there any way to get you to understand this need in me? Is it asking too much to consider a place we could live out our years together? A place our kids could continue to think of as home even as they are leaving the nest?*

As I intersected with the street that ran along the river property, I decided to turn down the long, secluded driveway. My senses stirred as I heard the first rumble of thunder in the distance. *Nothing like early thunderstorms. They move in so quickly.* Spring growth on the trees mixed with the deep, cooling evergreen shade of the few remaining hemlocks. Thick privet hedge, growing tall as some trees, formed a tight walled entrance into what was meant to be the proper yard for the house itself. Now a sky of gray showed above the tall oaks. The wind picked up, as evidenced in the limbs of forest growth. The place tugged at my heart, as it had on my first visit. The white of dogwood blossoms popped in abundance in sharp contrast to the heavy cloud cover blocking any glimpse of the sun.

I could not bear to pull up to the house itself. Instead, I got out of the car just past the privet hedge entrance. Now thick with the coming storm, the air weighed me down as I walked across a section of the side yard. Spring bulbs fought their way through the clutter of car parts. A groundhog scurried from behind a small bulldozer parked on top of a bed of daylilies working to push their way upward to the needed light. Squirrels scampered everywhere as if seeking shelter from the pending storm front. The old tin roof of the springhouse caught my attention. *I know where I need to go. Macy's bench should still be there.*

I sat for the longest, sometimes leaning back against the cool rock wall, often with my head hanging in despair. The thunderstorm came on full force soon after I sought shelter. Thunder sounded close and ominous. Through the screen section of the building, I could see giant trees swaying, sometimes creaking in defiance to the wind's strength. My tears started in sync with the heavy rain that pounded the tin roof. I sat, allowing myself to shelter in this special place. The storm raged. Once the bottom fell out of nature's fury and my own, twilight moved in, and soft-spoken rain wept from the edge of the roof.

The kids would expect dinner. I knew I needed to head back to the house. For some reason, as I stood to leave, I walked over to one of the springheads. Getting down on my knees, I began to let the water fill my cupped hands. Its coolness soothed my puffy eyes. I had to find a way to help Tim see how good it would be for us, for our family, if we put some time, some money, and some combined energy into making a home out of the old house. *I can live with a real estate office at the front entrance of the property. I can live with your next apartment project if you will give some effort for us to have a home that I can count on for years to come. Please, Tim, hear my plea. I long to live on this land.* As I got back in the car, I sat for a moment longer, listening to the distant river waters crash on the rocks below.

As it turned out, by the time I made it back home, both Macy and Duncan figured out dinner on their own. *This might be just what Tim and I need, a meal without the constant banter between the kids. A real conversation will do us both some good.* I should have known better. I couldn't complete a thought without Tim interrupting me with details involving the real estate office.

As he reached for a second roll, the other shoe dropped,

"Sarah, you are wrong about us being reduced to living in an apartment. I had not wanted to get into it earlier, but we will be finding another house to live in. I have yet another renter ready for this last, larger section of the house that we are now occupying once I get a few minor upgrades taken care of. They will need to start renting by early fall. Just think of the additional income we will be bringing in."

I tried my best to find the right moment to interject an idea that had lodged itself in my heart when I sat at the spring house earlier. I knew this was the time to let Tim know just how much I still wanted to live in the house on the river property. If I were ever going to bare my soul, it needed to happen now. *I'll tell him I can get behind the real estate office. I think I should just come out and ask if he will agree to start the much-needed clean-up and renovations on the old house so we can be in the warm by wintertime.*

He beat me to the opportunity to speak. "You know, Sarah, I talked to a banker friend of mine this morning. He had the idea that I should put some condominiums on the river property. You do get that people from Atlanta will pay good money for the view from that ridge? Let me tell you what I have in mind. Up at the head of the property, we will replace the trailer with an appealing gatehouse that serves as the real estate office. The first condominiums will sit right where the driveway now runs, so they capture that view of the water spilling over the rocks."

"Tim, are you saying that a line of condos will sit in front of the old house? You mean we will be looking at the backside of them from the house? I paused, trying to fathom what I was hearing.

He started again, "Sarah, let me just get all the cards on the table. I plan to tear down the old heap. We need the space for the new driveway and parking. Besides, we can build a brand-new house down at the far end of the property. I think it's time you get behind me on this and start thinking realistically. It's also time you walk away from that dead-end job of yours at the school. I could use your help in the real estate office. Don't even think for a moment we are going to discuss this all night. I've got to run and pick up something, then meet with some fellas to talk about these development plans. I am in no mood to hear you gripe about your precious ole house. Just button it and accept what I have said."

For the first time, I spent no time glossing over this kind of talk from Tim. *I can forget any ideas of my own. It's always Tim's plan.*

Without question, we were worlds apart. The river property served as a constant reminder of that sad reality. I did find myself hoping against hope that I could somehow just not say a word in response. *Maybe, in time, he will swing to yet some other brilliant idea.*

For the moment, I think he knew he had gone too far with me. He did toss one more quick promise my way. "Maybe if we can make enough from the sale of this place, I will try to start building us a house sooner than later. Once you get your mind on the house design, you will soon forget all about the old house. That should satisfy you." Of course, he did not wait long enough to find out any detail of my thoughts or feelings. The door slammed once again as he headed out.

What is driving you so? Why has it taken the events of today for me to realize just how few nights you are home for dinner? It often seems the moment you make it through the front door, you are ready to rush out again. Eventually, your yo-yo behavior collapses into several days of round-the-clock sleep. I stood at the kitchen sink, my brain on overload. I tried briefly to justify Tim's behavior. Then the questions started again. *Surely, he is not seeing another woman?* Somewhere in the depths of my being, I entertained, perhaps for the first time on any serious level, just how much my husband's behavior disturbed me.

There was nothing normal about the way Tim processed life daily. He bounced from one idea to another with an amazing amount of energy but rarely brought any of his plans to completion. Inevitably the dark days of retreating into the world of non-stop sleep took over. *What was I missing in this hodge-podge of erratic behavior?* Although nowhere near to looking the problem squarely in the eye, I took one step closer to being certain that Tim was in a crisis of some sort. It had not yet occurred to me that his nightmare would spill over into all of our waking moments.

I held to the belief for years that marriage should allow for the dreams of both husband and wife. At last, I came to terms with the error of my thinking. Tim couldn't consider any of my feelings and hopes for our well-being. I could either bury the pile-up of broken promises and pretend to be content or accept that each breach in my trust only served to drive the wedge deeper in our relationship. If I allowed full honesty, I would also acknowledge my fear that my husband was incapable of keeping his word. As I finished up the dinner dishes, I settled one truth. *Tim, your plans really do not revolve around me or the children.* I sensed the threat of the hairline cracks that compromised the foundation of our marriage. At the time, I had no clue how close I stood on the brink of making some decisions that would cause me to just about lose myself in the process.

§

The upgrades to the area of the house we still called home smelled of fresh paint when word came that the new renter needed to move in. Tim's whirlwind consumed our household. No down-time came with the car business nor the apartment renovations during real estate deals that seemed to close at record speed. Without forewarning, his endless energy, at last, crashed into days of sleep. He emerged out of his stupor, more convinced than ever that his plan was moving in the right direction. In the midst of all, there had been no more talk of condominiums or plans for building a new house. The extra rental income made life easier. Once again, I allowed myself a sliver of hope. *Could this possibly be the time when Tim will forego the idea of a new house and finally come through with a start on the renovations of the river house? After all, I have never wavered on how much I long to fix up every inch of the place. Oh, please, let's work to rescue the old jewel.*

§

Looking back, I now see in those days that it I took less conversation between Tim and me to be a good thing. On the rare occasion we did touch base, it seemed I always caved to his dreams. The dread of one more rental house steamrolled over me when I found out about the down-payment deposit on a place I had not yet seen. Dark and drab filled every room. I unpacked only the most essential boxes. The kids spent as much time away as possible.

Most women don't shut down in one fell swoop. Portions of our hearts stay pliable, determined to keep up appearances. Promises continue to be broken, decisions made by one instead of two. Many of us, particularly the strong ones, find ways to keep our fragile, tired relationships afloat rather than face another failure.

Survival came with smoke and mirrors. My raised-in-the-

South breeding adapted readily to the magic of surface miracles. A vase of flowers, the drape of linen under beautiful dishes on a well-set table could trick the eye into seeing enough lipstick and blush to make-believe my world a pretty place. With time, I realized this skill came at a price. My strength, mixed with eye appealing tricks to mask reality, made it possible for Tim to strike out on any tangent that interested him at any moment. I could be counted on to quickly clean up any negative consequences. I readily became the glue that held all the broken pieces together. Energy wasted on editing our reality drained me in unexpected ways. The consequences of my compromise slowly came into focus.

Although I was certain something would someday bring the craziness of our lives to a screeching halt, I seemed incapable of any real action. I drifted along with all of my husband's plans and schemes. It simply seemed easier not to question his decisions. I did not see a way to walk away from the nightmare. Eventually, the idea of a new trailer at the beautiful forest entrance of the driveway no longer repulsed me as much as it had when I first heard the idea. My mind went back to the first day I had turned down the long drive onto the property. I recalled the rusty, disheveled single-wide that sat on the riverside of the property. Getting rid of that eyesore proved the only step toward taking care of the land that Tim ever carried out. I worked to focus on the new and improved office space, telling myself over and over that it was not exactly the white-trash tin box of years back.

Still, I could not bring myself to share the details of our life with my mom and dad back in Mississippi. Excuses were always ready when it came to heading home during those years. I rarely called. *I can just hear the reaction from Mama and Aunt Beth Ann to the idea of any Baker having a trailer anywhere on their property. Of course, Uncle Jake would just roll his eyes and remind my parents that he had warned them that their late-in-life daughter readily marched to the beat of a very different drummer.* It was only with the thought of this assumed reaction that I thought of the entertaining story regarding how the old trailer happened to be sitting at the entrance of the long gravel drive to my beloved river property.

The strong, steely, red-headed female who had at one time run a moonshine distribution from the big house had the idea to add a single-wide at the head of the driveway. As the story goes, a local law enforcement officer pulled up, right as the trailer was hauled in place. He informed this landowner that trailers were not permitted in this section of town. I remain intrigued from the first time I heard the tale of this tenacious woman and her legendary response to the lawman's warning, coupled with the Smith and Wesson 38 she pulled from beneath her long skirt. "By God, Officer, why don't you stand back and watch me." *Maybe I need to find some of that spunk when it comes to dealing with my life. Now those words would shock my mama and aunt more so than me having a trailer on our property. Uncle Jake would, no doubt, get a good laugh.*

The idea of walking away from the classroom slipped into my life like a slow boil. Yes, Tim threw the thought in my face the night of our landmark blowup. The heat turned up ever so slightly when he came in with his first talk of me studying for my real estate license. Macy's second semester tuition payment cranked up the temperature well over the boiling point. Tim had come home well after midnight for the past two nights. The first time I feigned sleep and did not say a word. I cannot say the same for the second. My words met him in a rage. "What keeps you out so late, Tim? What's the great idea you've dreamed up this time since that always seems to be the case when you pull your string of late-nighters?"

Then he let loose. "Well, Sarah, we may as well face reality. Thankfully you got your real estate license. I need you to take over the office for me. I can't keep coming up with the tuition money if I am not out working some other angles."

"But I thought we were doing so well with the rental income that is coming in from all three apartments?"

"Get something straight. My ideas bring the money in, not your teaching salary." Before I had time to point out that he did not answer my question, he added, "With Christmas break coming up, it will be the ideal time not to go back."

I want to think I walked away from a profession that I loved to put my children's needs first. The thought of having two kids in college at the same time had its way of getting my attention. We supposedly had the second tuition money set aside. Instead, Tim insisted Macy apply for a student loan. Tim's version of our financial status shifted by the moment. None of his conclusions made sense. We lived in a rental. The purchase of one more house to turn into apartments, also the money for mobile home office…I could clearly take in the steady stream of cash being spent. It did not take long for the rental project to come to a standstill. Two perspective renters were up in arms. My paradigm shift started. *Against all odds, I've spent many of my days making whatever heap we were living in at the moment into a home. Maybe it is time I take over the management of the office? Tim and I might even see more of each other.* Unable to decide if more of my husband would be good or not, I at last found some comfort in one thought. *I will at least be on the river property during my working hours.*

§

Some days I took time to walk the property during my lunch breaks. Time's toll on the old house never failed to smack me in the face. The yard remained cluttered with used car parts. A new year came and went. The unkempt state of the beautiful river land paled in comparison to home life. After completing the last of the apartment rentals, Tim settled into a pattern of back-to-back highs and lows. Before what I now call the downhill-rush-to-disaster that I assumed would crumble our empire of slap-stick business adventures, I managed to close on a couple of sizable real estate sales. Within weeks after the influx of cash into the business, the state of the books that I kept at the office did not match reality. In one weekend of highs, the checks that were sent out in confidence to pay the current bills no longer cleared by the time they arrived at their intended destinations.

Chapter 7

A couple of years since the first dream caused me to wake with a jolt, another compelling night tale once again startled me from my sleep. Within moments of opening my eyes, I recalled similar details involving a walking tour of a small town. Two dear school teacher friends kept me company as I found myself enjoying the historic homes that stood proudly on different streets. My subconscious mind could not have populated this sleep adventure with better company. In real life, Alice and Mark remained two of my dearest connections from my time as a teacher in Mississippi. In this sequel, I found myself telling my friends about the first tour and my off-the-beaten-path find. Moments later the rutted, old side road appeared. We broke from the group at that point. As we made our way down the ridge, I spotted the same, large, two-story, rectangular house with the boarded windows and sagging porch over the lower entrance level. As we got closer, the three of us immediately put our heads together in an effort to figure out which board we could remove from one of the windows.

As I walked around the far side of the structure, I spotted yet another building, some distance away, very close to an old set of railroad tracks. Quickly losing interest in the first place, we all headed toward the new find. A weed eater would have been nice as prickly growth pulled at my clothing.

"Hey, what do you guys think? It looks like an old store to me."

Mark spoke up next as we forced our way around to what we concluded must be the front of the building. "I'm not so sure about that. Look at that small boarded window with the ledge running underneath. I suspect that's a window where some sort of business was conducted. Was there a post office or a depot around here?" As a history teacher, Mark had a knowledge base to draw from when he explained. "Many times, a general store served other aspects of community life. What do you think, Sarah?"

Nodding in agreement, I worked my way closer to the window. From the corner of my eye, I saw an old, green light attached precariously atop a vine-covered pole to the right of the building. "Look at that. We've just got to get a peek inside this place."

All three of us moved through the heavy growth till we stood directly in front of the window with the ledge that Mark had pointed out. Alice spoke first as she gestured toward the old window casing. "Look, right up there at the top right corner of that window. There's a small section of the board missing. Why don't you see if Mark can help you up?"

With both feet resting on the ledge, I pleaded with Mark to hold on to my legs the best he could as I got up on tiptoe to catch a glimpse through the opening. "Any one of these rotten boards could give away in a moment. Plus, you realize I am going to be looking into a building that is, more than likely, totally dark. Don't get your hopes up too much." No sooner had the words left my mouth than my body recoiled with shock. I almost fell backward in the process. "That light!" Grabbing for traction on the board's edging, I cocked my head slightly to the right toward the light that had, just moments before, caught my attention. "That same light," again nodding in the direction of the green fixture atop the vine-covered pole, "is also inside the building and it's on!"

Mark and Alice simultaneously cried in disbelief, "What do you mean it's on?"

Reacting to their response cost me my balance. I landed awkwardly, almost knocking Mark to the ground. Getting back on my feet, I worked to stammer a response. Time seemed suspended as my friends waited for some sort of explanation of what I just said to them. Alice watched me closely as I stared at the old light atop the pole. "What is it, Sarah? What did you see in there?"

"Guys, I know this makes no sense, but that same light fixture," pointing my hand in the direction of the vine-covered pole, "is in the building. This gets crazier. The inside of this building is bigger than the outside. For the brief moment I got to take in what I was seeing, it's as if I were looking down a corridor." Looks of total confusion met mine. "The light was on just like the lights in my house are on when I have turned the light switch on!"

Mark, always the logical one, spoke up first, "Sarah, that's impossible! Just look around. There's no electricity running to this old place."

"I did not say any of this made any sense. I'm just telling you that I know what I saw. There's more to this building than meets the eye. A green light fixture just like that one," as I pointed again at the nearby green fixture, "is inside that building, on a pole that is not covered with the thick dead vines from many seasons of growth. Nor does the light look as if it is about to fall off the pole. And, there's a bulb in it, and it's illuminated." Catching my breath in my hurried explanation, I added, "I cannot begin to tell you how any of what I have just said is possible. But one thing I know for sure, we've got to get inside this place."

I could sense hesitation in Alice as she shook her head negatively. Mark started examining the building more carefully. The front door had one board nailed across its upper half. Mark reached his hand up under the edge of the board and turned with a grin, "There's a door handle, and the door is not locked!" I laughed as I heard him mumbling the obvious question. "Why did the three of us not think to try the door first as opposed to scaling a rotting building?"

Alice may as well have saved her breath, for just as she started her warning to be careful, the old door creaked open as the faint glow of light started to show. Mark turned, flashed his best grin at the two of us, and said, "I would say ladies first. This time I think I should lead the way. I also suggest that whoever follows me should hold on to my jacket or pants leg. Then, whoever brings up the rear needs to do the same thing with the second person."

With one last mention of the absurdity of what we were doing, Alice offered to bring up the rear. Once we had all cleared the partially boarded doorway, we all stood speechless with arms interlocked for what seemed like an eternity as we stared at the scene in front of us. Disbelief and questioning showed on all of our faces. Just as I was about to break the silence and point out that I had not gone crazy after all, I slowly took in a scene just a short distance away that stopped me in my tracks. Holding on to both Mark and Alice a bit tighter, I whispered, "Do you guys see what I am seeing? The longer we stand here, the more I am taking in. Look at those two couples, each waiting in front of one of those windows. I think it is a post office. But, look over there. Do you see that paper listing a train schedule and ticket prices? Alice spoke in a hushed tone, "I know period clothing. These people belong in the 1920s. What have we stepped into?"

I stood in total amazement and then added, "I don't think these people have a clue we are standing here. The woman in that navy polka-dotted dress ought to be pointing excitedly at us this very moment, for she just turned in this direction. I could have sworn she looked right at us. You know we stand out in our jeans and jackets and winter scarves. Let's go closer and see if we can get their attention."

We moved slowly and quietly toward the four strangers. About to reach out toward the woman closest to me, Mark pulled my arm back. "Sarah, don't. I am not so sure we should make contact with these people. Let's think about all of this a bit more."

Even our breathing turned labored and calculated at this point. I, for one, did not know what to think. Mark broke the silence. "Look around this place. Sarah. You're right. It's much bigger on the inside than it seemed from the outside. However, the green light fixture on the pole is not the only thing that was outside and is now inside. See, there is that same window with the ledge. Remember, that was what made me jump to the conclusion the place must have been either a post office or ticket window of some sort. There's also a door beside it, just like the front door that opened so easily for us on the outside of this place. I know this does not sound like logical me, but I'd be willing to bet we're in some sort of time warp. It's just got to be some passage where time gets all mixed up or where one can travel from one time to another. I think I better repeat my warning. Hold on to each other. Be careful."

I stood in amazement as I thought more about Mark's conclusions regarding our location. All the while, my curiosity was pumping. I led us around the two couples and worked my way closer to the doorway that Mark had just pointed out. There was no old board tacked over the upper half of this door. The glass was intact. I had to get a look. *What else could I possibly see that could increase my already-heightened confusion?* With Mark and Alice peering over my shoulders, I took in the scene on the other side of the antique pane. A present-day office space with modern lighting, carpet, even a telephone on a credenza filled the room. I felt my eyebrows raise in astonishment as I took in the details of the article of clothing lying on the floor near the table. Alice regained her ability to talk first, "Look at that black jacket. You can even see the *Nike* logo right there!"

I woke suddenly, this time in a cold sweat. The details of the dream seemed hauntingly real. Within moments, I experienced the nagging feeling that I should recognize the location of these two old structures from my sleep story. Try as I might, I could not connect the setting of my night's adventure to any location in my real world.

I spent an equal amount of time mulling the fact that I now had dreamed two related tales. A sequel, I suppose. This second mystery unfolded as a continuation of the first dream from well over a year ago. *Have I ever continued a night tale before? If I have, I certainly don't remember.* Over the next week, I thought about the intriguing details more than not. I recalled that I had rather quickly let go of figuring out the location after the first dream. At that time, I could not seem to think about anything but the many problems that filled my marriage. After this second dream, I relished the thought of losing myself in this mystery. *It sure beats the heck out of dealing with the miserable reality that has somehow become my lot in life. I longed to live on the beautiful river property. Instead, here I am, working out of a mobile home, stuck in a job that does not interest me in the least. What really gets under my skin is the fact that I leave this amazing piece of property every day to drag myself home to a cramped, miserable apartment with more olive-green appliances.*

Single-handedly, I juggle the schedules of two, sometimes four children, who seem to be involved in every activity that kids can possibly participate in from middle school to college. Most days, I cannot find anything that resembles a spark of life in my marriage. Tim and I rarely see each other. He occasionally drops by the real estate office, only to shut himself off behind a door he cannot slam shut fast enough. When he does come out, the rush to leave always happens. He may as well record his parting words each time. They never change. "I don't know when I will be back tonight. I have a lot going on."

One day out from the mysterious dream, I concluded. *Figuring out the location of the second dream saga may provide me with the perfect out, at least mentally.* That same afternoon the repetitive door slammed in goodbye, coupled with the same song-and-dance words, caused a different sort of response to rise up in me. Even if my long-gone husband never actually heard it, I felt a newfound joy in venting my frustration. *Tim, don't let the door hit you in the backside. Stay gone, as long as you wish. In fact, the longer, the better. I can get my work done at the office, have time to walk around the property a couple of times as I unravel the mystery behind the many strange details of the old building with the green light fixture atop a vine-covered pole.* From that point on, I determined to hold sacred a bit of time each afternoon before heading back to the drudgery of my home life. During the carved out get-away, I did not think about Tim, the real-estate business, the classroom I left behind, or even the awful apartment that awaited me. Instead, I walked the land daily until I fell into sync with its heartbeat.

§

The ritualistic afternoon walk worked wonders to push aside, at least for a short time, the negative in my life. Soon I began to start my day in the same way. The relentless pace in the outdoors helped keep at bay the overwhelming fear that fought to take hold of my thoughts. Deep down, I knew it was only a matter of time before the inevitable collapse of our house of cards. This morning, I decided, for some reason, to try a different route to the office. Past the building supply yard, I took Oak Street down to the old lumber mill that adjoined our river property. The morning air, thick with fog, suggested an unseasonably hot day for early fall in the mountains.

In jeans, a loose-fitting cotton blouse, and a light jacket, I thought back to the funk that consumed me when I found only one pair of pants that did not require a great effort to squeeze into. *I've always heard that approaching fifty was sure to bring on the great fight with the waistline. Did that too have to plague me when the rest of my life proved a daily struggle? Truth be told, I've let my appearance go to pot. Maybe walking will do me some good in that department.* I took a deep breath, picked up my pace, vaguely aware of what felt like the energy that used to fill me as I took my daily runs around the old cemetery back in Mississippi. I jogged every afternoon after school back in those days. Something stirred in me that I had not felt in years. *Maybe it's time to look long and hard at myself. I can't change Tim. But can I do something different with my life? Is it possible it has taken me these many years to realize that happiness is my responsibility? I've waited on Tim day after endless day to serve up daily helpings of joy. Before Tim, I looked to Macy and Duncan's dad to give my life meaning. What happened to using my brain to figure out something that works for me?* At that very moment in my thinking, I spotted the abandoned railroad track that ran parallel to the street. *I know it's illegal to walk the tracks, but...*

My perspective of the surrounding area changed simply by

walking the tracks instead of the sidewalk along the street. Off to my right sat two small, abandoned houses. Looking ahead, I could see where the track split. Over to the left, an old, weather-greyed building looked close to losing the battle to years of growth that caused it to sag slightly under its weight. As I got more in line with the front of the structure, I spotted a green light fixture attached to a leaning pole, close to falling if not for the thick vines that held it in place.

A sudden chill passed over me. Early into my walk, I tied my jacket around my waist and rolled my long sleeves up as I broke a sweat in the morning that had warmed up quickly for early fall. Now I could not shake the bone-cold feeling. I knew with certainty I stood just outside the very building that still haunted my memory from my second mystery dream. The old green light fixture, the now partially boarded window with the ledge below it, the bottom half only showing beneath a boarded door just to the right of the window, all seemed to fit the second place that Mark, Alice, and I had stumbled upon in the sleep adventure that had unfolded in the intriguing sequel.

Unlike my dream, behind the board that covered the best part of the entrance, I could see the door stood slightly ajar. As I made my way through the briars, my mind raced with thoughts. *There is no way I will tumble into the building-within-the-building of my dream. Just calm down. I know good and well there will be no light inside the building.* Still, as I drew closer, not sure what to expect, my heart raced. *I'll need to crawl to get under this board. There's also a bit of light coming in through the broken board of the window. Maybe, I can get my head in and hope to see a bit of the inside. If I see a green light fixture atop a pole and people moving about, I may just pass out. What have I gotten myself into?*

As I wedged my shoulders under the board that blocked the full doorway opening, I let out my pent-up breath. I just had to go farther. As I stood up inside, the bit of sunlight showed the disturbed dust particles moving the air in front of me. It took a minute for my eyes to acclimate to the almost darkness that permeated the place. I accidentally kicked an empty bottle of some sort with my foot, then looked around. Over to my right, I saw what might have been an office. *Was that the remains of a window frame to the left of that doorway?* I struggled with details in the limited light. Although the doorway, the window frame, and the office area, in general, supported what I recalled from my dream, the space was small, nothing like the expanse that had met our eyes in my sleep world. In reality, the inside of this building was no larger than it appeared from the outside.

I stood in the quiet surroundings reveling for several minutes, in fascination with what my eyes took in. I knew I needed to leave. It was past time for me to open the office. My mind kicked into overdrive as I forced myself to head to work. *How could I have passed by this place time and time again and never really noticed it on any conscious level? The green light fixture atop the pole was admittedly lost in the overgrowth. Some level of awareness must have taken root in my subconscious for me to dream about it.* My thoughts filled with more questions. *No question, I never once entered that old building. So how did I dream about the inside with the accuracy regarding the window frame and office area in general?*

As I walked the slight ridge that led to the river property, I quickly began to look around for other signs that this was indeed the location of my second dream. The large, two-story building present in both dreams, the place I had assumed to be some sort of boarding house, could not be found in my line of sight. I got so wrapped up in "of course, there wouldn't be such a place" that I almost missed taking in the fact that the trail that led off from one side of the old lumber mill property across the main road, lined up perfectly with the abandoned pathway that I had taken twice in the sequel tales. Details began to fall into place. The home toured twice in its holiday glory had to be my old house on the river property. My dreams had given me the privilege of seeing it in its prime. *How could I not have made this connection earlier?*

I walked the rest of the distance to the office hand in hand with remembered details from the two dreams. My heart continued to race with excitement. The love of an abandoned site felt comfortably familiar. The old curiosity lay like a bed of buried hot coals. The spark now begged to be fanned into a fire.

§

I could not concentrate on work. Thoughts of the old building with the green light fixture on a nearby pole played in my head, making it nearly impossible to get even the simplest task completed. Later in the afternoon, Colin walked into the real estate office for the first time. I, of course, had no idea this total stranger would eventually play a major role in my life. Thinking back as I so often do, trying to remember every detail of our first meeting, I recall I had stepped outside the back office door, leaving it open. I needed to be aware of the phone ringing or anyone entering through the front. The distraction left by my morning walk remained with me. I enjoyed the gentle breeze and perfect blue sky of the early fall day. However, even the intriguing revelations of my walk to work could not squelch the nagging awareness that my husband remained trapped in a struggle that seemed impossible for me to really nail down. The more I watched his cyclical patterns of behavior unfold, and with some answers found through a local counselor, I began to suspect the classic symptoms of depression.

The manic days of round-the-clock running from one idea to another had continued to perplex me until the situation unfolded with Tim back in the early summer. Until that crisis surfaced in the light of day, I remained in awe of the spells of my husband's unstoppable energy. Then, almost like clockwork, his drive would come to a screeching halt as he hit the brick wall of fatigue and then collapsed into days of deep sleep. While he slept, I busied myself with the clean-up of whatever work he left in limbo for a now irritated client. I soon learned, on the fly, the details of how to close deals that Tim had been working. If I could keep up the real estate work, the weekly bills could be met. I did not know how to begin to find any real help for Tim. He simply refused to talk about what had happened. Even when asked questions about the juggling act of managing the business, Tim would grab another beer from the refrigerator and walk out the door. I no longer wondered how long it would take him to surface again. I called the crisis of the summer a wake-up call. Tim apparently saw it as one more opportunity to rush headfirst in his downhill journey.

The water crashing on the rocks below soothed my troubled mind to some degree. Hope for any meaningful relationship with Tim had blown out the window many weeks back. I had accepted that I would live through hell and back rather than face another divorce. Maybe I could at least hold the business together, take care of the kids and their needs to the best of my ability, and somehow manage to keep the river property from foreclosure. Why did this property seem to almost dare me to believe my life was not a total mess? Still caught up in the play of the white water breaking over the rocks below, I realized I was a bit too close to the edge of the steep cliff. At that moment, I heard his voice for the first time. "Hello! Anybody here?"

The question startled me. Moving back from the rocky ledge, I turned to see a tall man step out onto the stoop of the back door of the office. I rushed back toward the doorway in time to see him reach up with one hand to brush his hair back from his eyes. It might have been that movement that caused me to notice the strange ring first and his eyes second. The silver ring twisted into an unusual shape and looked as if it had to be a symbol of some sort rather than a mere decorative design. As his hand stopped midway in brushing back the sweep of thick silver hair, I took in the penetrating blue eyes that locked momentarily with the coppery brown depths of mine. Fate's first nudge was gentle and lasted only for a brief time. Our stammering efforts to speak to each other resulted in an extra-long handshake. In a deep-South accent, unfolding slowly like a rich bass note, he added, "Colin Michael Stewart."

With my hand still wrapped in this stranger's grasp, I responded, "Sarah Baker Bryant." Pausing briefly, hopefully not long enough for him to notice the sadness in my voice, I added my married name, "Novak." Then, I invited him into the office.

We talked for some time that afternoon. He talked freely about himself once we both got past the awkwardness of trying to speak at the same time. A subtle shyness showed throughout the conversation. An English professor at UNC-A, an extension of the University of North Carolina in nearby Asheville, Colin enjoyed exploring the mountains in this far west section of the state. "My parents live in Sylva. Most weekends I drive over to see them. Often, I am out roaming these mountains with my camera in hand. I want to think I am a fairly accomplished photographer. I always thought I would be a writer. Now, it seems I write stories with my pictures."

As the conversation flowed easily between us, I soon realized this most interesting man had no interest in buying property. The sharp cliff that jutted up from the Valley River below fascinated him. Colin interrupted my thoughts. "I promised myself the next time I was in the area, I would drive onto this river property. I had no idea the old house even existed until I pulled up the drive today. I took shots from the other side of the river on a couple of different occasions. With your permission, I would like to get some pictures. Do you mind if I explore the property on past the real estate office? I've just got to capture that house. I cannot begin to explain my fascination with old structures."

With that comment, I raised my eyebrows as a subtle smile spread across my face. Then embarrassment took over as my thoughts went inward. *How can I explain that the clutter just should not be around what had been a lovely home at one time? Can I get this stranger to understand that the house should have been restored many years back? I wish I could at least tell him I had done everything I could to take care of the place.* When I finally came out of my deep thoughts, I managed to say, "My husband, well, we're…"

I started to tell this total stranger that my marriage was falling apart. *Who am I kidding? "Falling" is not the correct word. In reality, my marriage totally collapsed earlier in the summer. Why is this so clear to me at this moment?*

I forced my thoughts back to Colin's interest in photography. I finally found some words. "My husband and I own the property." I then added quickly, "I have no objection, but I must confess that I hate what you will find as you head down to the old house. I'm afraid my husband…well, never mind. I just wish you could see it without the clutter. Pausing briefly, I then added, "I love this property. I still dream of saving the old house from total ruin."

My visitor said nothing for a brief time. Our shared silence seemed to carry far more weight than ought to be there when no words were exchanged.

Chapter 8

My sister Emily always reminds me of the date when she comes to visit. Just this morning, she announced. "Finn Pinkney Campbell, II, I can hardly believe my bull-headed brother has managed to stay hidden all this time. Here it is almost the end of December. Before you know it, 1906 will roll in."

I know I can't stay forever in this makeshift dwelling of tobosa grass hay. Papa, my brothers, and I sweated throughout the summer heat to cut, bale, and stack the winter feed here on our Cienega ranch in these rugged Chiricahua Mountains of Arizona. I'm awfully glad family members sneak in and out of my house of straw. I suspect the silence could be my undoing if one of them did not find a way to come visit regularly. Sometimes I wish we could talk about something else other than the Saturday night back in August that is sure to change my life forever. Truth be told, if it wasn't for all the rehashing, I'm not sure I would remember much about my actions from my recollections. Only the nightmares seem real enough. The sting of birdshot, old Doc Neely working on my neck and shoulder, those first hours after I came to back in the jail… all comes galloping in when sleep takes over.

Some thoughts stay lodged like a heavyweight well into my waking hours. *Even drunk, my skill with firearms enabled those shots to find their marks and leave two men dead and my boss seriously wounded. That damn Palace Bar gets me in trouble every time. I don't remember leaving the bar. My brother Charley claims I eventually rode my horse Bonita right out through the swinging saloon doors. They tell me there is no question that I fired my gun three times. Just because I don't remember anything much on my own does not make what happened go away. I know now that I wounded a man who I respect. According to Papa, I took down Constable Hernandez next. I've been told Hernandez just walked into the Palace because he heard the ruckus. I guess you could say he was in the wrong place at the wrong time. Now that lowdown Marshall Collins, hell, I wish I could remember shooting him. He always goes after any girl I take an interest in.*

My wounds, still rough to the touch, usually cause another thought to surface. *I am one lucky son-of-a-gun since that last lawman only fired one round of bird shot. Otherwise, I might not be here to think about the mess I've got myself into.* After they doctored me and moved me back to the jail, blurred pieces of the events rolled back in slowly. At that time, I figured I would hang. Even the wild-west law that tried to keep peace on the streets of Silver City, New Mexico, would not overlook two murders caused by shots fired for no reason other than drunkenness.

I guess I underestimated the strength of the Campbell blood that runs through my veins. Family takes care of family. I should have known my fate would not be left to the law. I've never been so glad to see my sister and brother as the night they busted me out. We all rode hard through the star-lit sky to make our way back to the ranch. When we finally came to a real stop in the wee hours of the morning light, Henry motioned to follow him. My sister reached out to embrace me quickly. My brother and I then walked the rest of the distance to the area of our land that forms a broad fan where two creeks join. At last, he hurried me down on my knees through an opening leading to a small bay that had been created in the middle of a large stack of hay bales. The entrance opened and closed quickly by simply moving one of the bundles.

Day after day, in the silence and monotony of this confining space proves a heavy burden. My thoughts never quite shut down. *What's taking so long to firm up the plans to get me to New York? Here it is almost Christmas. Henry says it might still be two weeks.*

A couple of weeks has now turned into another month. The confinement dredges up the burrowed-down-deep hard thoughts. *I am nothing but trouble waiting to happen. Pa and Ma are good folks. They raised all of us with a sense of right and wrong. I grew up on the stories and values of my Campbell ancestors Great Grandpa Angus, Great Grandma Mary, Grandpa Finn, and Grandma Maggie. Grandpa Finn did not always represent the best of the family. Still, decent behavior was expected from all of us. My pa, Joshua Angus Campbell, more than made up for the roughness of his father. No one questions his good character. Known as a fair man not to be reckoned with, he's the perfect combination for one who calls the Arizona Territory home. His name carries weight in these parts. He taught all of us boys the art of being a cowboy, also the whiskey distilling business, and, of course, how to use a gun. Shoot, my sisters can hold a candle to any one of us boys in any of these skills.*

I can almost hear him speaking now, "Son, whiskey, cattle, and horses are our livelihood. Guns are our survival. All need to be used wisely." Pa and Ma believe if they instill us with piety and insist on some education, that maybe, just maybe, we will learn from the past.

When Pa refers to the past, especially when talking to me, I always figure he has one name in mind, Finn Pinkney Campbell, his father, my grandfather. More times than not, I am certain my parents have regretted naming me after Grandpa Finn. Just about everybody I know has one consistent remark to share. "Finn, you are a carbon copy of your Grandpa Finn down to the name, the tall, dark-haired, Scotch-Irish good looks, and the quick temper and angry edge that seems to fill your every move."

The only difference I can figure is that, unlike my grandpa, I have no apparent reason for my anger. Any misery that I am caught up in is of my own making. I've heard all my years that Grandpa Finn died without ever being able to do one thing to change what bothered him in his heart. He lived out his years at odds with a world that kept him from the woman he loved. He, in turn, had taken his anger out on those nearest to him. *Now here I sit, 26 years old, thinking just how much I am like my namesake, without any real reason for the shared traits. I've got a lot of life in front of me. Why do I suspect I feel about as lost as Grandpa Finn did when he and his family first headed west?*

At sixteen years of age, Finn Campbell, the man who would later become my namesake grandfather, left western North Carolina with his family. My ma often told us his story to soften our reactions to his harsh behavior. Pa didn't care one bit for Ma taking up for the old coot. In Pa's opinion, there just was no excuse for a man to show his temper to everybody who crossed his path. No doubt Pa found it hard to forget how his Ma and all the siblings put up with the undercurrent of his father's unhappiness day after day.

Pa's frustration with Grandpa Finn is easy to recall. How could a man's life be consumed with some Indian girl who he never hoped to see again? Ma, on the other hand, was moved deeply by the story of her father-in-law's years in the North Carolina mountains, where he had first met the Cherokee girl named Maidena. I can easily remember my ma adding in Grandpa Finn's defense, "Kids, there's a lot more to Grandpa Finn's story than meets the eye. After all, your grandfather watched his family pull up the roots that had meant so much to all of his family. He also realized that the Cherokee he played with and lived so near to faced the loss of their land, their homes, and their way of life. From all that I have heard, your grandpa used to be a kind, sensitive young man. Too much injustice piled up at his feet at an early age. I cannot be angry with him over that fact. Yes, I do hate that his unhappiness made for a sad life for your grandmother and your father. As your grandpa lived out his years in the West and saw the white man continue to take from the Indians, I figure the constant reminder of what he had witnessed as a young man back in North Carolina got too much to shoulder. He never figured out a way to quieten the rage."

Shaking his head in frustration over the memories of his namesake, Finn recalled just how long it took him to take in that he was serving a sentence, even if not in a prison cell. The days piled up in a seemingly endless heap. *My careless actions cost the lives of others. By all rights, I should hang. I know this without question. I swear, this confinement tugs and works in me hour by hour. I can either ride it out or give myself up to the law.* Just when I think I can't take living like this another day, a family member shows up. Sometimes it's thoughts of Grandpa Finn that pull me through the nightmare. Ma still holds to her belief that my grandfather had a gentle heart buried somewhere deep inside him. *Is it possible I am capable of such?* As much as I can't wait to leave the confines of these hay bales, I do find myself dwelling on one concern most of the time. *What exactly will I do when the word comes that I am really heading to New York?*

Emily brought the news in early January. Plans came together for me to leave the land that I had always called home. I knew with certainty my life would change in ways I could never dream. *I am leaving behind my family, everyone I know. I figure I'll never see them again.* In the three days leading up to my departure, every family member found a way for a few moments with me. I hated seeing my mother cry. The first leg of the trip included long hours on horseback till we made it to Vicksburg, Mississippi. My brother Charley stayed with me until the first switch to a river barge. Travel sometimes happened in borrowed space in supply wagons, then back to horseback until I made it to New York.

As February 1906 comes to an end, I am feeling rather lost in a small bedroom off the pantry of one of the brownstones in the Upper-Westside. Thanks to a family connection, I can lay low in surroundings very different from the bay inside the stack of hay bales on our Cienega Ranch. I've just come back from meeting the man who will supply the papers with my new name, the ticket that will assure me passage on the steamer to South America, and also the contact just outside Rio de Janeiro, Brazil, who guarantees me work on a large cattle ranch. *Something in me wants to sneak back to those Chiricahua Mountains and hide out in hay bales the rest of my days. I know that is no way to live.* I don't find it easy to think about all it will take to *survive* as a wanted man.

Chapter 9

The nightmare of my life reached a new level of despair several months before the crisp fall day in September of 1999, when Colin first showed up on the river property. My daily walks on the river property provided the one self-care act that I allowed myself in those days. Somehow the endless steps around the various trails on the wooded acreage gave me the strength to continue putting one foot in front of the other in a marriage that failed miserably as a union of any sort. By mid-morning of this particular workday, I could hardly wait to finish the work on the closing that consumed me for days. The phone rang, interrupting my thoughts of my afternoon escape. "Sarah, it's Rick. Are you with a client?"

Rick, Tim's lead construction man in the apartment renovations, rarely called the office. "No, I am by myself. What's going on? Everything okay?"

The hesitancy seemed to hang in the air. Finally, Rick spoke again. "Sarah, Tim is in the hospital over in Franklin."

"What's happened? Was he hurt on the job? Tell me what is going on? And, why Franklin? I know nothing about a job over in Macon County." As soon as the words came out of my mouth, I realized the disconnect that others must pick up on between Tim and myself. Most of the time, the schedule that I pulled together for the office did not resemble reality. I collected my thoughts and added quickly, "I am closing the office and heading over there."

Rick added quickly, "Sarah, I think there is something you need to know before you walk into the hospital. "First, Tim is okay. I found him soon enough. I did not call an ambulance. I took him to Angel."

Concern moved over me. "Rick, whatever it is, you need to tell me." As I paused for Rick to answer, a long-buried thought pushed to the top of my memory. Tim had made a disturbing comment as he left the river house one day many years back. At the time, I was just taking in the fact he could not seem to focus on the much-needed renovations. His heavy words about blowing his brains out washed back in like water from a spillway. I needed to know. "Rick, did Tim try to kill himself?"

Again, Rick hesitated, "Sarah, I do not believe that was his direct intention." He paused yet one more time as if he needed to figure out how to say what needed to be said. He took a deep breath and then explained. "I take it you are not aware that Tim is struggling with drugs. I know you know he is on medication for depression. But he is messing with other drugs on top of those meds."

I could find no words for what seemed like an eternity. My brain slowly began to absorb what Rick shared. I could almost hear the subtle clicks in my thinking process, much like someone working the back and forth turns in an attempt to open a safe. Finally, I found my next question. "This has been going on for some time, hasn't it? This explains so much." I could not go further. I started to tremble as my thoughts turned inward. *I have so underestimated the nightmare. Managing depression is bad enough, but drug addiction on top of it? Is there any way Tim can survive the onslaught of this challenge?* I then asked one more question. "What makes you so sure he was not trying to kill himself?"

"Sarah, I knew the need for a fix was driving Tim early this morning as soon as we met up. After he left me several times to make phone calls from his truck, a man drove up. There was a brief exchange of some sort at the man's vehicle. Tim then walked around to the back entrance of the apartments we are working on over in Clay County. When he did not come back after about fifteen minutes, I decided to check on him. It did not take me long to locate him in the bathroom of that apartment on the lower level. Flat on his back on the floor, I feared he was close to unconsciousness or worse. He held four more pills in his hand. I told him I was going out to the truck to call 911. He managed a few words. "No, you drive me. Franklin, not Hunterstown." Sarah, I know now I probably should have called for an ambulance. Hell, I figured if he could talk, he would pull through. As I made the drive, I heard him mumble a weak explanation. "I think I've taken too many.""

Rick's haunting words played over and over in my brain. *Tim almost overdosed this morning.* The question that followed in my head simply had no easy answer. *Where do we go from here?*

Chapter 10

By the end of 1906, Finn knew he found his niche working for the large cattle plantation deep in the interior of the Brazilian state of Mato Grosso. *I suppose any enterprising young man could figure out a way to impress the investors back in New York who own this growing ranch. I'll do just that. My Portuguese gets better by the day. Shoot, I'll be negotiating deals for grazing and water rights with some of the neighboring landowners in no time. What have I got to lose? It's not the time to hold back. Plus, staying busy helps keep the memories tucked down out of sight and out of mind.*

§

The ranch stood several days' distance from the closest train station, then well over many hours of travel to any significant population. Even so, I understood the need to be careful regarding my identity. When I first arrived in South America, my newly acquired name didn't get much use. Ranch hands fell easily into the quietness of the long cattle rides, the desolate range. "Hey, cowboy" produced the needed response from any one of the ranch hands who accepted me without questions. Now my growing status as a rancher forces me to stay alert and careful. As I become more established in the region where names are used and questions are asked, there is never a time when I am not reminded of the stack of hay bales back in Arizona. *I'm fortunate. I know that.* Many people from the States have made their way to South America for all kinds of reasons. *Many have their secrets as I do.* My contact in New York cautioned me strongly about the need to keep my real name to myself. Most days, I manage. I have long accepted that it will never be natural to live as anyone else other than Finn Pinkney Campbell, II. Memories of my deeply rooted family tree remain strong even with the passing of the years.

The lie does rest easier with time. When I met Sarah Louisa San Juan, a guest at a dinner gathering of landowners in 1915, the transformation into Carl Martin, successful ranch manager, made for a good fit. I still longed to use my given name when we eventually married. As I grew in my respected leadership position among the ranchers, I wanted my parents to know and be proud of me as a Campbell. Nothing prepared me for the struggle that forced its way to the top on February 2, 1917, when Anna Isabella, our daughter, came into the world. It pained me to write her last name as Martin in all the family records except for the family Bible where the truth was written. The moment I held the tiny infant in my arms, the whisper rose in English. "You are first a Campbell, my little one. Never forget that. I will share the story someday."

§

Except for the need to use the Martin surname, Anna's birth seemed to smooth so many of the rough edges in my life. The nightmares that still push their way into the dark of night, calmed to some degree. Even the memories of the endless travel that left me with the deep loss of family dulled with the arrival of my own flesh and blood. *The disturbing thoughts of the two men I killed may never leave me, but I am determined to make a good life for this little girl.*

What surprises me the most is how much Anna is a living reminder of Grandpa Finn and my Great Granny Campbell. Something about her brown eyes that flicker with hints of copper, triggers the memory more often than not. As she gets older, her outspokenness speaks even more to these family ties. Many times, I've suspected this intriguing child has the second sight. Great Granny Campbell believed in such. I recall my father sharing the tales that had been passed down by Angus Campbell and his wife, Mary. Mary, or Great Granny Campbell, as my family called her, seemingly had this gift of inner sense. Like many Scotch Irish people, we held to our background rich in Druid lore. I knew my ancestors relocated from Northern Ireland with the hopes of finding religious freedom. I never quite understood any real difference between our religion and our lore.

For great grandmother, the second sight meant having more responsibility than others. She felt like she had no choice except to see the past, the present, and the future so she could help point the way. Great Granny Campbell knew that she and her husband, my great grandfather, should move to the mountains in North Carolina. It was also her insistence that caused the family to leave those same mountains and head west.

Anna also seemed to see and understand with a certainty far beyond her years. My perceptive daughter moves beyond the pretense of many people long before others have an inkling. Then there is her obsession with the two Indian women who cook for the family. I know she heads as often as she can to the large adobe kitchen located just behind the hacienda. She sits at the feet of these women as they work, listening to every word they say. No question, the native tales of mysterious gifts and abilities settle deep in my child.

§

Time seemed to stretch as far as the horizon as I made the long journey to the Catholic boarding school just out from Rio, where my thirteen-year-old Anna and twelve-year-old son William were enrolled. I headed straight toward the Mother Superior's office. The news would be hard on the children. We had to get back to the ranch immediately. The carriage trip to Rio De Janeiro had been long and hard, but I could not send one of the men on this task. I should have sent a letter earlier to the children about the complications of the birth of their youngest sibling. Instead, I had hoped against hope that my wife would be able to recover. Sarah did make it through childbirth but never regained her strength. Now I am here to share the sad news in person. My mood matched the long, dark wood of the covenant hallway. Admitted quickly into the Mother Superior's office, I was not prepared for the words that met me before I could even speak.

"I thought about contacting you, Mr. Martin. Thank God for this unexpected visit. I had about given up on finding a way to calm Anna down. Nothing I said convinced her that her over-active imagination needed to be reigned in."

Shocked and confused by these words, along with the heavy burden that would soon spill over to the two oldest, I answered back rather harshly. "What on earth are you talking about? What is the problem with my Anna?"

Mother Agnes then proceeded. "Several days back, your daughter was outside with the other children, playing and climbing along the brick wall that runs along the backside of the gardens. Several of the Sisters saw what happened. During her play, Anna suddenly started screaming uncontrollably. Sister Monica went to her side immediately. She at least got her to climb down off the wall. She indicated it took several minutes to calm your daughter enough to get anything out of her that made sense.

Finally, amid her hysterical sobbing, the Sister made out her words. "Papa will be here in the carriage soon. My mother has died."

The Mother Superior continued, "Nothing the Sisters said convinced your daughter that it was just her imagination playing a cruel trick on her. She kept insisting she saw you coming in the carriage. She's been inconsolable for the past several days. Even young William failed to talk any sense into her."

Anna would only say over and over, "But I saw it. You will see. He will come soon."

Perhaps Mother Agnes picked up on the expression on my face that confirmed Anna's story, or maybe she simply began to wonder why I had come to the convent, unannounced, during the middle of the school term. About to begin another sentence, she took in a deep breath, unable to hide the look of being visibly shaken, she asked. "It is true, isn't it, Sir? Your wife has died, hasn't she?" She continued in a low, hushed voice, "No doubt you've come in the carriage to get the children."

§

Anna rarely talked about what happened on the garden wall at the convent. When she did discuss the subject, it was only with me. I told her what little I remembered of the stories told to me about people who can see something that will happen in the future. In many ways, Anna's first vision ushered in responsibilities left undone in our home full of young children and no mother. My daughter rose to this task without hesitation. I regret the mound of work that falls on my eldest, even in a house with many servants. The months after Sarah's death unfolded with an empty awareness compounded by all I left behind in Arizona.

After the death of her mother and my eventual sharing most of the truth about my former life, my insightful daughter soon brought up the subject of going back to the states. She insisted we would indeed make the move. My internal struggle could find no peace. *Now I question whether I should have ever spoken of the family ties back in the states. How do I begin to tell my daughter that going home is not a possibility? What will she think when she finds out I am a wanted man? What will they all think when they find out Martin is not really their family name? When they take in that I am truly Finn Pinkney Campbell, II, wanted for double murders back in the Arizona Territory, will they ever forgive me?*

Chapter 11

Almost a year after Tim's near overdose, our relationship seemed permanently stuck in hopelessness. I knew my husband spent most of his days teetering on a cliff of depression mixed with drug abuse. The idea of counseling served as a band-aid that popped off with his next fix. Without question, the care of family and home rested squarely on my shoulders. We last saw his boys briefly around the Easter Break. Met them at a halfway point and visited for under an hour. The twins had not spent time in our home during the past year.

The children and I sensed the daily balancing act we all played out. Unexplained shortfalls of money continued. Meeting weekly payroll and accounts payable always proved to be a crapshoot. Macy knew student loans were a given if she wanted to continue in college. Although my bookkeeping showed us at least with our noses barely above water, the money that just disappeared into thin air without explanation left me scrambling weekly. Most nights, I did not see Tim. I no longer found it impossible to sleep when he did not come in at a decent hour. I even quit calling our friends with the age-old questions, "Have you guys seen Tim tonight? Do you have any clue where he might be?" By this point, I treasured sleep and the opportunity to forget what was so apparent in my life when awake.

Loneliness clawed at me, but I quickly learned to treasure the half-assed peace that surfaced with Tim's long absences from home. Hard work and long walks helped to force aside the sense of failure that threatened to flood back over my shaky self-esteem.

§

June seemed to drum up enough heat for the entire summer. By the middle of the month, temps resembled what we typically expected in August. Nighttime hours brought no relief. Tim walked in the door just as Duncan and I sat down for a late dinner. My thoughts focused on the window unit we added in the kitchen area. *That dilapidated air conditioner does not stand a chance against the heat from cooking. Now look who has waltzed in for a night of home life* Somehow, I buried what I wanted to say to Tim. Instead, I added, "I'll grab another plate. Do you want some sweet tea? I'd go heavy on the ice in this ...”

Tim's green eyes glared at my son. Then his words added to the already hot summer night. “Duncan, don't think you are going to sit around for the next couple of months. We need every cent we can scrape together if we are going to turn our money problems around.”

I watched the shock spread over my son's face. His reply was soft-spoken.” I worked last summer with you. I stayed on at school with my work study job at college until a couple of days ago. Just today, I have found work with...”

Again, an interruption, “Don't' talk back to me, young man!”

I feared the downward spiral that was sure to come. Thank God, Macy stayed at school for the summer. I hated to think of her reaction to the situation that brewed in our kitchen. The kids often witnessed Tim being verbal and heated over some detail of business that did not go his way. It was rare that he riled Duncan so openly.

After a moment, as I handed Tim his drink, I dared to intervene. “Let's get some dinner and hear the details of Duncan's new job.”

Tim grabbed the drink from me and slammed it onto the table as he added, “I need a beer, not your damn ice tea.” As he turned toward the refrigerator, he kicked his dining chair across the cramped space where it landed on its side. The chair hit with enough force that a vase of flowers bounced off the rolling cart at the end of the bank of cabinets. Glass shattered across the floor. With no effort to clean up the damage, he grabbed a beer and headed back out the front door. Duncan and I heard the truck start up. I feared the long summer storm that I saw brewing.

Duncan and I navigated wide paths around Tim. Whenever one of us carelessly stepped in the line of fire, Tim's anger and discontent lashed out in lightning swiftness. I often thought back on the days when my husband's world consisted of two extremes: highs of unbound energy and lows of endless sleep. I had, at the time, never really appreciated the reprieve that came to our household with my husband's downtime. Now Tim seemed bottled up somewhere in the middle ground with all of his rage. I unconsciously moved as much furniture out of his way as possible as I cleared items that he could throw in a moment. Duncan and I typically found excuses to leave if at all possible. At my recommendation, Macy came home only toward the end of the summer. She and Duncan packed their belongings for the fall semester but also helped me move absolute essentials over to the river property. I assured them I would be living in the real estate office the moment they headed back to school. I let go of the fear of yet another failed marriage. The deep need for peace won out.

§

By early December 1999, the upcoming new millennium created an air of expectancy far beyond the usual anticipation that filled the holiday season. Many people worried for a variety of reasons about what entering the new century might mean. My struggle focused on a whole slew of other challenges. After the tragedy just a month ago, I could not muster any concern over the Y2K situation. The overwhelming pain woven into the endless "what ifs" asked in my personal life made the festive season seem a mockery. Sadly, every day since the phone call that came mid-morning back on November 2, it seemed it was all I could do to plod through one day at a time.

Since the near overdose back two summers ago, Rick Dawson communicated regularly with me regarding business details and my concern regarding Tim's struggle with drug addiction piled on top of depression. To get a call from Tim's lead construction man during the middle of the morning on a workday was nothing unusual.

"Sarah, it's Rick. Are you with a client?" Always polite and never wanting to catch me at an inconvenient time during work, I did not pick up on any concern. Then he used my name once more. "Sarah, I found Tim's body out here at the Hanging Dog job. This time, I did not get to him soon enough." He paused long enough to realize no response had come from me. "I have already called the police. Although you never said a word, I know you guys have been separated since Macy and Duncan went back to college in late August. No matter, I knew you would want to be told by me first, not an officer in uniform. Also, your friend from school, Belinda Naples, should be there any minute. I called her. You don't need to be alone."

Finally, I spoke. "Rick, do you think it was drug-related?"

"Sarah, there was an empty bottle of Oxy lying next to him."

I forced the next question out. "Do you think it was suicide?"

"I do not know, Sarah. We need to wait on an autopsy to

know the cause of death."

Then the slow deep sobs started, coupled with the questioning, "Tim, why? Why? Would it have made any difference if I had stayed?"

§

The temperature, severe for an early December day, chilled me despite my layers of clothing. I made myself concentrate on an almost certain sale as I forced aside the sad mood that lingered as I forced myself to make a few more phone calls. *If I can stay focused, I can wrap this up.* As I plowed my way through the calls, I took a look at the calendar. *Now, find a time for the prospective buyers to come in. Remember, this deal pays the bills for the next several months on top of the double tuition payments that are due.* Just as I was writing the confirmation date and time into my calendar, I heard the vehicle pull up out front. *Oh no, I do not think I can face another client. I have had my fill of real estate for the day.* Instead, I longed to pull the blinds and curl up with a good book in the bedroom that had been Tim's office at one point.

My feeling of dread quickly changed to surprise as the front door opened. Colin shut the door quickly to keep out the cold. Thinking back on the first time I met Colin Stewart, I recalled how easily the talk flowed between us. Before I could speak, his deep melodious Southern drawl started, "It seems this place attracts redheads!"

"What on earth are you talking about?

"I turned up some interesting information while trying to find out something about the people who sold the property to Floyd Logan years back. It seems the owner was a redhead. Something in common there, wouldn't you say? Her reputation seems a bit more colorful than her hair. According to everyone I've talked with, she was a character and a half. Through a moonshine business right here on the property, she served all of Junaluska County well into the 1900s." The sheriff and his men seemed to turn a deaf ear to all of her operations.

I felt the smile rising in me. As I let this intriguing English professor continue with his tale of the former property owner, I allowed myself to take in the sad fact that I had not felt like smiling in a long, long time. Perhaps it was for that very reason that I did not bother to stop this still somewhat a stranger from telling the story that I already knew quite well. As he continued, my thoughts went to the envelope of pictures I found in my mailbox only weeks after I left Tim. The shots captured the lush summer growth of the trees that clung to the rocky cliff leading up from the river. The note had simply stated, "I thought you might enjoy this collection. It is one of my favorites from your property."

Then in late October, another envelope appeared at the front door of the office. This group themed around the beautiful fall colors on the property in all their glory. The note contained only one word: Colin.

Finally, I interrupted the story that obviously intrigued him. "Did you also discover that the red-headed Betsy Casey gave a big party once a year to honor the local law enforcement? Moonshine flowed freely at these events, and, in turn, the law found it easy to ignore the steady stream of people who made their way to the big house with their deliveries of white lightening or their coins to purchase a pint or a quart."

Colin sat down in the chair across from my desk. Without missing a beat, he went right to the topic of the parrot that had served to welcome the moonshine population to Betsy's front door. I then countered with the story of the man who lived right up the street across from this property in an area called Booger Holler. The man had first visited the property as a young boy, tagging alongside his father's whiskey run.

"Needless to say, the young boy was fascinated with the parrot that greeted him with *What'll it be? Quart or Pint?"* The boy visited the place year after year. He admitted he was even more intrigued with red-headed Mrs. Casey than the talkative parrot. Only as he became a man did he realize his father had perhaps made his regular whiskey run as much to see Mrs. Betsy as he had for the liquor itself."

Talk flowed freely between us. My eyes eventually took in the clock on the wall. *Have I really been sitting here swapping tales of a fiery redhead and her moonshine business for the past hour? Why does it feel like a burden has lifted off my chest?* Then in moments, the weight of guilt came rolling back over me. The question pushed into my thoughts once again. *Would it have saved Tim if we had not separated?*

Colin must have noticed the change in my mood. His tone

turned somber as he added, "I know." He paused as he caught the questioning look I gave him. "I know what you are going through. I read the local paper. I am very sorry. Do you want to talk more? Or shall I leave?"

I answered his question by jumping circles, sharing something I had not told him during our first visit. "I recently left the teaching profession. I, too, taught English."

Again, he kept the conversation going. "Why did you quit?"

"You know, I am not at all sure why. I guess you might say I got caught up in circumstances that led me to believe I had no choice."

"You don't sound as if your heart was in that decision. Am I right about that?"

"Oh, you are so right. If you don't mind, I now don't want to talk anymore about that subject either. I am where I am at present. I guess, I guess…." My voice faltered. I knew if I didn't stop, I would find myself in tears. Years back, I had become good at shifting the topic of my personal life. I did so again. "Are you native to North Carolina?"

"Yes, but we moved to Tupelo, Mississippi, when I was twelve years old. I lived there throughout my high school years, and eventually attended college at Mississippi State University, then went on to Auburn for my graduate work."

I looked at him with surprise. "I'm from Mississippi. Everyone in the Baker family went to Ole Miss except me. I'm not sure my parents and their siblings ever missed a Rebel football game. My father managed to give a small nod of approval to my decision to attend a small college in the Delta known for turning out the best teachers. He would have gone into shock if I had decided to attend Mississippi State. Hey, as an English professor, you'll find this bit of family trivia interesting. My grandfather and William Faulkner were at the University of Mississippi at the same time. Grandpa Baker worked at the University Pharmacy, right next to the post office where Faulkner had a job."

"Faulkner happens to be one of my favorites."

"I did my master's thesis on that genius. A friend of mine, also an English major, lived in Ripley. We spent weekends in Oxford and the Ripley area visiting all the old Faulkner haunts. The more I traipsed the world the intriguing writer made famous, the more engrossed I became."

Looking a bit quizzical, Colin asked, "Is there anything else we have in common?"

"Well, what's your family background? I'm a strange mixture of Spanish on my mother's side and Scotch Irish and Welsh on my father's. You couldn't possibly have that unusual mix."

"No, I don't. I do happen to be a tartan-wearing Scot through and through. There is something about that fiery expression in your eyes that should have told me that Scottish blood also runs in your veins."

We both fell silent. Our eyes locked much as they had that first day Colin stopped by the office. I began to feel much too aware of his piercing blue gaze. We both broke the connection by turning our heads down. Silence moved in like a thick cloud covering. Colin found his voice at last. "I didn't realize it was so late. I really need to head back to Asheville."

As I moved away from the desk to follow him to the door, I did manage to add, "Thanks for stopping by."

§

When my parents came to be with me and the kids after Tim's death, plans unfolded for Macy and Duncan to fly to Mississippi for Christmas break. I adamantly refused to go. The kids flew out on the 12th of December. Mama and Daddy both tried to get me to at least consider joining them later. I used the excuse of the real estate business. And, admittedly, our cash flow would come to a screeching halt if I had not jumped right back into that selling fray. Truthfully, I could still change my mind. With two days left in 1999, I had closed out enough deals to at least breathe for a few months. However, I knew I would never pick up that phone to catch a last-minute flight. I could not face the rest of the family with the questions that were sure to come about the cause of death. No question about the overdose of drugs. One question continued to haunt me. *Did you try to end your life, Tim? Or did your drug-induced bad judgment convince you to go after the ultimate high that unknowingly would be your last?* I had no desire to discuss that burning question with family.

Temperatures dropped considerably during the late afternoon. I talked myself out of my ritual walk around the property. Instead, I retreated into a book. By the time I could bring myself to put the good read down, the evening slipped into night. At the kitchen window, as a wolfed down the last of a tuna melt sandwich, I noticed the stars off in the distance. Deciding to brave what was sure to be a crisp, cold December night, I put on my walking shoes and grabbed my heavy coat. As soon as I stepped out the back door of the office, the canopy of skylight pulled me to it as I spotted the full moon. I had long enjoyed the Carolina moon in all of its phases. Although I knew that it was the same beacon my children would be seeing at Mom and Dad's place in Mississippi, this wonder of the night sky had the power to make me believe it was custom designed to light the skies of these breathtaking mountains.

The silvery, white glow bathed the area, showcasing the outline of trees, even the lay of the land surrounding the river. The previous day's snow glistened on the branches of the tall oaks. I moved closer to the cliff. I longed to see the moon's magic at play on the waters below. I stood for some time and watched the breathtaking scene of river water moving over the rocks below. Despite the sheer loveliness of the moment, my thoughts turned inward to the weighty matter of my life.

I gave up on love in my marriage many years back. I believed for several more years that I could live with any amount of misery, anything to avoid another failed marriage. Tim's actions eventually chipped away any shred of respect that I held for him. When I finally understood the sin against myself, the loss of all self-respect for tolerating his downright awful actions toward our family, I stepped away. Tim's death dissolved the marriage in one way. In other ways, the weight of our chaotic union still threatened to choke me even from his grave. Failure tried its best to own me. *Could I have forced you to get help? I know I tried. It just never seemed to work.*

As I continued my night walk around the property, the thoughts washed over me. When I first moved to the office, Tim hounded me day and night. The calls, the volcanic eruptions of anger, sometimes in front of clients, threatened me at every turn. My walks around the property seemed to unleash the built-up frustration. Tonight, the circle that enclosed the old English garden pulled me into its well-worn path. All the while, the full moon bathed me in its light. The sound of an owl met the night's silence. Crisp air, painfully cold as it rose from the waters below, caused me to tighten the hood around my head. Slowly I found peace.

The limbs of the giant oaks appeared to move in response to my thoughts. I reflected briefly on the trees created by the words of C.S. Lewis in his *Narnia Chronicles*. For the first time in a long time, I set aside the nagging fear of failure and loneliness. *The river property is mine to walk whenever I want. It is up to me to find happiness. Yes, it is also up to me to finish sending my kids through college.* As I made the turn to head back toward the office, I walked by the old house. *Is it possible to save you? Can I somehow turn your neglect around?* Fleetingly, I questioned whether my moonlight wisdom would be around in the light of tomorrow's day. As I turned my attention back to the fullness of the moon, I knew I would find a way to live life on my terms. Peace and purpose would be my companions.

Chapter 12

The details that unfolded on New Year's Eve of 1999 changed my life in ways I may never fully understand. Colin Stewart, the professor from UNC-A, walked to the property for his third visit. I admittedly found the man intriguing and intelligent. As he now stood in front of me holding a picture of the boarding house that I had now dreamed about twice, I moved several steps beyond intrigued. I took the picture from him. I stared in amazement at the familiar structure. I had never laid eyes on this structure in real life. Yes, I had dreamed about it, twice now, in what I refer to as my sequel dreams. *How is this possible?* After a few seconds, I decided to put the question out to Colin.

As a confused look spread across his face, he asked, "Sarah, what are you talking about?

"I may as well walk you through this bizarre tale a step at a time. But rather than freeze to death out here, let's go in. This is no short explanation. I will warn you. When you hear me out, you may very well think I am crazy."

Colin smiled as he reached to help with the grocery bags sitting in a tangled heap at the front entrance. As I put away the groceries, I asked, "Are you ready to hear what I have to say?"

"Not until you have answered a question. "From the looks of the groceries here, one would think you live here."

"Yes, one would think." I offered nothing more.

It did not take me long to get Colin's attention back to the details of my dream. Soon I made it to the part when I first came across the long, two-story building with the front porch across the lower level. I explained the resemblance to a boarding house. He reached for the picture that he had brought. He continued to study the picture even as I moved to the story of the second dream. As I paused to seek a reaction, he blurted out quickly, "Sarah, you mean you had no clue this place existed before I brought this picture today?"

"Now you are listening. I had no clue." He shook his head in disbelief. "You've got to hang with me through the explanation of this second dream. It is an understatement to say the story gets better. I worked my way through the details of the mysterious building with the green light fixture on a nearby pole. "I awoke from each dream certain I should be able to recognize the property on which my sleep adventures took place. No success initially. But then, some time back, I solved the mystery behind the location. That is another story unto itself."

"Sarah, I am close to speechless."

I continued, "Colin, I understand. The only piece to the puzzle that remained missing at that point on my walk when I spotted that green light, was this place." I reached over to take the picture from his hand as I shook my head in disbelief.

"This picture in my hand makes some sense of the dream. Obviously, there used to be a boarding house on the lumber mill property that joins my land. The new mystery is that the structure had been torn down long before I ever saw the building. That's what I mumbled about when you first showed me the picture. How could I possibly dream about something I have never actually seen?"

I could see confusion in his look. "Hey, instead of trying to explain this any further. Are you up for another walk? If you think all I have told you is fascinating, just wait till you see what I am about to show you."

I locked the door behind me as we stepped out into the cold air. Reminded of just how short the days seemed this time of year, I said, "Let's head down this trail by the springhouse. Then we will cross the street. We need to get a move on it, so we still have some time to explore in the evening light." As we continued our walk, I told him just how stunned I felt when I first saw the old green light fixture atop the vine-covered pole. "It was just like it had been in my dream when my friends and I found ourselves directly in front of the place." A look of bewilderment covered Colin's face.

He asked in a voice full of excitement. "You went inside, right? Don't tell me the inside of this place is also like it appeared in your dream."

"Oh, Colin, come on. It was a dream. Nothing more. I have to admit I was somewhat nervous as I entered the building initially. And, yes, I have been back several times. Every time there is only a dusty, old, deserted building waiting for me on the inside."

Colin stood for some time, taking in the details of the outside of the building. "I cannot believe I left my camera back at the bed and breakfast."

I motioned with my head toward the old door. "I could kick myself for not grabbing a flashlight. Ready to go in?"

Colin followed behind me closely. Upon entering the building, I experienced the strange, hopeful sensation that I had now felt every time I walked through its door. We stood there for some time, speculating on the details of my second dream. Then, this inquisitive man turned back toward the doorway and said, "I am heading back out. I want to walk around the building. I also want to see for myself where I think the boarding house would have been on the property across the street."

I had made my way to one of the back corners of the building, then turned to head back out with Colin. "That might not be possible since the ridge the board house was built on has..." I stopped my words midstream as I tripped on a slightly raised board and fell to one knee. Colin immediately turned back and reached out to help me up. The moment I grabbed his hand, my fingers touched the silver metal of his strange ring that had caught my attention the first time I saw him outside the back of the office. While using his helping hand to get back on my feet, I noticed the warmth pulsating from the silver ring. About to ask about the sensation, I experienced something that I can only describe as a slight ripple of movement.

For a brief moment, the whole ambience of the room seemed to change. Awkwardly aware of doing so, I held on to Colin's hand to steady myself. It did not take long to take in his tight grasp on my hand. *Did he notice my embarrassment?*

He spoke carefully. "Sarah, look around. We are no longer in the old building."

It seemed an eternity before my mind stopped racing in its effort to make some sense of what was going on. We were not inside, period. No question about it; we were standing outside with the night sky up above. In fact, the fullness of the moon showed clearly from the darkness. The way it lit up the surrounding area reminded me of my moonlight walk on the property just the night before. I knew then my brain struggled to make sense of some detail. I could not, however, bring the concern to the surface enough to talk.

Colin commented with a shaky voice as he pulled at the sleeve of his jacket to peek at his watch. "It's 5:38 p.m. That makes sense, according to when I think we left your office to head down here. No weird time loss or gain according to my faithful *Bulova.*

But now "here" isn't where we were, just minutes ago. Obviously, it is no longer evening. It is now well into the night. Sarah, we need to figure out where we are. Is there anything around here you recognize?"

Forcing my thoughts back to the scene around me, I began looking for any landmark that calmed the fear building up in me. The brilliant moon revealed, off in the distance, a cluster of buildings. But nothing I saw seemed quite right.

At that moment, I realized I still held on to Colin's hand. I thought briefly about the comfort and security that came with another person's touch. Then, reminded of the warm sensation I had felt from the silver ring, I purposefully touched the ring one more time. Cold silver met my finger.

Colin spoke softly and hesitantly. "Do you realize we may not even be in Hunterstown? Have you noticed those buildings are not showing any lights? I find that strange. Makes me wonder...." His thought dropped. Then he started again. "Look around. Do you spot anything you know?" Instead of answering, I still toyed with nagging questions about Colin's silver ring. *Had I imagined the earlier pulsating heat? I first felt it at the same moment as the slight ripple of movement. I know now it just had to be when we changed locations.*

I took a step back from Colin. We both began to walk in the direction of the cluster of buildings. Once again, I bumped my foot on something. It took my eyes just moments to take in the strip of railroad track. I stood in place, hoping some familiar landmark would come into focus. "Look, Colin, look at that building. I think it might be the depot here in Hunterstown. It is a far cry from the building I am referencing in modern times, but with a little imagination, I can convince myself it sits in the same location as our present-day depot."

"Sarah, at last, I see one dim light off around that side of your supposed depot. It's got me thinking. We've got to be some years back in time. After all, our modern tendency is to light up our public buildings. I cannot take in how quickly I have given over to the conclusions that your friend Mark came to in your second dream. If we are indeed somewhere in the past, I prefer we are in a town that is at least familiar to us." Pointing in the direction of a slight hill, he said, "Why don't we head up in that direction and see what we can find?"

Second thoughts filled my brain. "Hey, just hold on a bit.

What happens if we run into somebody? With this full moon and maybe more lights, if there really is a town up ahead, we could be in trouble. At least I am wearing this cape-style coat, which may pass for something that would have been worn years back. You, on the other hand..." My voice trailed off as reality sunk in. *Our situation is unbelievable. We are standing here wondering about which timeframe of history we are in presently.*

I forced myself back to the problem at hand. *Yes, my black cape with its lamb wool collar could pass. Colin's bright red, nylon Eddie Bauer jacket and jeans might get the attention of the wrong person.*

"Colin, I have to admit that I'm scared. I mean..." pausing to gather my thoughts. "What will happen if somebody questions us?"

His solemn tone was obvious. "Well, I'd be lying, Sarah, if I didn't admit that I am a bit worried. Perhaps even fearful. But we can't just stand here. If we are in Hunterstown, the town you live in, then it seems to me we have to try to get back to the old building with the green light fixture out front, although I suspect we will not see such a fixture if we are indeed in the past. We left our time from that building. It is my hope we can get back from the same location. We will never get back to that location if we just stand here. Let's veer around this way. His hand pointed toward the left. Maybe we will see something that makes us believe we are indeed in the same town, even if it is not the year 1999. Or is it 2000 already?" He looked at his watch once again. "Sarah, if the old building down from your property was a time warp, I think it is fair to say my watch is keeping time in a world we are no longer in. You know good and well it is not 5:45 in the evening where we stand at the moment. It is too deserted."

We both walked in silence for a bit. My mind kept going back to the fact that I had on many occasions entered the old building with the green light fixture out front. I knew Colin must be focused on whatever mystery his watch captured. *Why had nothing ever happened out of the usual the other times I had entered the old building? What if we make our way back to the location, but nothing happens? Or worse still, what if there are people inside?* Then I spoke. "Oh! Colin. What have I got us into? What if we never make it back to the world we know?"

Colin reached out and put his arm around me as we continued to walk. "Let's just stay close. Maybe your cape will distract attention from my clothing. We can hope no one is out this time of night. If we do see someone, we keep our heads down and talk to each other in hopes that no one interrupts our conversation."

As we crossed the street toward a building on our right, I took in the outline of the structure. A thought struggled to surface. My mind latched onto the fact that it was built right into the side of the hill. *There is something familiar about this place. It's on the tip of my brain.* Stopping to take in the scene better, it finally hit me. "Colin, it has to be the Ramsey building. It has always held a certain fascination for me. Typically, in the summer, its walls are covered with vegetation." Just as I was about to tell Colin what I had concluded, I spotted the path leading up a hill with the stonewall built alongside it.

"Hey, look up this way! This stone wall exists in our time. It runs right up the side street by Dickey's Hardware. I often cut through this way to avoid the stoplight in town."

It seemed to take forever to make our way up the hill to what I now assumed was Hunterstown. To my left, I could make out a faint outline of a good-sized building. It did not look familiar to anything that I knew about in the present. *Was there any structure that I had heard about in the town's history that once occupied this spot?* As we got closer, the obvious sign brought the stories of this place back into play in my memory. "Colin," pointing off to my right, "Look. It's the old hotel that sat here in the middle of town years back. I can never remember the name of it. I don't know the town's history enough to recall when it was torn down. It perhaps burned. I do know it drew a crowd back in the day when Hunterstown was a sought-after location for those who traveled by train from Asheville." We stood in silence as we took in the faint lights inside. Just up from the hotel, I could see the outlines of several more buildings. My heart raced. We just had to be looking at Hunterstown at some point back in time. "Maybe we should think about getting rooms for the night?" As soon as I gave voice to the thought, I shook my head in disbelief over what I had just said.

Colin spoke in a hushed tone as he stayed close by my side. "You are joking, right? Plus, I left most of my cash back at the bed and breakfast. Do you think they would take a credit card?" He went on to point out more details that were obviously coming into focus in his mind. "Sarah, no paved streets, only a couple of sparse lights, probably oil. I would say it has to be late 1800s, maybe right at the turn of the century."

My brain rushed to absorb what he had just said about the turn of the century. "Do you think there is a connection? You know, there are many beliefs about strange happenings tied to the turn of a century. Colin, as much as I am trying to sound lighthearted at the moment, I admit a chill just went up my spine as I mentioned the thought of the inexplicable. Do I sound a bit dramatic?"

"Sarah, I think 'a little dramatic' is an understatement for anything that has happened since we set foot in that building you took me to earlier in the day."

As I smiled and shook my head in agreement, I turned to the right.

"Where do you think you are going, Sarah? We can't go on into town. Look around. It's getting light. I'm not sure I want to take the risk of running into someone, not until I've figured out a way to get some clothes that don't stand out so much."

"I agree, Colin. We have got to think about every move we make. Even in present-day, *different* stands out on the streets of Hunterstown. I can only imagine the reaction if we are right about this being the late 1800s. I'm not even sure what I am so fearful of. I doubt seriously that some person from this time in the past is going to look at us and ask if we have traveled from the future. But I do suspect it is best if we remain very careful." I seemed to need a moment to take in what I just said. I finally spoke again. "If we don't go into town, where do we go?"

"I still think our best move is to get back to the building that jump started this adventure."

"Are you serious about getting back to the present? Boy, that sounded strange…"back to the present." How can you resist looking around just a bit?"

"Sarah, I never said I didn't want to look around. In fact, I keep bemoaning the fact I have stumbled back in time without a camera. And I call myself a photographer. For some reason, I am convinced we need to see if we can at least find that building with the green light fixture out front. I also would like to get back to your property. I cannot explain why I feel so strongly about doing these two steps first. Anyway, we probably stand a better chance of stealing some clothes around homesteads, not here in the middle of town."

"Just think. We could probably be hung for thievery back in these times. You know, just as that came out of my mouth, I could imagine my kids hearing this conversation. I am not sure which would shock them most, the thought of time travel or me stealing clothes."

We headed off cautiously to our left, hoping the light of day would come slowly on one hand, yet longing to see our surroundings a bit more. Colin broke our silence, "You know, I just found myself wondering if time will have passed when and if we make it back to the present day. Will my watch track the passing of time correctly? How is it possible? Even as I have accepted that we traveled back in time, I can make no sense of anything we are discussing. Most of us know so little about time. I wish I had read more of Einstein's works."

"Speaking of time, as I watch a new day dawning, I should be heading back to Asheville today. My, my…well, let's just leave that thought. I had already done the unthinkable when I refused to go to the New Year's Eve party and headed out this way to shoot some pictures of a new century unfolding. At most of the parties we attend together, she rarely notices whether I am there or not."

I realized as Colin spoke that I somehow assumed he was not married. The strange ring he wore on his left hand did not resemble any wedding band I had ever seen. I finally commented when I figured he had said his piece. "You have never mentioned any family except your parents. Do you have children?"

"Yes, I have a daughter from my first marriage. Listen, I think you know that I know you are not one to talk about your personal life. I am aware of those awkward moments in our conversations. Apparently, I am as guarded as you are. I hope you will understand if I change the subject. I've noticed before that you jump circles very easily. Please allow me to do the same."

Silence engulfed us. I toyed with the fact that Colin had known all too well that something was amiss in my personal life. The pain of my marriage to Tim, then his awful death, all came rolling back into my thoughts. At the mention of Colin's daughter, I soon moved to a state of heightened panic about my two children. *Yes, they are young adults, but what will they do if I can't get back to our time?* My brain ached with the uncertainty of our situation. *What if Mama calls from Mississippi? How long will it be before she officially starts to worry about why I am not answering her calls?*

The silence of being lost in my thoughts enabled me to hear the familiar sound of the river. The light of early morning had helped me get oriented as we sought our way from the town. Logically I agreed with Colin that we needed to get away from the town. Something in me wanted to hold on to the bits and pieces of Hunterstown that I recognized. Off in the distance, water lapped the river rocks. Comfort washed over my tired brain. Even if just for a moment, I could easily pretend I was out on an early morning walk around the river property listening to the familiar rhythm of water breaking over the hard, rocky surfaces. It made sense that the river should lead us to the old store Colin was intent on finding, the very place we had just hours before explored back in our present time. The thought of home, the river property itself, filled me with a sense of longing.

As comforting as the river sounds proved to be, I could not get my bearings. I knew I would not see the familiar silver bridge that connected town to the area of my river property. *But there is no sign of a bridge at all.* Thankfully, the pale pink of early sunrise showed its face slightly off in the east. Again, familiarity in nature proved to calm the panic that tried its best to rise in me.

Colin stepped out ahead of me just a bit when we first hit that awkward point in our conversation about his personal life. I noticed his tall form stopped quickly in the early shadows. As I caught up to him, he put his arm around my shoulder, then dropped his head, hiding behind me as much as possible. I started to ask what was going on. Then I noticed the figure heading in our direction. As the man got nearer, I feared he would hear the sound of my heart beating wildly. I, too, dropped my head and talked in a whisper to Colin in hopes the man would walk right on past us.

"You folks may as well save some walking. That ferry ain't running first thing this morning. They say it will take most of the day to get her repaired." He continued walking as he talked, moving at a fast clip. He turned back to us one more time as his voice trailed off in the distance. "I'm heading on back around the other way to the ford. Guess that river water will be freezing, but I've just got to get to the other side."

Colin and I were speechless for just a moment. As we moved forward at a safe distance behind the man out in front of us, his thoughts surfaced. "Sarah, we have to find that ford. We best follow him. We need to at least understand the general direction."

"Colin, the man that walked by us and spoke, belongs to the past. Are you taking all of this in?" I could not begin to answer how or why we had somehow stumbled into another time period, but the voice of another human brought that reality up close and personal. "Like you, I think we will feel a lot better if we can at least find the building where all of this started."

"Sarah, what if the old store or post office, or whatever you think that building was…well, what if it did not yet exist at this point in time? There certainly will not be an electric light out to the side of it. At best, we can hope for one of the faint oil lights we saw in town. I just hope we can find the location."

"Let's worry about finding the ford first."

Colin's next words surprised me. "Look, hanging over there on that fence post. There's an old blanket. Sarah, I'm going for it. I stand out like a sore thumb in these clothes, and it's getting lighter by the moment." The moment he grabbed the cover-up, he added. "This thing stinks. No wonder it was left out for the night. He then laughed before adding, "Maybe it will help to steer people away from us."

No sooner had Colin reluctantly wrapped the filthy wool around him, he got right back on track with more questions. "Do you know anything about a ford anywhere near your property?

"Well, the legend of the leech…" my mind trailed off in thought for a few moments. Knowing how much you have explored the property around my place from across the Valley River, you are probably aware of that second bend in the river. There is a spine of rocks, just noticeable beneath the rushing water. It runs pretty much from one bank to the other. I assume the path of the river has perhaps altered over time from natural causes and man's interference, but is that location possibly the ford? If so, it leads right up to the backside of my property and the TVA land that surrounds my place. That would be convenient, I suppose. I have to admit I am not looking forward to the cold river water lapping my feet as we attempt to cross. Never mind that we could easily fall into the river."

We pushed along the path. "Look, Colin. The man who spoke to us, can you see him? He is crossing over the river on foot. From here, it looks like he is walking on water. We've got to do the same if we are ever to get back to my property."

"Does that land on the other side look familiar to you?"

Taking in the property across the way, still in the early morning light, my heart plummeted. *Was I confused? Is that the land that surrounds my property and the old lumber mill? The woods are so thick with growth, even in winter.* I finally found my voice. "Colin, let's just cross this river."

The rocky path of the ford was treacherous in many ways. Thankfully both Colin and I wore shoes with decent tread. The ice-cold water forced us ahead. There was no sense in thinking about the danger. The quicker we could get across, the better.

The deep shivers started well before I reached the shore. As soon as we stepped out of the water, Colin pulled me into the warmth of his body as he wrapped the smelly blanket around us. "We've got to get to the cover of that stand of growth there. Your shoes are soaked. Let's get you out of them. We need to use each other and the warmth of this wool cover to keep from freezing."

§

The stand of evergreen and rhododendron provided just the shelter we needed. Colin laid the wool blanket out on the ground, then sat down. His long legs stretched out the length, with wet hiking shoes resting on the ground. "Now, Sarah, hand me your cape first. Then sit down here beside me. I will arch my legs enough for you to tuck your legs up under mine. Try to get your cold feet wedged between my ankles so we can stop your shivers." A few minutes later, I was wrapping the remaining portion of the smelly wool around both of our lower extremities. He then basically tucked me under his arm as he used his free arm to wrap us both as tight as he could in my cape. I resisted for a few minutes but soon gave over to the close warmth that started to penetrate my cold body. My head nestled under Colin's chin.

"Sarah, for once since we started this adventure, I know exactly what I want to do next. There is no question about it; I need some breakfast. I hoped you were eventually going to cook me some dinner last night with all those groceries you had at your office."

"Now you have me thinking about all the possible meals with those ingredients. Funny, I had not thought about food, but now I'm sure to start. I wonder if they would hang us twice? Once for stealing clothing and again for stealing food." We both laughed. Fatigue and worried thoughts of our next move overtook me. My head fell into Colin's chest as my tired mind gave over to sleep.

Colin spoke again before I totally gave over to the much-needed rest. "Sarah, have you thought about the possibility that your property may be nothing like you know it, now that we are back in time? We might be walking into nothing but woods. We'll need to find food eventually."

I could not take on one more worry at the moment. Sleep overtook me.

§

"Now, chile, you just listen to ole Sadie. You know I know what I'm doing when it comes to babies. You got no business out here planning to cross that river to get into town. Look at you. Back hurtin' and achin' a tad. I'm telling you that's a sure sign baby is on its way. If that ain't enough a reason not to go traipsin' round, you know that water of yours done broke late yesterday. I'm here to say you be asking for trouble. It's a good thing I just happened out here on the porch. Lord knows, you need some sense talked into that stubborn head of yours."

Her wild, dark eyes filled with fear as she replied, "But I've got to get some goods from town if I'm about to have my baby. I also want to be with Charles. I need to get him to come home." Her voice trailed off as she tried to ignore the sort of sick feeling that had been rearing its head for the past hour. It reminded her of the many mornings she had lost every bite she tried to put in her mouth.

"Now, Savannah, you just gotta' listen to me. Ole Mistah Pierce ain't bout to let Charles out of his sight until the end of the workday. He could care less if one more Indian baby make it into this world without his daddy being home. Why it being the day after New Year's, Charles be having two time the work to do. You know for certain, that boss man of his be determined to make twice as much money this year as he did last. Besides, you just be grateful Charles even got a job. Not too many will hire you folks. When it comes to you Injuns and us Coloreds, we better count our blessings that one of us has regular work. You just never mind Charles getting home for the birthin' of his baby."

The awful feeling of being sick to her stomach refused to leave. Still, she argued. "But, Miss Sadie, you seem to be forgetting that I ain't had no real pains yet. I know for a fact there is going to be plenty of that for a long time before this baby is ready to be born. I can make it into town. Anyways, it's still early in the day. I promise I'll be careful. If Charles has to put in his day, I'll just wait it out in the back of the store. We can head back home together."

"Suit yourself, but ole' Sadie knows best. That baby be on its way."

§

A blood-curdling cry broke through my sleep. It only took one look at Colin to realize he, too, had given over to getting some rest. I motioned with my fingers to my lips in a shushing manner and mouthed as quietly as possible, "Did you hear that?"

As he nodded his head, he whispered, "I think it may be what woke me up."

Pulling my legs out from the warmth of Colin's long frame, I found my shoes and socks. They were by no means dry, but at least I had warmed up. As we both got to our feet and Colin once again wrapped himself in the old wool blanket, we moved from the shelter of the thick woods. At that same moment, we heard the cry a second time. "That sounded like a woman in agony. We've got to find out what's going on."

Colin and I moved quickly through the heavy, old growth. As we made our way through the rough forest, the agonizing cries continued. I know that I never thought once about the danger we were possibly moving toward. At the moment, it seemed we simply had no choice except to find the source of what we had heard. I sensed we were close.

Collin shouted out, "We've come to help. Where are you?"

Even though the response did not come immediately, we continued to move in the same direction. The sobs seemed closer. Then a muffled response came within moments. "Over here."

Colin reached forward to pull back the twisted limbs blocking our way to the mysterious voice. The dark, shiny black hair caught my attention first as I moved forward through the evergreen growth. My instincts kicked in quickly as I spotted the young woman down on the ground with her arms stretched behind for support. Her eyes, filled with anguish, locked with mine. I recognized her reaction to pain coupled with her short intakes of breath. The mound of her belly left no question. I knew with certainty she was in the throes of labor.

Without hesitation, I moved to kneel down by her, looking full into the almost black depths of her eyes. Her high cheekbones reminded me of a Cherokee woman that I knew back in my time. As I looked down at her, large and round with life, the memory of childbirth forced me to focus on the urgency of the moment. Her eyes met mine with a plea for help as a low moan started to escape her mouth. I knew a contraction was starting. My mind raced to the now old memories of labor and all I had learned from those Lamaze classes taken so many years back.

"You are doing fine." I questioned quickly. "Is this your first?" As she quickly nodded yes, I added. "I know it hurts. Just ride it out. It's like going up to the top of the hill with the pain. But, then, you start coming down that hill. Come on now. I know you can make it." I could still see panic starting to rise in her. I kept talking. "That's good. Try taking deeper breaths. You will be down at the bottom of that pain in no time." As I watched her body relax, I decided to talk her through what was sure to come. "Another contraction will come. Just try to get some rest in between."

Colin moved behind the young woman to be out of the way. I looked directly at him. "Figure out a way to keep up with the time between contractions. It will help me to figure out what to do next." I then reached over and rubbed her forehead gently but briefly. I recalled how I had not wanted anyone touching me too much. I then said, "My name is Sarah." Pointing back behind her, I added, "This is my friend Colin. What is your name?"

Ever so softly, she replied, "Savannah."

"Savannah, just rest for a bit." In the quietness of the woods, my mind went back again to the birth of Macy and Duncan. With both, I had gone into labor hard and fast. I did not have the luxury of resting very much between contractions. Duncan's labor had started as I walked through the woods that late fall day. I recalled the fear that consumed me when I thought I may not make it back to the house before I gave birth alone in the woods. With that thought, I noticed Savannah start to lower her head and arch her back. *Is it possible this baby will be born right here in the middle of what certainly seems like nowhere to me? Well, at least you are not alone, my dear.* Then I spoke, "Savannah, the next contraction is starting. Let's try those slow, deep breaths again. And, Colin, can you tell me the time between contractions?"

Colin worked to conceal his watch beneath the sleeve of his red jacket. I figured he certainly did not want Savannah to see the strange device. "Just under five minutes, Sarah."

I waited for this young woman, laying on the cold ground in front of me, to ride out the contraction. As soon as I could see her body relax a bit, I decided I better ask some questions. Reaching up to move a strand of her dark, black hair from her face, I started. "Savannah, we need to get you out of these woods before you get any closer to having your baby. Can you tell us where to take you? Colin will carry you." I looked up pleadingly at this man who had burst fully in so many ways through the front door of my world. He nodded in affirmation. "We will work around and through the contractions. Just, please, tell us where to take you."

Again, almost in a whisper, she answered. "Just get me to Miss Sadie's."

Lost for the moment in a state of worry over the fact that we were in a time when we did not know people by name nor where they lived, Colin startled me when he spoke and began to point straight ahead. "Now, if I remember correctly, Miss Sadie lives right up this way? I see a trail up that way. Can we just follow that way?" I had never been so grateful for Colin's quick mind.

Savannah could only nod her head in response. Signs of yet another contraction had started. Colin spoke quickly. "A little under four minutes this time."

"Remember what I told you before. You've got to get up the hill of pain. You know it will get worse as you make the climb. But then you start back down. Try to relax. Here, watch me breathe. Try to do just what I am doing."

It surprised me that after so many years, I retained the ability to move from the quick short breaths to the deep, slow breathing patterns that would help me get this woman through her labor. Even as she made her way through the downside of the contraction, my mind raced ahead to the fact we needed to get her some real help. I reached up to move a strand of curly red hair away from my eyes as

Savannah showed signs of relaxing. I knew exactly what needed to happen next. "Colin, we have to move her."

"Savannah, Colin is about to lift you into his arms. Relax as much as you can. We will see if you can handle being carried as the next contraction comes on." For a brief moment, when I grabbed the big blanket that had been hiding Colin's clothes, I saw the young Cherokee give us both a strange look. But just as quickly as I had become aware that she perhaps had questions about the two of us, she seemed to quickly dismiss whatever thought had crossed her mind. She simply gave over to being carried by a stranger.

As we climbed a slight ridge, I still could see nothing but the winter woods in front of me. Something about the lay of the land seemed familiar, but I had trouble focusing on anything except Savannah. It seemed we had barely been on the move when I saw the signs of yet another contraction. "Am I right? This one has come on pretty quickly."

There was no doubt that the movement and being held had made the recent contraction very difficult. Colin moved ahead at the fastest clip possible. I dropped behind just briefly. I found myself looking at the man moving in front of me. *What do I really know about this man? I've known him for such a short time.* I did not have much time to dwell on this thought, for he yelled back at me. "Should we stop this time?" I knew then the contractions were hammering in hard and heavy, maybe two to three minutes apart. As I moved around to the front of the two, I could see Savannah writhing in pain.

"Yes, we have got to let her recover a bit as this labor picks up even more." Also, I could now clearly see the trail had veered to the left. There is a stand of rhododendrons up ahead of us. Let's put this blanket on the ground here. Let her down gently."

Savannah reached out and grabbed my hand with incredible strength. I knew we had not stopped a moment too soon. As I worked with her through the strong contraction, I noticed Colin down on his knees. Eventually, when the grip on my hand began to relax, I took in that he used his cupped hands to drink from a nearby spring. *God knows, I could do with some water myself.* When he looked up and saw me watching, he smiled and added. "Here, take a brief break." He motioned me over as he moved toward Savannah. "We need to keep moving toward Miss Sadie's."

At that same moment, he reached down to pick up Savannah once again. He looked down at the bundle he carried. "You may need to help me with directions at this point for the trail forks."

I first brought a small handful of water to Savannah as Colin had her in his arms. I dabbed a small amount on her dry lips and used the rest to cool her forehead and push the strands of dark hair back. Fatigue showed on her beautiful face. Her black eyes opened only for a moment as she nodded toward the ground. "Take the trail by the second springhead."

Confusion spread across both of our faces. It only took a moment to spot the second springhead and the right fork in the trail. "You guys get moving. I need to splash some water on my face and get a quick drink. I will run to catch up." As the icy cold water renewed my energy, it took only a moment for the thought to rush over my brain like a tidal wave. *We are on my property. I have stood on this spot many times. This is where the springhouse will someday be built.*

The sound of Colin's plea brought me out of my revelry. "Sarah, another contraction is starting. I say we try to keep moving. It has only been a couple of minutes since the last one."

I fell into stride alongside Colin and immediately started to coach Savannah. No doubt, being on the move did not help the situation. *Are we running out of time? I sure would like to get to Miss Sadie's before she starts pushing.* The drink from the spring worked wonders to clear my head. I allowed my worry to land on the potential problem we faced if she had to deliver here on the ground. Then my brain grabbed at a thought that came out of nowhere. *What are the chances we would find a passageway through time and, then, stumble upon this young Cherokee woman in the throes of labor?* I felt certain that Colin and I were caught up in something too complicated for easy understanding.

The trail broadened, then veered off to the right. Again, Colin's ability to think under pressure amazed me. "Savannah, we are getting near Miss Sadie's, right?"

Once more, she raised her head that rested against his chest. "Cross the road. You'll see another trail…" Her voice caught before she could finish her thought. Another contraction moved in. The closeness to the last one alarmed me. Very little time to recover. I tried to wrap my head around the plan for delivery on the cold ground of an open trail. In the meantime, we moved forward.

Colin's voice provided the relief we all hoped for. "Well, here we are at last." A small cabin peaked out just around the bend. In the time it took us to get to cover the distance, another contraction had rolled in. At the same moment, a white-haired, black woman came from the other side of the house. She carried a load of wood in her arms. Her course, curly hair was pinned back in a bun, with a wisp or two loose around her face. The high neck and bottom edges of a faded, floral-print dress showed beneath a dark, heavy coat. The details our brains latch onto amid so many urgent happenings. *That has got to be a man's coat. The shoulders are disproportionately large, and the sleeves are cuffed several times.*

Deep lines formed across her forehead as her dark eyes took in the sight of Savannah being carried. Feeling a little uncomfortable in her presence, I nervously added in explanation, "We found her just up from the ferry crossing."

The piercing eyes seemed to do some quick assessing as she neared Savannah. She placed her sure hands over the distended belly that tightened again under her knowing touch. While moving up a set of rickety steps, she motioned us forward with a cock of her head. I had a sudden thought pass over me. *If I am not mistaken, this woman has just managed a brief moment to give both of us the "once over." Do I dare think about what conclusions she just came to?*

As she opened the door, she mumbled. "Chile, Miss Sadie done told you got no business traipsing off to town today. Anyone with a grain of sense could see you be giving birth before dark."

§

The moment I entered the warmth of the cabin, I felt exhaustion mingle with the relief of knowing that Savannah was at last where she wanted to give birth. As I stepped inside, my tired brain kicked into overdrive. *We are from the 20th century. No, now the 21st century. Should we be running off toward the woods at the moment, not stepping into someone's home?* The smell of what had to be apples cooking on the wood stove overrode any good sense. As Colin, with Savannah in his arms, followed Miss Sadie toward the bed, I found myself staying close by the warm stove filling one corner of the small room that served as a kitchen, a living space, and a bedroom all in one.

Within moments of propping a pillow and a rolled blanket behind Savannah's back, Miss Sadie unbuttoned her big coat, handed it to Colin as she shooed him out the door with instructions. "Lordy mercy, you need to put that on. Grab that big pot sitting on the other side of the stove and head on outside." As she leaned over to grab the old wool blanket commandeered from the fence post earlier in the morning, she added, "Throw this filthy thing out on the front porch to air out some. There's a well out back. We be needing plenty of water keeping warm on that stove. Once you got that, you may as well bring in more firewood. I guess your woman can help me with this birthin' and keep my stewed apples stirred. Those apples be some of the last ones in my root cellar. I sure would hate to see them go to scorching.

I smiled and found my eyebrows arching upward at the reference to "Colin's woman." This man, who stumbled into my world as surely as we found our way into this timeframe, looked back in my direction as he made his way to the door. No question, an impish grin spread across his face as he headed out.

My amusement lasted only briefly. *Why had Miss Sadie insisted Colin put on her big coat? Am I overthinking this? Did his jacket not look like it would keep him warm against the cold day? Or…*

I knew I needed to just throw myself into helping. I reached to unbutton my cape as the stove's warmth worked its magic. Miss Sadie once again gave me a questioning look. Thankfully Savannah's next words shifted our attention.

"Oh! Miss Sadie." We both turned in her direction. "I feel like I'm 'bout to push this baby right out of me." Savannah arched her back away from the pillow as another strong contraction took over. Every fiber of her being seemed to give over to the urge to give birth.

Miss Sadie's stern voice took over. "Now, child, no pushing' just yet. Give me a minute to see if you be ready."

"But I can't stop myself."

Before I had a moment to question whether I should throw myself into this situation, I spoke sternly as I locked my look on the dark eyes in front of me. "Yes, you can! Follow my breathing again, Savannah." I began the pattern of short, quick breaths, following each by quickly blowing the air out. I stopped when I saw she had caught on enough to allow me to add, "Keep on till you get past that urge to push." Savannah and I continued together.

Miss Sadie moved with experience as soon as the opportunity presented itself to determine just how far along Savannah was in the birthing process. Just when I managed to let go of some of the worry about my presence in this cabin, the knowing eyes looked directly at me and laid in with an unspoken question that I knew would eventually come out. The awkwardness of the moment made me feel as if I needed to say something. "I can help get her past the urge to push till you give the word." Sadie simply nodded. She then brought me into the ease of working with her. My experience kicked in. Miss Sadie moved like a graceful swan in her familiar world of assisting with childbirth. *The questions may start later. For the time being, I am not her priority.*

A draft of cold winter air rushed in as the front door opened. I continued to coach Savannah through another contraction. Miss Sadie directed Colin to the stove with the water as she shifted the apples to the top and added, "You see that wash basin hanging there? Put it here. I need a bit of fresh water in it. Then get back out there for more firewood." Then she reached for a small leather roll from a nearby shelf. When she opened it up, I saw the instruments of her trade. She turned and added a stack of folded cloths to her set-up.

I watched as Collin seemed to access how close birth had to be when he heard Miss Sadie's next words. "Now, we in business." Nodding her head to me, she added. "Get behind her. You know what to do. Savannah, let me see you give that push you been talking about." It only took seconds for the front door to close behind Colin.

Miss Sadie's sure but soothing voice began in a singsong rhythm. "Ain't gonna' be long now, ain't gonna' be long. In a shake of a rabbit's tail, we'll have us a baby. Ain't gonna' be long now, ain't gonna' be long."

Time seemed to fly. "You 'bout got the head out. Let's keep working. Give me another good push." I could feel the strength rise as the blood-curdling cry came from Savannah." Miss Sadie's sure hands guided the baby on out. I watched as tears formed. *The miracle of birth unfolded before my eyes. I can hardly take in the fact that Colin and I are somehow a part of this experience.* Miss Sadie's voice, coupled with the hearty cry of the newborn, stirred me from my reverie. "Why, Savannah, you got yourself a baby boy. Charles gonna' be one proud papa when he gets home before long. *Oh! No! What if Savan-*

nah's husband discovers Colin out in the yard?"

Miss Sadie's strong, knowing hands held the tiny infant toward Savannah for that first glimpse. My mind shifted from my concerns. I watched this wizened elder place the baby in his mother's waiting arms. *No doubt this woman had been about the business of birthing babies for many years.* She quickly moved to the task of the afterbirth.

Looking at me, she instructed further. "I gotta' figure out the best way to get word to Charles."

Savannah's exhaustion showed, but her radiance and joy won out. As the scene of mother and child in those first moments of bonding took place, my heart filled with the joy of coming across this young Indian girl as we had crossed the ford earlier today. The fact that Colin and I had somehow traveled back in time paled in comparison to what I just witnessed.

As Sadie continued to move in a smooth rhythm around the mother and child, propping the pillow just so, adjusting the rolled blanket to assure every detail of comfort was in place, I focused on a thought that had played in my brain earlier. *This wise, wise woman has the knack of reading people and the situations they are caught up in. Who am I kidding? There will be no "pulling the wool" over those knowing eyes.* With no clue why the next thought came to me so clearly, I let it wash over my troubled thoughts. *This insightful woman just might not be as shocked as I anticipate. What if I just tell her the truth? Is it possible that Miss Sadie's closeness, probably many, many times over the years, to birth, to new life, has made her open to the inexplicable in life?* Whatever the reason, I embraced my sudden assurance that Colin and I had found the best possible place to take shelter until we found our way to some answers as to how to get back to our time. Now, I just needed to get outside to Colin. *What will he think of my latest idea of putting everything out on the table with Miss Sadie?*
I watched as Sadie changed the soiled bedding, working her way around mother and child. "I need to check on Colin and that firewood. He's had a long day. I suspect he could do with some time warming by this fire. I'll be right back to help in any way I can."

§

Colin leaned the axe against the fence post as he spotted me on the small porch. I could feel a smile spread across my face as I neared him. "Well, Savannah has a son."

"Is everything fine with both?"

"Yes, it appears to be. Miss Sadie is a seasoned midwife. I suspect she could deliver a baby with her eyes closed. She seems satisfied that both came through the birthing process just fine. But listen, Colin. Before we head inside, I want to talk about our situation. I can't tell you why I am so sure of what I am about to say, but here goes. As I worked alongside Miss Sadie, I could not shake the feeling that she might be able to handle the truth of the circumstances that have placed us in the middle of her home and Savannah's birth. Her intuitive ways and years of wisdom would spot the holes in any story we tried to spin."

"Sarah, the thought of just how we will explain ourselves to Miss Sadie has been almost the only thought on my mind as I have chopped firewood. I think my clothing triggered some questions in her the moment she laid eyes on me. Maybe you are right. Do we go back in and offer up the truth or wait for her to ask?"

"Even as those words come out of your mouth, I find myself almost shaking on the inside at the thought of actually telling another soul how we happen to be standing here at the moment. As you and I know all too well, we don't have a clue how we got here."

We didn't have time to take our conversation further. The cabin door opened. Miss Sadie walked directly toward us with a water basin in her hands. Her light-skinned face showed the dark spots that some of her age carried. Wisps of silver-grey hair strayed around her dark, knowing eyes. No question, her penetrating look worked to take in our details. She remained silent for a brief moment. I continued to take in her appearance. As she stood close by Colin, her full hips and ample bust no longer distracted me from the fact she stood his equal in height. *Even if she were short, I think possibly I would see her bigger than life based on her age-old wisdom with the birthing process.* Her commanding voice interrupted my thoughts. "I need some fresh water. I used up most of what we had cleaning up those linens."

"We were just heading in with firewood and more water. Colin also needs to sit for a minute. Here, hand that to me."

As I took the large container from her, she turned abruptly and headed back toward the house. I could hear her mumbling under her breath. Only one phrase that she repeated twice came across clearly. *Strange goings on. Indeed, strange goings on.*

I stopped long enough in the deep darkness that moved in to see the stars that shone far-brighter than seemed normal. The same observation caught my attention almost twenty-four hours earlier when we first time traveled and ended up at the location near the depot. *The plentiful electric lights that ward off darkness in our time are not yet in existence back at this point in history.* In seconds, another thought became clear. *We have now been caught up in this timeframe of the past for close to a full day.*

I rushed to catch up with Colin before the door closed. Miss Sadie walked straight to the wood stove and lifted the lid from the apples. The heady aroma of the cinnamon-seasoned fruit quickly filled the room. Hunger overcame me. Without even turning in our direction, still intently stirring the tantalizing apples, she spoke. "I expect you folks might be gittin' right hungry. Why don't you take a leftover biscuit from this basket?" as she pointed to the shelf above. "There's some bowls up there too. Some of them stewed apples, even with cold biscuits, are sure to hit the spot. I got some ham bone here with beans that I'll get warmed up before long for supper."

Turning abruptly, Sadie turned and looked me square in the eyes. "Go ahead. Get yourself a biscuit. I imagine your man be wanting something to eat too. I 'spect we got some talking to do. We may as well do it over quiet stomachs."

Colin and I shoveled the food into our mouths. Our obvious hunger also provided a reprieve from responding to Miss Sadie's words. The old woman then pointed toward Savannah and the child sleeping on the nearby bed. "Let's keep the talking on the quiet side, for those two need to sleep when they can. I'll head over to fetch Charles here before long. I suspect I better get there before he comes home to an empty house. My, my, he's gonna' be some kind of proud of this son of his." Then she moved to another topic very quickly. "I feels like I better go ahead and ask you what be on my mind. Do you folks have someplace to go? I don't think…" then she paused. "Well, I just think it might be best if you two stay here tonight. There's something a can't quite put my finger on about the two of you. I think you are good folks. That's not the concern. I think it might be best if…" Again, she dropped her thought before adding, "Sho think we need to do something about them clothes of yours." Then, changing her tact before either of us could recover enough to respond, she looked directly at Colin and asked. "So, your name is Colin?" Turning to me, she added. "And you are Sarah."

Knowing this would be the first of many answers we would give this interesting woman, I almost whispered my answer. "Yes, I am Sarah."

Sadie nodded her head. Then headed off into the lean-to room that extended off the main portion of the small house. Colin spoke quietly. "You are right. Miss Sadie sized up our situation down to the details of our clothing. I can only imagine the questions to come."

Colin no sooner finished his comment when Miss Sadie stepped back into the room. Reaching up to the nearby peg where her big coat hung, she wrapped herself in its oversized warmth as she turned the collar and added a man's hat to her interesting outfit. "I need to get Savannah's husband. Better check on these two before I leave." She touched her hand lightly to both foreheads so as not to wake them from their needed sleep. I immediately thought I saw a look of concern as she lifted her hand from the baby. She looked at me immediately and added. "I'm counting on you to keep your eye on everybody here. Savannah and Charles live just right around the bend. I'll be right back."

Sadie no sooner headed out when Colin asked. "Do you think she would mind if I took another helping of biscuit and apples? I'm still hungry."

I smiled as I answered. "I don't think she would mind at all. I plan on getting out of these wet socks and shoes while Sadie is gone. Maybe a bit of time close to the fire will make it easier to put them back on." I looked forward to having a moment to talk to Colin. As he wolfed down the extra serving, my mind filled to overflowing. *What a day. I am worn out. We are caught in a downright crazy situation. Yet, I feel totally content.* Within moments of relishing the fulfillment of the day, my heart turned to thoughts of Tim. *He had so many reasons to live. Why, why did he...* I pushed the memory down. *Tim's choices were Tim's choices. If nothing else, this day, so full of the unexpected, has fanned my faith in life. It is so worth the living.*

The baby's whimper brought me back to the rest of the people in the room. Savannah opened her eyes in response. The fretting picked up in earnest. I took in the worried look spreading across the new mother's face. "Let's try putting him to your breast. You'll have to get better at that sooner than later. It may be just what the little fella needs. Here, let me hold him a bit. Colin, why don't you pour Savannah water. There are some tin cups up on that shelf."

As I paced back and forth around the stove area, I bounced the little bundle carefully in my arms. The fussing continued. Then I wondered about whether he might need his diaper changed. No sooner had the thought formed than I questioned whether the term "diaper" had yet surfaced at the turn of the 19ᵗʰ century. As I placed the baby at Savannah's feet and unwrapped the blanket, I did feel dampness. "What shall I use to change him?"

Savannah answered quickly. "Miss Sadie keeps a stack of cloths ready right over there." She pointed in the direction of the wood stove. I decided I better pay careful attention before taking it off. I questioned my skill would be enough to keep the rag diaper wrapped around anything as tiny as this infant. My thoughts quickly jumped to a bigger worry. As I touched the soft, baby skin, I reacted to the warmth. *A bit feverish? Is that why Sadie looked concerned when she checked on the baby earlier?* I stroked the dark head of hair gently, trying to squelch the worry that could easily show on my face. My next thoughts sent me plummeting down a dark hole. *I do think thermometers have been around for a long time? Does Sadie have one? No emergency room for sure. From what I've picked up, we may not even get a doctor to make a house call.*

The baby continued to whimper. "Savannah, did Miss Sadie talk you through feeding your baby?" She nodded yes. Even so, her awkwardness was obvious. *I better talk her through the basics of how to position her fingers so the little mouth can find the nipple.* The little guy latched on easier than I anticipated. The small cries continued to come. Frustration showed in both mother and child. I reached for the infant. Savannah offered me a slight smile of thanks.

My hand stroked his black head of hair. I recalled the memory of placing my colicky first child so her little stomach rested on my shoulder. That move, coupled with enough walking, eventually, calmed her down. *Hey, it's worth a try.* I began to pace back and forth in the small cabin. Eventually the baby quietened. Savannah spoke softly. "Thank you. I am also very thankful you folks found me at the springheads. I was so afraid nobody would hear my cry for help."

"I'm glad we got you to Miss Sadie's when we did. Now,

that dear woman knows what she's doing when it comes to birthing babies. Is there a doctor you would have gone to if you had not been so close to birth when we found you?" I thought I knew the answer to my question but hoped to find out more about a doctor we might call on.

"No, Miss Sadie planned on coming over to our place. No doctor round here gives much time to birthing Indian babies. I guess we should have stayed close to some of our people that live on up in the mountains a ways. But I sure like it down here near the river. My family's history has been linked to this land for as long as I can remember. Besides, Miss Sadie is family to me and Charles. She knew best. I should never have gone off into town." I could see a questioning look move across her face. "I don't think I've ever seen you folks around these parts."

In an effort to move to another subject, I answered quickly. "No, we're not from around here. By the way, is your place close by? Do you think Miss Sadie and your husband should be back soon? Also, I think your little fellow has settled down at last." As I handed the quiet bundle off to his mother, I added. You better get some rest while you can."

"We live right around the bend. It won't be long."

I took the opportunity to talk with Colin. "Give me a moment to put my shoes on. Then let's step out on the front porch so these two can get some sleep. A shot of the cold mountain air will do me good at the moment." Colin grabbed his red Eddie Bauer jacket, as I took in for the first time, the black under-layer he had on. *No wonder he got out of his jacket once he came inside.* A troubling thought crossed my mind as I took in this reminder of the time we left behind. Try as I might, I could not hold the disturbing thought that tiptoed across brain., Instead, as soon as we were out of earshot, I poured my worries out. "I am convinced the baby is feverish. To make matters worse, Savannah just confirmed another concern. Getting a doctor over here is not going to be easy. Do we have any options if something is seriously wrong with this infant? Oh, Colin, I miss our time a great deal at the moment."

"Hopefully, Miss Sadie will be back soon. Maybe she will know what to do. Many of these old-timers are gifted in the healing arts. Any idea how long it will take Miss Sadie and Savannah's husband to get here? I have to admit, I worry about him being a bit suspicious of the two of us.

"Oh! I meant to tell you. Savannah said they live nearby. So, I suspect any time now. Colin, if you think about it, what can her husband do if he has serious questions about us? Savannah reminded me of the shameful truth that all too often Indians were treated deplorably during this time. I guess what I am trying to say is her husband may have no place to go with any concerns. Who would listen to him?"

"You're right."

We both heard the voices. It had to be Sadie and Charles. *Should we just wait out here? I want to talk to Miss Sadie without the new father around.* By the time the thoughts formed, Miss Sadie and a tall, slim young Indian man dressed in dark wool pants and jacket appeared on the path leading to the front porch. I took in the broad shoulders and handsome good looks. *What a striking couple he and Savannah made, both capturing the dignity of their Cherokee heritage.*

Miss Sadie did the talking. "Charles, these here folks got that wife of yours to me in time today."

Colin reached out his hand and added. "I'm Colin." As he gestured towards me, "This is Sarah. Thankfully she knows something about childbirth."

Charles seemed almost stunned as he looked at us for a bit. Miss Sadie did not give him a moment to get side-tracked, however. She spoke with certainty. "Charles, let's get you in here to see your wife and son." Looking at the two of us, she added. "Let me check on everybody, and then we will give this young family some privacy. I'll be back out in a bit."

§

As soon as she returned, I started my litany. "Miss Sadie, the baby has been fretful most of the time since you left. Although he latched on once, it did not last long. It took a great deal of walking and bouncing to calm him down. I suspect he is running a fever. Is it possible to get a doctor? What do you think might be wrong?"

"Now, just hold on, child. Babies can have all sorts of lil' problems. Usually, Miss Sadie here has just the right touch to make them better. I told Charles how you folks just happened to hear his wife's cry for help down at the springheads. He was sure grateful someone found her. I told him you folks are not from these parts." I could not help but notice the penetrating look she gave the two of us before she spoke further. "Guess I better be getting them beans on the fire to warm. Probably should make us a batch of cornbread since there's so many mouths to feed."

Before I stopped to think, I asked. "Is there anything I can do to help?" No sooner had the words come out than I realized I might find it quite awkward to cook in a kitchen without modern appliances. *I think baking powder came about earlier in the 1800s. But I certainly would not bet my life on that detail. Of course, I do not have a clue about baking in a wood-fired oven."*

Miss Sadie again gave one of her all-knowing looks. "Why don't you just help your man fill that water on the stove. I guess we could use some more firewood inside. Feels like it gonna' be a cold one. Seems like the day after the New Year always be on the cold side."

Sadie headed back inside. Colin and I looked at each other in astonishment. I spoke first. "Somehow, it is the day after the New Year. Yet it was New Year's Eve when we headed out on the walk to see the building of my dreams. Of course, it had been daylight, early evening, at that time. Yet, we arrived here in the middle of the night. Colin, I assumed it was the morning of New Year's Day. Somehow, we gained or lost a day, depending on how you looked at it."

"Well, it's obvious your brain is doing double time just like mine! It's not New Year's Day, at least not here at this time in this location. I wonder if a gain or loss of time always occurs in time travel? We have a lot to keep up with for the next time."

"Whatever do you mean by "the next time"?

"Sarah, we've got to get back to our time."

"Of course, you're right. Who cares what time it is or which day it is, as long as we make it back. Colin, we could drive ourselves crazy trying to make sense of all of this. I have to admit I've been so caught up with Savannah and the baby that I have not given the return to our time much thought."

"Remember, I've been outside with nothing but a pile of firewood to distract my thinking. For the most part, I've thought of nothing else. I'm still convinced we need to get back to the building or at least the location of your dream. That location did pull us into this time travel situation."

"Colin, I don't disagree. If there is such a store in existence at this time we are presently in, we should be able to find it. When we do, how can we be assured we will travel through time once again? How do we know we will go to the future, to what was our present time? What if there is some connection to the time of day? We can't exactly walk in the place time and time again, waiting for the right moment. I can only assume if the place exists that people will be hanging around it."

"Sarah, I, of course, have no real answers for your questions. I catch myself still thinking time travel is impossible."

"I can relate, Colin."

We both stood silent in the cold night air. I knew there was still one more question on my mind. "What is the story behind your ring?"

"What are you talking about?"

"Colin, remember, back in the building that we explored. You wanted to go back outside to figure out the location of what we thought of as a boarding house in my two dreams. We turned to head out. I tripped, and you reached to steady me, or maybe I grabbed your hand. Anyway, when I touched your ring, there was a strange heat radiating from it. I started to tell you about it. Instead, that ripple occurred as if the whole set-up of the place somehow changed. Of course, you know the rest. We were not only in a different location, never mind a different time. When we first arrived here, in this time, I still held your hand. I remember I no longer felt the warmth of your ring. Is it possible you or your ring are connected to the ability to travel through time? Remember, I had been in that place many times before. Never once did I go traveling through time."

Colin showed a quizzical smile before he spoke. "I think my grandfather will appreciate this theory. Not that he knows anything about time travel, but he does believe certain legends about the ring. I remember as a little boy sitting up at night, scared to close my eyes as I recalled some of the strange stories about the Stewart clan and this ring. Up until now, I always figured he was an old man who enjoyed the telling of a good tale. Sarah, I don't know if I can make myself believe in a magic ring. There has to be some logic behind all of this. Again, how I wish I studied Einstein's theory a bit more thoroughly. All I know are a few basic terms about black holes and time warps. Did we get caught up in such? Can we manipulate any detail of our world to control the ability to warp space and time enough to travel back and forth in time? Is traveling forward even possible? I reach that point in my thoughts and have to take a break."

I could not allow my thoughts to linger on the idea of not getting back to our time. I added quickly. "It could be that pure metals simply react when such a warp is occurring. Diana Gabledon's Outlander Series makes use precious gemstones in her time-travel adventures. Of course, that is fiction. We've stepped into time-travel non-fiction. I'm beyond my knowledge base. I don't know anything to do except wonder what the conversation around dinner will turn into when Charles touches earth again. The excitement over the birth of his son will settle down enough at some point for him to take in two people sitting in his presence who somehow do not fit quite right in his world."

"Sarah, should we walk in there right now and say we need to get on our way? I'd like to get to that store during the night when no one is around."

"What if we get to the building and nothing happens? We don't even know if there is a building. Maybe we need to go back in and somehow work some questions into the conversation about the possibility of a general store nearby. Worse still, what if we get there and nothing happens? Then what? Where would we go for the night? I think I would feel better staying here until we know more."

"Wise words. Can you carry a few more pieces of wood if I stack them on top of what you've already got there? I'll get the bucket of water and then come back after one more load."

§

Sadie had managed in the short time we talked outside to have the cornbread in the oven. The warmth of the cabin wrapped around me as we entered. Charles, holding the baby close, stood near the bed. He and Savannah looked our way. "Miss Sadie, you folks, I'm so grateful you found my wife when you did. I'm proud of my son, Charles William Martin." He stepped slightly closer to Colin.

"That's a fine young man you have there."

In a matter of seconds, the baby began to cry. The new father tensed and looked at Sadie. As Savannah reached for her child,

Sadie intervened. Charles handed his son over to her experienced hands. "He cries a lot. Is something wrong?"

"Let me walk him about a bit. Sarah, keep your eyes on them beans. The bread's got more cooking. I need to work with little Charles here. I suspect we need to get this fever down."

Probably not knowing what else to say, Charles added, "We will call him William."

Colin, again with a good, quick response, said, "Charles, can you give me a hand with more firewood?"

Between stirring the beans, Sadie put me to work getting the next batch of cold compresses ready. The ice-cold water Colin had brought in earlier caused me to warm my hands by the stove any opportunity I found. When at last Sadie seemed satisfied that baby William's fever was down, I asked. "When do you think this cornbread can come out? I thought I'd fix Savannah a plate. I think she could use some nourishment."

Sadie placed the sleeping baby at his mother's side. "I'll be gettin' it out right now. After you get Savannah situated, you can put the food out on the table for the men folks and yourself." Within a moment of speaking, she let out a sigh as she looked down at little William, "Now, lil' fella', just rest a bit. Hopefully, we gats that fever down for a while. I need to go to the springhouse real quick-like. Sarah, you watch over mother and baby."

Charles and Colin made their way in with the last of the firewood. Sadie walked in moments later with a pitcher of cold milk.

Charles turned toward Sadie quickly. "What's the matter with my son?"

Sadie hesitated before answering. Both parents looked at her with worry. "I be worried about your son. He is sleeping now. That's good. As soon as Savannah finishes her food, she needs some rest also." Before she joined us at the small table, she leaned over the infant. She touched his forehead gently with two fingers.

I hoped against hope that I was wrong. But Charles must have also noticed the look of concern that moved over the kind face, for he asked strongly, "I can tell you are worried, Miss Sadie."

"Charles, this fever seems to have a vengeance to it. He is already warming up again. I can keep working with him, using the cold compresses and some of my other remedies."

The young father had no intention of sitting and waiting. He pushed back from the table, grabbed his jacket as he headed toward the door.

"Charles, you may as well grab Jeb's old hat and that wool scarf. The wind is whipping out there. And you knows sure as you are standing that if you can even wake ole' Doc Mills up, he may not be willing to come out till morning."

The door slammed behind the determined young man.

§

Miss Sadie sat back down with the now whimpering baby in her arms. "His fever be rising fast. Sarah, I need your help with some more cold compresses. That bucket back in the storeroom has the coldest water. I suggest you folks also try to eat a bite while you can. I also got something to ask you. I don't mean no disrespect with that ole' Doc Mills, but he can't do what I can do with my remedies. I be worried about this little one." Then with a slight pause, the wizened eyes locked on us both and asked. "Where you folks come from, be there any help?"

For a brief moment, the silence of the pause hung heavily over the room. Colin spoke first, "Miss Sadie, where do you think we come from?"

"Well, I don't rightly know. I don't 'spect it be anywhere I ever been. I never seen clothes like yours." She passed near me as she continued to work with the fretting baby and reached in the direction of the zipper tab at the neckline of my sweater. "Too much is… well, a bit strange with you two." Her voice trailed off. "You folks don't have to tell me what ain't my business to know, but my Gran Mam used to say that along this river here, anything can happen. She knew for a fact that the Cherokee believe those double springheads, along with the two bends in the river, and the creek that wraps the other side of this land, make for a mighty force. Gran Mam once heard an elder of the tribe speak of strangers that had traveled the circle of time. She never got the whole story but did know a young Indian who came across such a stranger at the very spot you'ens found Savannah."

"Miss Sadie," my voice faltered. "You said that you have probably never been where we come from. It just so happens I live nearby. But," then my voice faltered. "We don't live in the same time. In our time, it was the advent of the year 2000, not 1900. That is the correct year at present, right? We don't know how we got to your time. It was an accident." My mind raced ahead to a thought that had now filled my brain twice. *Is there possibly some purpose behind this trip, this wild adventure?* I forced my response back to Miss Sadie. "What do you mean when you ask if there is help from where we have come? What are you thinking?"

"Yes, it be 1900. I just have a strange feel about this baby. He ain't gonna' make it. Even if Charles gets that doctor, I fear he can't save him. My bones tell me something really bad be wrong with little William. I guess I'm wondering if you know ways to get him help. I made a promise to Gran Mam. Savannah is the great-granddaughter of the woman who saved my great-grandmother's life. I be obligated to this new mother and her child. Can you help?"

I shook my head in confusion. Once again, Colin responded when I could not. "Miss Sadie, is there a general store nearby?"

"Well, for sure, Mr. Billy's place be in walking distance."

"What are the chances you can get us inside that store?" Then he paused and added. "Tonight?"

Colin's boldness stunned me.

He continued. "Miss Sadie, we have doctors, medicines, hospitals, so many possibilities for saving an infant's life. Are you suggesting we try to get little William to our time?

Miss Sadie nodded yes as William began once again to cry.

I found my voice at last, over the infant's wailing. "Miss Sadie, that store is the location that brought us here. We can't offer you an explanation. We have no assurance we can even get back to our time. And what makes you think Savannah and Charles will let us take their baby down to that store to even try out this crazy idea?"

"Listen to me. I got to get this fever down. We got no time to waste in my opinion."

I tried to comfort Savannah as Sadie worked with the baby. At last, there was only the sound of the infant's whimper. Then Miss Sadie pushed ahead with Savannah. "I guess you done figured out that something be wrong with your child. I can't keep this fever down. It'll be hours before William gets back here. Even if he has that doctor with him, I don't think there's a thing he can do. I think these folks might be able to help." With those words she nodded in our direction. "You know when I gets an idea, I just have to give it a try."

I dared not speak. I could not fathom how this incredible old lady would sell this new mother on an idea that would most assuredly sound like insanity.

"Sarah," she brought me to attention with the sternness in her voice. "Get Savannah ready. Dress her as warm as you can. Your man, here, gonna' be carrying her, for she in no shape to walk. Savannah, Sarah, here will carry little William and the little bundle I fixed up for the two of you. We gonna' head down to Mr. Billy's store. You just got to trust me."

As my brain started making at least some sense of Miss Sadie's plan, I asked, "But what about Charles?"

Miss Sadie shot me a look that made it clear that I, too, needed to let her take charge. This woman continued to amaze me with her gentle strength. Within moments, we all followed her instructions without question as we headed out into the cold winter night.

§

Colin eased up alongside Miss Sadie who led the way with lantern in hand. The soft lamp light showed Savannah sleeping soundly in his strong arms.

"Miss Sadie," Colin spoke softly. "Your ideas about what we can do to help keep weighing on my mind. If, somehow or the other we can manage to travel back to our time, I agree both mother and child need to go." Colin paused.

In that moment, Miss Sadie confirmed one more detail in her plan. "Well, I am here to tell you that will be the only way you take this baby. No mother worth her salt would let you take her newborn. So, you better be getting your ideas together on how to make all of this happen."

Colin shook his head in questioning confusion. At the same time, I had one clear thought. *This strong-willed, determined woman is at least one step ahead of us at every turn.*

I remained silent, taking in the more direct path we took to the store instead of swinging back towards what I would call "my property" in our time. *It seems like a week's worth of challenges has unfolded in this one day. Thankfully, we at least had a chance to warm up, dry our socks and get some food.* No time for more thoughts on all that took place since Colin and I stepped into the old building just down the hill from my office home. The baby started crying in earnest once again.

Colin shifted Savannah's weight in his arms. She awoke in response to her child.

Miss Sadie spoke at last as she unwrapped from her shoulders the old wool blanket we had stolen earlier in the day. "Here, set Savannah down here. Sarah, see if you can help her try to nurse this little fella just a bit." Then looking directly at Colin, the intriguing old lady blew out the lantern as she added. "Let your eyes adjust. Thank the Lord there's a good moon tonight." Motioning her head toward Colin, she added, "Come on. Follow me. We gonna' figure out the best way in." As they walked away, I swear I heard her words clearly. "Sho be nice not to get caught breaking into Mr. Billy's store with the likes of these two by my side."

§

My mind filled with possible problems as I sat beside the new mother and her child. William nursed fitfully but at least allowed me some moments to think. *What if this time travel just does not happen again? Does Miss Sadie get that we can't exactly make it happen on demand? And what if we do manage to get Savannah and little William into our time? What are we supposed to do? Walk in the nearest ER and try to explain how we happen to be in the company of a strangely dressed, young Cherokee mother and her newborn?* As I started to tackle the many questions that were surfacing in me about how much time would have passed in our time and whether or not my children had tried calling, Colin came back.

He gently picked up the mother and her sleeping child held tightly against her chest. He spoke solemnly to me. "We got the front door of the store opened. Come on. All we can do is try. You hold on to me. If we travel at all, hopefully, we all go together."

Thankfully Savannah did not say a word. Her big, dark eyes, however, could have bored holes through us. *No visible signs of panic. Maybe she does not know enough to be worried.* Just as that thought leveled in my brain, another, deeper feeling moved in. *Maybe she is drawing on strength and knowledge that are simply beyond my under-*

standing.

My heart raced as we made our way around the building. Miss Sadie moved in close to us as we neared the front door. My mind was busy comparing the entrance to the old, dilapidated building of our time when I took in the hushed words being shared with Savannah. "Child, there's no other way. Let's just see what about to happen here. I made a promise years back I would protect you with all I got."

Collin got my attention next. "Sarah, let's step in here together. Miss Sadie, if you will, stay outside, several steps away from the door. Savannah, I want Sarah to hold your baby, so I can get a better grip on you." As I linked my left arm through Colin's, I noticed the lamp light flickering on the silver of Colin's mysterious ring. "Miss Sadie, can you place the lantern into Sarah's hand here near me, so we can at least see inside the place?" Looking over to me, he added. "You got a good grip on little William?" I nodded. "Then, let's move to the center. Wouldn't you say that's about where we were when it happened before?"

My eyes immediately started taking in the details of the well-stocked store, so different from the dust-filled building that I had first come across as I had walked the tracks last spring. Off to my left was a neat display of several sizes of small, black shoes that fastened with tiny buttons. The lantern light played off the glass candy jars lined up neatly on the counter. Nearby, a large wooden box filled to overflowing with marbles of all sizes. A scoop rested on top. I could imagine kids standing in anticipation in front of the counter. I looked at Savannah as I could see her eyes taking in Mr. Billy's store. She did not say a word. Her eyes darted from my face to the sleeping bundle I held on to.

"Colin, the heat from the lantern is getting a bit...."

My first thoughts went back to the dream where I had so clearly realized I stood in a world within a world. The couples sitting on the bench simply had no awareness that my friends and I were standing in their midst. My brain then began to sort through my surroundings. I saw neither the general store we had just stepped into nor the old structure just down from the river property. Instead, for just a brief moment, I took in what seemed to be a long passageway filled with the eerie light. Try as I might, my tired brain could not seem to think fast enough. *Why is this lantern so warm? Or is the heat radiating once again from Colin's silver ring just inches down from my hand?* Next, as I pulled little William even closer, I remember calling out, "Colin, hold on. It's happening."

Chapter 13

"Are you sure you have not misunderstood? We never invite company for dinner here at the ranch. Grandma Campbell certainly feeds the occasional ranch hand in the kitchen, but…"

Ola, anxious to set her older sister straight for once, interrupted. "Anna, I heard Papa talking with Grandma. It's true, his friend, called Doc, will be here for dinner."

Of all the times, William and I have to head back to Bisbee. I won't even get to meet this mystery guest. Back in Brazil, visitors filled the large dining room regularly. The kitchen, a small house unto itself that sat separate from our big house in South America, bustled with activity before such dinners. *I close my eyes, and the memories of that lost life come rushing back. The smell of bread baking in the massive stone oven, my pet monkey swinging mischievously from the rafters, mix with thoughts of the many hours spent sitting on the floor listening to the tales shared by those wizened cooks. The two native elders were the first to share the* mystery of the *second sight* with me.

I thought then that Papa would think me a silly young girl for listening to the prattle of the old women. For that reason, I did not share the stories from the big kitchen with my father. When Mother Superior told him about what happened on the garden wall of the convent, I was astounded that Papa had grown up hearing tales from Grandpa Finn about Great Granny's gift of the second sight. Now he reminds me often. "You are cut out of the same cloth as your Great Granny Campbell. Her Scotch-Irish blood flows powerfully through your veins." According to Papa, his Grandpa Finn often told him about his mother, who came from a long line of women with this unusual gift. Long before I saw the image of my father coming to the boarding school to tell William and me of our mother's death, I had a vague awareness of events about to happen in my life. At Papa's encouragement, I learned to treasure the gift and accept the responsibility that came with such sight. The stories from the native cooks continued to fill my head.

More thoughts stirred, buried deep in piles of treasured memories learned while sitting on the tiled kitchen floor: native workers and their intriguing thoughts about life, the healing plants from the jungle itself, the power of the moon and surrounding bodies of water, even the alluring idea that the events of life unfurled in a circle rather than in a line of progression. More intriguing had been their sincere belief that sometimes these events folded back and forth on themselves, mixing time in the strangest of ways. *I was so young when I first took in these tales. It all seemed possible when I sat at their feet and let my imagination flow with the talk. Now that I was getting a more formal education, I assumed I had outgrown my childhood innocence that had been hungry for their fairy tales.*

Memories of warm, muggy evening life back in Brazil could, however, turn my heart to those treasured stories in no time. Other recollections found me in one of the finest garments designed and sewn by the seamstress that provided the dress clothing for all of our family. The memory of my coming-out ball always rested just beneath the surface of my special memories. This traditional rite of passage event from Mother's beloved Spain was common to the wealthy landowners of the area. The dinner that followed the gala still lingers as a treasure in my mind.

Upon turning thirteen, I was expected to be a hostess for such dinners alongside my elegant mother. The ritual was a learned art passed from mother to eldest daughter. First, we met in Mother's dressing room. She gave her final approval of my appearance. My dark hair coiffed into a low-lying bun with wisps trailing loose as was the fashion, was meant to be just like hers. I, too, dressed in silk, practiced sitting straight and poised. Before we headed out to dinner, Mother always asked that I fasten the beautiful garnet necklace set with small diamonds and pearls around her neck. *Now, this single piece of jewelry, a gift from Papa to my dear mother, is the sole treasure brought from our home in Brazil. Life in Arizona provided no occasions for such finery.*

The dinner parties invariably moved through the floor-to-ceiling double doors of the dining room to the veranda that wrapped the hacienda. This welcoming expanse to our home drew the guests to a shawl of lush garden growth that wrapped the grounds and greeted the eye at every turn. Neighboring ranchers and their families were a common sight. As the eldest, I understood that one ranked in the Brazilian ranching world if invited to the home of Carl Martin II and Sarah Louisa San Juan Martin.

A smile accompanied the many thoughts that surface as my mind wandered through memories of the first thirteen years of my life spent in South America. A rite of passage celebration, my coming-out ball, marked the point when Papa felt he should tell me his real name: Finn Pinkney Campbell II. Of course, he also explained why he had come to Brazil under an assumed name. I easily remember how honored I felt that Papa now considered me a young lady, an adult in many ways. Even now, I find it hard to think about my Papa as a reckless murderer. He had shown me the studio picture taken not long before the shooting spree that soon made him a wanted man: Handsome college student, dressed in suit and tie, shoes polished, with a gun hanging in the holster off his right hip, near his shooting hand. Crack shot that he is, even intoxicated, he had not missed. One thought always won out. *He is such a good father.*

I told him at the time that we would someday move back to the states. Again, I had known that something, some twist of fate, some turn of events would draw us back to father's homeland. He had not believed me. He clung to his doubt. I could easily see that Papa would never be able to fully forgive himself for the senseless shootings. The heavy burden of his guilt always robbed a portion of the freedom he had gained. Papa's sister's marriage into the family of the Governor of Arizona Territory would eventually gain his pardon that the Campbell family sought. I've always known Papa would never be able to grant such a gift to himself.

Now, here I am, sixteen years old, and we live on a portion of the family ranch in Arizona. Papa, along with his eight siblings and his parents, share what had originally been a massive Cienega that stretches along the Rio Grande River in both Arizona and New Mexico. Gambling debts on the part of Papa and some of his siblings were behind the reduction in the family's acreage. Nonetheless, the Campbell land remained vast. The rugged Chiricahua Mountains, with Granite Peak off in the distance, hold our family together.

Presently, the States, as Papa calls them, are recovering from the Great Depression. Here at the ranch, the harsh facts and many hardships of this time are in some ways not as noticeable. We raise our own food and continue the work of the ranch day in and day out. I am in school in Bisbee. Like my Papa and my older brother William who are often out and about, I understand more of the impact of this dark time. One thing I know for sure. *I have already accepted and conformed to the differences in our lives here as opposed to how we lived in South America. Could any results from the depression really be any more challenging?*

The presence of young men flooding into the nearby Civilian Conservation Corporation to find work helped bring the reality of this economic downturn to these remote regions of Arizona. Papa came across his new friend at this CCC Camp. Although I've never met the man in person, I am intrigued with the friendship that exists between Papa and this "Doc" character. My father, Finn Campbell II, is known around the area as a quiet and private man who does not wish to share the details of his life with others. The suggestion of a temper no one wants to provoke makes it easy to keep most folks out of his business. To head off for a night of poker and beer at the Camp is one thing for Papa. To invite this young man for dinner intrigued the entire family. *Apparently, second sight fails me when it comes to understanding what prompted Papa to extend this rare invitation.*

§

"William, I've hardly said a word the whole way to Bisbee. Since Ola told me about the invited dinner guest, my mind has been caught up in the life we left behind in Brazil. Now those memories are dredging up the days of endless travel as we set out into the unknown. I'm sure you, like me, will never forget that long voyage from Rio's port to the States." I drifted into silence again as the memories moved in.

At every turn, excitement filled us older children. What will it be like to be on a ship? Around the dinner table, we often begged Papa to tell us all he knew about sailing in the open seas. Sometimes he added details of his trip from New York Harbor many years back. The thoughts of our new adventures kept me going through the relentless preparations for the move to Papa's homeland. In the sad months following our dear Mother's death, I took her place in many ways. Care and concern for baby Francie consumed me. I longed to somehow help this sweet baby someday understand something about our mother, who had died days after childbirth. I clung to the hope that Mother would be proud of me. I managed the servants and cooks and my youngest siblings. Papa told me over and over that he could not have been prouder of the big sister I had turned into when our family needed me most. Nothing prepared me for what it would be like when we left the comforts and extensive help that had always been a part of the life on our Mato Grosso ranch.

Papa explained the evolving plans nightly. Finally, the time came for the two carriages to pull out at the break of dawn for Rio De Janeiro. That morning I looked back at the only place I knew as home. Excitement soon gave way to bouts of loss and fear. The curve of my baby sister's head, peeking out from the blanketed bundle I held so tight, brought me back to the task at hand. I knew much depended on me. *Papa counts on me to help with the younger children. The baby will never know Mother if I do not stay strong. I've always known we would make this journey. Just keep looking forward.* Try as I might, nagging questions kept filling my head. *What will our lives be like in the new world we will eventually reach? Will I like my grandmother? Papa promised me she will be unlike anyone I have ever met. He also assured me I will love her deeply.* I could not help but think how complicated it would be, when the timing was right, to explain to all the younger children the many twists and turns of the real story of our father's life, from his tragic, sordid past to his assumed name.

§

Days and nights of travel took their toll as we crossed the great expanse of ocean that stretched alongside South America. The river passage inland would eventually bring us to the Gulf of Mexico but not before confinement and the monotonous movement of the ship wore us down. Papa forced us to find ways to pace ourselves through the ups and downs of what seemed like endless time. The sight of New Orleans off in the distance brought relief mixed with that same sense of worry I had experienced when we left the ranch.

The wharf teemed with the hustle and bustle of throngs of people. The French language mixed in with Spanish and English reminded me of my studies at the boarding school back in Rio. *Will I be able to go to school in this new place?* Papa quickly, using Spanish, negotiated hired help to work with my brothers and the stack of luggage and boxes we had packed. I managed the girls and the baby. We stayed close together, taking in the sights and sounds around us. Even little Francie seemed to sense the excitement of the moment.

A night at the boarding house would give us the food and rest we needed to continue our journey by train. Leaving the older girls in charge of the baby, I came back downstairs to talk with the cook about our family's need for an evening meal and breakfast before we left the next morning. Papa sought directions from the owner to the train station. He used Spanish again. As I quickly remembered to do the same, I knew I had a question for my father. *Why is he not speaking English?*

The following day I purposely moved close to Papa as he purchased the train tickets and made arrangements for our luggage and crates. Once again, he used only Spanish, even repeating several times to the clerk the correct pronunciation of the last name Martin. I heard clearly, "Marteen" said over and over.

Apparently, my eavesdropping was not overlooked by my father. He also had a way of reading the expression on my face when questions or concerns overwhelmed me. As he finalized the arrangements and motioned to my brothers to meet him with our belongings, he asked, "Anna, dear, what is troubling you?"

In Spanish, I asked, "Why are you using Spanish? You have insisted we all speak our native tongue since we have arrived in New Orleans."

A heavy look moved over his face as he answered. "My dear, perceptive daughter, I am not yet a pardoned man. Until I reach Arizona and go through the official act, I prefer to continue to be Carl Martin from our Mato Grosso ranch in Brazil. Spanish is more common here than Portuguese. So, Spanish it is."

"We will all speak Spanish, Papa. Just leave that to me."

§

Grandma Campbell, as she was called by almost everyone in the area, often said her old heart mended the day my father came back from Brazil with her slew of grandchildren. I suspected within days of meeting Kendra Campbell that the family's need for a mother no longer rested solely on my shoulders. Father and the older boys were quickly absorbed into the work of the ranch. I tackled the task of getting to know the strange world we landed in. This grandmother could not be more different from the stately elegance that I remembered so well of my mother. Yet, there was a strength that impressed me from the moment I met her. Grandmother's first words would always be remembered. "You are indeed pretty enough.

Do you know how to cook? Can you ride a horse and shoot a gun?"

I stood dumbstruck, unable to speak for a moment. Finally, I managed a few words. "I can ride a horse."

Kendra Campbell held the reputation of being one of the most outspoken women of the region. There was no question in my mind that this strong-willed woman intended to have the last word when it came to the running of her household. Her physical appearance alone got our attention even when she did not say a word. She had to be close to six feet tall, with a head full of silver hair, still faintly streaked with red. The wild mass of curls rarely stayed in place, even when pulled back in a bun. I stood in awe the first time I saw her rope a calf and lift it off the ground by herself. Her ox-like strength combined with rough-cut gracefulness unexplainably brought back memories of my elegant, stately mother. It did not take me long to latch onto this intriguing woman as if my life depended on her companionship.

The thoughts of our first night at the ranch will probably always stay with me. I offered to help Grandma Campbell with the cooking. It took about a minute for this wise woman to figure out that I had never cooked a meal in my life. Within a few seconds she declared, "Well, my eldest, it just won't do for a girl of your age not to be able to cook. Since the chances of any servants showing up in this wild country are pretty slim, I suggest you stay right by my side in the kitchen. I'll have you cooking in no time." As it turned out, kitchen work was only a small part of all that I learned in the day-to-day contact with Grandma. She made sure everyone started the day with breakfast, then, without fail, headed outdoors to work alongside the best of the men on the ranch. Horseback riding and shooting a gun were a necessity with the work out on the range. At the end of every long day, Grandma still found the energy to make sure we all got one more big meal before the day was done. Before long, my sisters and I worked right alongside Grandmother, whether in the kitchen or out on the ranch.

Many tales circulated around the countryside about our grandmother. I concluded quickly that the daring and the spunk attributed to this lone woman were not exaggerated. In addition to soothing many a dispute between the local ranchers with her chocolate cake, which was undoubtedly the best in the territory, Grandma Campbell, in her younger years, had managed to survive a raid led by Geronimo. Years later, she fed a meal to this revered but captured chief, along with his men, from the very house she now lived in. Although Grandma seemed evasive about one particular topic, Anna knew there was indeed a tale that could be told about Grandma hiding Will Cody in her home. In short, this woman shaped by the Wild West itself soon won a place in my heart. No doubt she could do about anything she put her mind to doing. Papa assured me more than once that it was his mother's relentless efforts that swayed the Governor of the Arizona Territory to act on his long-awaited pardon when, for several months, it seemed like it may not come to pass.

Here it is 1934. I can hardly take in that three years have passed since my family and I made the voyage to the States. I think Grandma's tenacity rubbed off on me within minutes of meeting her. Like her, I don't think twice about tackling any job put in front of me. I enjoyed Papa educating me as much as he can, so I, in turn, can teach my siblings. I am very pleased, however, that William and I go to Bisbee to further our education through the local school. My acceptance into classes at the University of Arizona in the upcoming school year is a dream come true. The life that revolves around my home, my siblings, Papa and Grandma Campbell, still pulls me back into the love and care that took our family in the day we showed up at the ranch. Before giving it much thought, I spoke in earnest to William. "I sure wish we could have stayed at the ranch today. I'd like to meet this friend of Papa's."

William took in the small-boned build of his sister and the dark hair that coiled at the base of her neck. She had the flawless olive skin characteristic of her Spanish ancestry. He never looked at her without a faint memory of their mother stirring in him. He knew the strong resemblance to Anna's mother often produced the same look of loss on Father's face. The sadness did not last long with Papa. Instead, laughter always took over as he reminded Anna. "You may look like your dear mother in many ways, but those eyes are from your Scotch-Irish side." Anna's brown eyes were not the almost black of her mother's. Instead, the streaks of copper, sometimes revealing just a hint of green just like Grandma Campbell's, seemed to bring to life anything she had on her mind at any given moment. Papa often joked with her that she would make a terrible poker player.

Still watching his sister ride her horse, he recalled just how much ranch life had molded and shaped the lives of Anna and all of his siblings. Our sister Ola gives us brothers a run for our money at being one of the best ropers in the area. Even little Francie, who often rides with Anna, is always tugging at the reins, eager and ready to take charge. Grandma Campbell had a way about her that had grown all of them in ways they had never imagined back in Brazil. Ranch life, along with the care and feeding of a big family and ranch hands, kept everyone predictably busy. Anna is right. Papa threw in the unexpected with his dinner invitation. Papa's move had everyone in the family astir in one way or the other. William added with a grin. "Anna, I'd be willing to bet you will someday meet Doc."

Chapter 14

Finn Campbell's contract work with a cattle company, along with managing the family ranch, often took him to different areas of the surrounding territory. As he headed home on one such return trip from the nearby town of Douglas, Arizona, a single burning thought played in his head. "Son, I want to stop by the CCC Camp set up just off the Montezuma Road that leads back to Ash Canyon. It's that place everybody is talking about, set up by the federal government. This Civilian Conservation Corporation Camp that I keep hearing about works with the U.S. Forestry Service to provide work for almost 400 young men whose families had no hope of a decent job anywhere else across the country. I've heard these fellas are building trails up Ash and Ramsey Canyons. I've been told all their daily needs are met right here at the camp. I'd like to see this for myself. What says we stop in for a little visit?"

As we approached on horseback, I only saw one person in medical whites milling about. I spoke first to the young man. "What the hell goes on at this place?"

The young man fired an answer back to me quickly. I would eventually know a great deal about this Lowery Jackson Baker standing in front of me in his pristine medical garb. Like many a college graduate in the early years of the Depression, Baker found himself caught in a time with no prospects for work. The struggle for money was no new notion to his hardworking family. He had accepted that he would attend the University of Mississippi only if he worked every evening after school, over his weekends, and throughout the summer months. In the fall of 1926, when he finally landed steady work in a drugstore in the town where he attended college, he had been certain his newly earned pharmacy degree would take him far in life. Then the flood of 1927 washed in, piling misery on top of a path of destruction. A year later, the Wilson Banking Company of Greenwood closed for liquidation. By noon of that historic day, people rushed on banks throughout the state. Baker returned to the old home place, figuring he would at least never go hungry working the family farm alongside his father.

Frustrated with the day-to-day routine keeping him away from the towns where he might pick up work in a drug store, Lowery Baker decided in a moment of desperation in late December 1930 to head west with a friend and let luck take its course. Bumming rides, eventually jumping freight trains, Baker and Wallace McGee spent the next years following whatever work could be found. The two covered some miles through Texas and Kansas, even some short stints in Colorado and California. 1932 found the two heading to Douglas, Arizona. Baker's luck landed him a job at a drug store. McGee moved on to other parts within two weeks. It felt good to be back behind the pharmacy counter again. At the job for four weeks, Russ Sellers, the man who had hired him, surprised him with a question.

"Lowery, I've been impressed with your work here in the store. Having said that, my question just might surprise you a bit. Would you consider taking another job?" Sellers did not even give Baker a moment to recover before he continued right on with more explanation. "You see, I'm involved in Arizona politics. I have been behind the effort to have the federal government locate their CCC Camp here in our area. There's a real need for a first-aid man in that camp if they are planning to take care of all those men for the long term. I think you are probably just the man for the job."

A day later, Lowery Jackson Baker left Douglas by way of Bisbee and the border route to Bisbee Junction, and then on to the CCC Camp at Ash Canyon. As it turned out, young Baker was the first to arrive, soon followed by three big trailer trucks, all driven by Mexicans. Even with his limited knowledge of Spanish, Baker figured out the supplies needed to be unloaded. Within moments of realizing the drivers were close to turning around and leaving, Lowery took charge with broken Spanish picked up in his travels across the country. By the time those in authority started pouring into the camp, all took notice of the young man who had managed to make a decent start at some much-needed organization. Within the week, the first aid station was up and running, and Baker heard himself called "Doc" more than once. As he settled into the world of camp life, the name stuck.

Now, September, a good year after he arrived at the CCC, Lowery stood, with a letter in his hand, facing two rough-looking cowboys on horseback. The letter contained devastating news. Both his father and his oldest brother had died one day apart. Deep in thought over the dilemma that he could see no way to make the long journey home at this time in his life, Baker took one hard look at the two men, stepped just a bit closer toward the man who had asked the question and shot off a quick answer. "Get off that horse, cowboy, and I'll straighten you out as to what the hell is going on here."

Campbell came to a quick conclusion. *A fellow does not hear this kind of full-of-spunk answer often.* He found himself glaring at the young man and continued thinking. *This kid is either a damn fool, or he just might hold his own with the best of men.* With that thought, he slowly got off the horse, returned the young man's hard look as he swung his reins around a nearby tree. William stayed on his horse with his hand resting near his gun.

Lowery took only a moment to access the younger man's position who remained on his horse. *It's time to cut this possible situation off at the pass.* "You two cowboys want a beer?"

Finn's eyes perked up as he looked the young man square in the face and answered, "Now, that sounds like a good idea. "Come on, William. Let's go."

§

A couple of hours later, after several more rounds of beer, the talk continued. Finn fell comfortably into using the name "Doc" as he not only told this stranger dressed in medical whites about his work with the cattle company but moved easily to details about the family ranch and his family. Lowery offered a tour of the CCC Camp. Although the son said very little, Doc could not help but notice that the older cowboy in spurs and chaps with a pistol at his side asked one question after the other. Eventually, late into the evening, when old man Campbell decided they better head back to the ranch, Lowery surprised himself as he offered the invitation. "You fellows are welcome to stop back by the camp when you happen to be in the area."

Needless to say, Lowery Baker was taken back when the next day at a camp staff meeting, Tex Moore, one of the older members of the Forestry Service team, looked right at Doc and said, "I know that cowboy you were walking camp with last evening. He's that Campbell fellow who is fairly well known around these parts for a temper that has certainly caused him some troubles in his time. Most reckon he comes by his hot-headedness from his grandpa. Everybody says he is the spittin' image of that man in more ways than looks. There's lots of talk about why Campbell fled the country several years back, totally disappeared for many years. Now he's shown up with a passel of kids from South America. No question, time has mellowed him a tad. Whatever the unembellished truth is about that night he went on a drunken shooting spree years back, I reckon it would be best, just in case, to never cross him. You just might get a taste of man behind the gossip that has only grown over the years."

Lowery had not easily made close friends with the younger men in the camp. Surprisingly he did feel very comfortable with Finn Campbell, who over the next couple of months, took him up on his invitation to stop back in for a visit. The unlikely friendship that formed between the two men over the first year of Baker's work finally led Finn to suggest that Baker come to the house and meet his family. By this time, in their unusual camaraderie, he knew quite a bit about Campbell's past. He knew the sad details of the wife who died in childbirth back in Brazil. The talk around the camp confirmed the seven children had been taken under the wing of Finn's mother, known as Grandma Campbell, around the territory. She too, had all the makings of being perhaps even more of a character than her son. *Even though I've been away from my own family for some time, coming from a long line of Scotch-Irish and Welsh, I do not quickly forget strong blood ties. In fact, the thought of visiting the Campbell ranch immediately makes me long for a home-cooked meal. I've heard many a tale about Finn Campbell's mother. Supposedly she can cook as good as she can shoot a gun. No question, she is a dead ringer. One of her meals alone would be worth the visit.*

§

The visit to the Campbell's home in April of 1934 proved to be more than a much-welcomed meal. The rancher's children, who ran the years with their ages, immediately found it easy to laugh and play with their special guest. *I suspect they don't see much company. Glad I can entertain them with my southern brogue. Course it brings to mind my siblings and their kids back in Mississippi.* He enjoyed the chance to catch up on news of William, who now worked as a ranch hand over in Sulphur Springs Valley. The kids also talked nonstop about the oldest daughter Anna. He quickly learned she was an honor student at the high school in Bisbee, where she served as a teaching assistant for the younger students. One of the sisters, Ola, quickly added, "On top of that, Anna has plans to start college classes next year. We think our sister might be smarter than the teacher."

My curiosity stirred as I asked about Finn Campbell's eldest daughter. "Just how old is this impressive student?"

Several voices around the table provided a quick answer. "She's just turned sixteen."

Quick thoughts filled my head. *Here I am twenty-five years. I can't say with any honesty that I've ever had any serious interest in a woman.* He surprised himself with the questions he wanted to ask regarding the eldest Campbell. He realized he regretted the absence of the opportunity to meet this daughter before she headed to school. "Tell me more about this sister who is smarter than her teacher." He noticed Finn shake his head in amusement. Grandma Campbell looked directly at me for the first time.

The time in Campbell's home passed quickly. I lingered longingly in the family atmosphere. Grandma Campbell's meal surpassed my expectations. But on the other hand, the older woman was just plumb "stand-offish," a term my Grandmother Baker often used.

The entire Campbell clan followed me to my horse as I left late into the evening. Some of the younger children wanted goodbye hugs. Mixed voices added, "Papa, can you bring Doc back to see us soon?" It was at that point that Grandma Campbell said her first words to me. "Hope you come back to see us sometime."

The invitation surprised me. Ola then totally threw me further off guard as she chimed in with her parting words. "We want you to like Anna. She sure is pretty!" Ola's remark brought on a serious look from the family matriarch. *Those coppery brown eyes could bore a hole into the ground.*

I turned my horse quickly, hoping no one noticed the blush that must be running up my neck and onto my face.

§

CCC Camp work filled my days and many of my nights. Young men from across the nation poured in to join the workforce. If one of them was not hurt in some way daily, I could be assured one of the horses or other animals would need my care. Never would I have dreamed this would be the work my pharmacy degree would land me. Some days I don't think I can give another shot or force another horse pill down a throat. I do enjoy Finn Campbell's frequent stops for a round of poker and a night of beer drinking. I've only been back to the ranch one more time since my first visit. Again, I enjoyed myself. Old man Campbell continues to intrigue me. No question, the man is a dedicated and caring father of his large family. On the other hand, the rough and tumble cowboy is one of the best poker-playing, beer-drinking, gun shooting fellows I've ever met. Lowery looked up from the injured horse he was working on. Both Campbell and his son William headed his way. *I've not seen much of William since he started full-time on the Sulphur Springs Ranch. It'll be good to catch up.*

"Howdy, fellows. This injured leg needs my attention at the moment."

William jumped from his horse to give a hand in calming the agitated mare. "So, William, it's been a while. About time you got a break from ranch work."

"Don't bet on that, Doc. Papa has me back at his place helping with the late spring branding. You should have figured out by now there is no downtime for a rancher."

Finn Campbell, still on his horse, chimed in. "It's a good thing I keep you busy. Maybe you'll stay out of trouble." We all chuckled with that remark before Campbell added quickly. "Doc, I hate that we can't stay. Looks like you got your hands full there. Wish I could leave William here to help you. We are just passing through, on our way to Bisbee. We're moving my daughter home for the summer. I stopped by to say that I would like you to meet my Anna Isabella."

Damn, here comes that flush of embarrassment. Why does the mention of Campbell's daughter get me blushing every time? This sixteen-year-old, who I've never laid eyes on, seems to have some sort of power over me. Only glancing up, I made my response strong. "Well, Finn, I would like to do just that. I'll make a point of coming out to the ranch sometime soon."

The injured horse required my attention throughout the night. The nightly vigil allowed me plenty of time to think about Campbell's invitation. The insistence that I meet his eldest daughter continued to baffle me. Just when I figured I had come about as close to figuring out Finn Campbell, II as any man ever would, the ole cowboy found a way to surprise me. I concluded sometime back that the community gossip was accurate for the most part. No question, the tall, lanky cowboy took it seriously if anyone dared to cross him the wrong way when it came to his family. Just as he did not take kindly to questions about his mystery years in South America. Yet, he's just told me he wants me to meet his Anna Isabella. I suspect that is as close as it gets to understanding the intrigue behind the man.

No doubt Anna, the oldest, holds a special place in Campbell's heart. On more than one occasion, I've heard many a local cowboys ask Finn when his pretty daughter would be coming back in town. The ole cuss set every hopeful male straight in a matter of seconds. "Let me assure you, young man. My daughter no more has time for the likes of you than I do. So, don't waste your time coming out to my place."

Back in the pharmacy tent to catch a little sleep, my brain stayed wide awake as I mulled the situation. *Who would have thought Finn Campbell would come out with such an invitation?*

§

About a week later, I found myself putting on a new suit of medical whites and heading across the canyon to the Campbell ranch. Several of the kids were outside helping with the wash. A feisty, young woman who just had to be the much talked about oldest daughter directed the whole ordeal. I stayed on my horse and watched the whole scene. She knew just how to get all the younger girls to finish the chore in record time. Looking at her dark, wavy, shoulder-length hair glistening in the sunlight soon found me taking in more. Her attractive, shapely body was evident in the riding pants and fitted blouse she wore. In that same moment that my thoughts were about to take me further with desire, Finn and his son headed my way. I got off the horse at record speed but still had trouble breaking away from the vision that I still took in from the corner of my eye. Glued to the spot, with her father and brother getting closer by the moment, I felt the flush of beet-red embarrassment move up my neck. The younger girls' shouts of excitement spared me from myself. "Anna, Anna, it's Doc. The one we've been telling you about. You know, Papa's friend."

My mind quickly jumped to other thoughts. *She won't even so much as look up from that laundry. I may as well not even be here waiting for her to take any notice of me. What was I thinking to head out here with any hopes of making a great impression on this young woman?* Time would eventually help me to understand that even though Anna was very comfortable in the classroom working with students, at sixteen, she was still shy when it came to men.

Little did Baker take in that Anna was caught up in her own mixed feelings at the moment. From the corner of her eye, she managed to steal a couple of glimpses of this *friend* of Papa's. Something about his smile and the hint of mischief in his eyes certainly got her attention. The words still caught in her throat. As this intriguing guest stood there as her dad and brother moved closer, no words formed in the midst of her emotions. *If I just keep hanging the laundry, maybe he will head off and talk to Papa and William so I can gather my thoughts.*

§

Fortunately, Grandma Campbell stood nearby on the porch. She read the situation like a very familiar book. Her commanding voice got everyone's attention. "Now, kids, stop messing around with this clean laundry before it all ends up in the dirt, and we have to start all over. Guest or no guest, I'll have every last one of you out here with the scrub board instead of sitting down to the dinner table. Now, Anna, girl, where are your manners? Set that work aside, and let me make an introduction." As she reached her rough hand toward Lowery, she added. "This is Lowery Baker. He's in charge of the clinic over at the CCC Camp. He's become a good friend of your Papa's. What amazes me is that he keeps coming back even though he has to put up with all these Campbell kids running around like they have never seen company in their lives."

An eternity seemed to pass before she could make herself look up. "Good to meet you." As soon as the words were out, she went right back to her work.

In that brief glimpse, Lowery noticed her eyes. Not at all the almost deep black of her siblings. *Was it the glare of the sun? Or did her brown eyes really appear to be streaked with copper? I could get lost in those eyes.* He knew at that moment he had to stop staring at her.

As he would later admit to Finn Campbell's dear daughter about the day, he first met her. "I fell in love with you in that instant. You were the prettiest girl I had ever seen. Believe me; I've seen a few in my travels."

This visit to the ranch proved challenging. I spent most of the time trying not to look at Anna Campbell. *What will Finn Campbell think if he figures out I am infatuated with his daughter? She's sixteen. Campbell will not put up with anything but the most respectful of interest in his eldest. Why did he make a point encouraging me to meet her?* I surprised myself with an apology to the family soon after the meal ended. "I hate to eat and run, as my grandmother often said." Then I told a big ole' lie. "I've got an injury back at the camp that I can't stay away from very long." I could not help but notice that Anna had kept her distance from me throughout the visit. *I've got to get away from here. Clear my head. Who knows, maybe I'll find a way to think of something else other than Anna Campbell if I can manage to get on my horse and ride.*

§

Only a few days passed after the visit to the Campbell ranch, both of Finn's sons showed up at the camp. As the three of them passed their time in the canteen, William turned the talk toward his sister Anna. "You know, Doc, my family has taken a liking to you." Then with mischief lacing his voice, he added. "And to beat it all, Anna Isabella is sweet on you!"

I blurted a shocked response. "Well, she sure didn't act like it! She seemed to enjoy that damn laundry more than me."

Douglas didn't offer a word. William only looked at me and grinned. *What am I supposed to read into that grin?* Lost in confusion, I gave up on making any sense of the situation. My words poured out. "Well, if the truth be known, I sort of like her too, but I see a problem. Fellows, I am soon to be twenty-six. Anna is only sixteen. Those are grounds for your father to shoot me if I even think about ever doing anything to hurt her. That seems a dangerous spot for a man to be in."

William and Douglas seemed to focus on their beers for a bit. The older brother then offered his words of wisdom. "Sounds like you got our ole' man pegged. As to your other concern, just keep coming out to the ranch like you did before you met our sister. I would have thought you've been around enough to know that most women act just the opposite of what they are really feeling." With those words, the Campbell brothers finished off the last of the beer. One headed to Sulphur City and the other back to the Campbell ranch.

I decided I may as well follow William's advice since I couldn't think of anything else except heading back to Campbell's place. *I do want to see Anna again. Maybe get to know her a bit.* I had concluded sometime back that I have to figure out a way to see her without the passel of her younger siblings being in the midst of us. They have a way of getting me to tell one story after the other of my adventures, hopping trains across the country. Then there's her papa to contend with. How will I ever find a way for some alone time with her? *Anna, although you are openly cordial and nice, you show no interest in anything I have to say.* Down the road a bit, I would learn that she often stood just inside another room listening to every word I said with what she calls my easy Southern accent. Instead, two visits in a row, I left the ranch again with my hurt feelings in tow. *That damn William sure does not know a thing about his sister if he thinks she's sweet on me.*

§

In late July, Finn Campbell finished up a poker game with Lowery and some of the fellows at the camp. He then looked directly at Baker and asked, "I know you manage to get to and from the ranch on that old mare, but would you be able to stay on a spirited horse and look anything like a real cowboy?"

"Hell, Finn, growing up back in Mississippi, I could stay on a mule without a saddle."

Baker did not see Campbell's next words coming. "Well, I've got a little outing planned for you and Anna. You two are going horseback riding two days from now when you come out to my place."

Lowery, at first, thought the beer was talking. "Does Anna know anything about this plan of yours?"

"Sure, she knows. Just be there around two o'clock. We will have one of our horses ready for you." With that comment, he raked the rest of his winnings off the table and prepared to leave.

Doc blurted out one question. "Does Anna know how to ride?

Campbell responded by laughing and shaking his head as he ambled out the door.

§

I arrived at the ranch well ahead of time. Anna waited ready in the same riding gear she wore the day she was working on the laundry with the kids. This time she looked at me directly as I noticed the fitted white blouse in contrast to her olive skin and dark hair. No time was given to talking. Anna led the way by mounting her horse. As we headed up Ash Canyon, I quickly took in that Anna was at one with her horse. She rode with ease and command that explained Finn's reaction when I had questioned his daughter's riding skills. *I better pay less attention to Anna's beauty and more to staying on this horse. Did she purposely pick the rockiest terrain she could find?*

As we made our way past a couple of homesteaders' places, she slowed her pace and rode by my side. "Just up ahead, there is an old mine shaft near the top of the next ridge. From that spot, you can see the Huachuca Mountain Range in one direction and the Catalinas from the other." As they approached the area, I easily saw why Anna had mentioned the view. Without sharing another word, Anna got off her horse, tied her Paint at the entrance, and motioned for me to do the same. Anna turned and walked into the entrance to the shaft. In a bit, I found her sitting on a little rock shelf right inside the entrance. Without hesitation, I sat right down by her side. Before I could find a reason not to, I wrapped one arm around her and kissed her.

At first, Anna drew back and started to act shy and disinterested. Then she melted. The first kiss turned into a second one. Lowery could think of nothing else. It was Anna who pulled away and added softly, "We better get back down the mountain."

Following this outing, and considering it had been instigated by Anna's father, I found all the courage I needed to make my way to the Campbell ranch regularly. Many days I would finish work at camp and head out for a short visit, often riding back late at night under the light of the moon. Most evenings were spent on the porch swing with Anna, talking and holding hands, stealing a kiss when we could.

The younger children continued to be in the thick of my visits until Grandma Campbell would issue her warning. "Now, kids, it's time you got yourselves into bed. Doc and Anna, you can talk a little longer, but not too long, you hear?" As often as possible, we headed off on the horses. I always found the right moment to give Anna a serious kiss. As the fall progressed, we were doing more kissing and hugging than horseback riding. I remained mindful of Anna's age, a fact intensified by my healthy respect for what Finn Campbell may be capable of if his daughter was wronged in any way.

The month of August passed in record time. It seemed no time at all before Anna had to leave once again for school. She would be attending her last year of high school in Tombstone instead of Bisbee. She would be able to come home more often. We agreed to write while she was away.

§

The remainder of 1934 brought a lot of talk around the camp about the government work program coming to an end. When I heard about a job at a pharmacy in Nogales, I decided I better take it if I hope to stay anywhere near Anna. As soon as I had the new job secured, I knew it was time to take another big step. I headed to the ranch with a purpose. Dinner never seemed to last so long. At last, as Campbell led me out to see the new colt, I worked up my nerve. "Finn, rumor has it that the camp is about to close down. I could easily move where the government work takes me." He could not help but notice that Campbell had not yet turned around to face him.

He continued. "I've been offered a job at a pharmacy in Nogales. I accepted the position." The tall, lanky rancher stopped walking, turned slowly, and looked him in the eye. Now, somewhat nervous, Lowery stammered out the next words, "I am in love with Anna. I would like to marry her someday. I know she needs to finish high school. In the meantime, I can work in Nogales, save a little money to settle down, and make a life for your daughter. I also need to go back home to Mississippi. I need to see my mother. There are some loose ends to tie up after the recent family deaths of my father and brother. I have some responsibility to put the homeplace in order for her. In my way of thinking, I need to put that obligation behind me before I come back here to settle down. My new employer knows about my need to get back to the South for a few months. He assured me he always needs a good pharmacist. My plan is to work for a bit to build up the money I need for my trip back to Mississippi. With your blessing, I would like to ask Anna to wait for me."

"Son, I guess you know if I had not liked you, I would have never insisted you come out to the ranch to meet my daughter. Of course, you can marry her. Besides, if I did not say yes, the rest of the family would never speak to me again. I suspect you are a smart man. Smart enough to know you better treat her right." As they headed into the barn, Campbell concluded, "Now, let's take a look at this little fellow. He'll grow up to be a fine horse someday."

§

Anna and I stayed in touch throughout her last year in high school, writing letters back and forth. We saw each other whenever she was in from school, and I could get away from my work at the pharmacy. The year passed quickly. The summer of 1935 brought Anna back home. I visited the ranch as often as I could. By the middle of June, the official marriage proposal came. My trip back to Mississippi could fit perfectly with Anna attending the university in the fall on the scholarship she had received. In my mind, the plan came together. I should be able to wrap up all that I needed to help with back at the homeplace, then be back to marry Anna in the late spring after she finished her first year of college.

Anna left for Tucson and the exciting new world of the University of Arizona. I returned to a Mississippi homeplace that I hardly recognized. Economic conditions remained grim in the deep South and left their mark even on our family farm. The death of both our father and our oldest brother, left my other two brothers with the responsibility of working the land and managing our farm. Our mother's health added one more layer of need to all that met me as I made my way back to the homeplace. The responsibility that faced me moved over me with a heaviness that I had not expected.

Within days of my arrival, I went job hunting. I knew the

extra money was needed until we could get the farm back up to productivity. Fortunately, I found some every-other-week work. The travel back and forth to the Delta town of Belzoni proved challenging, but I knew I needed to give equal time to the old homeplace. On my week off from my job, I worked alongside my brothers on the farm. Anna wrote several times a week. I answered as often as I could. Although most of my earnings went to the desperate family situation, I did manage to buy an engagement ring. For the first time in a while, I felt a little spunk in my step as I thought of Anna's excitement when she would eventually open the box that I put in the mail as left the pharmacy before heading back to the homeplace that evening.

§

As soon as I entered the doorway, I knew something tragic had happened. My older brother Thatcher rarely came in from the fields until dark. There he sat, holding Mama's hand. No question, she was in tears. "What's going on here?"

"Lowery, Daniel is in the hospital over in Winona. His leg is broke bad. He's lost lots of blood. I've just made it back home myself from getting him over there earlier. The two of us were up before daylight this morning. The cattle need to be moved to another pasture. You know the work it takes."

My head hung heavily. I could see all too clearly the mess we were in with my younger brother, now unable to do the heavy work required to keep the place going. Finally, he asked, "Where are Jessie, CD, and the kids?"

Mama finally spoke her first words. "They're all out working to move those cattle."

Thatcher looked at his brother. No words were needed. They both knew what had to be done.

§

The next morning, Lowery headed to Winona to the only hospital in the area. He thankfully found Daniel stable. The doctor had little in the way of encouragement as to any quick recovery. After visiting briefly with his younger brother, Baker headed into town.

Thatcher and I talked late into last night. I knew I had to find work close enough for me to help every morning and every night back at the homeplace in Poplar Creek. At the Winona pharmacy, I heard about a job in the drug store in Kilmichael, the town closest to our Baker homeplace. After a quick stop back at the hospital, I headed out to sort more of the details of our predicament. Two thoughts weighed heavily on my mind. *Will I ever get back to Arizona and my Anna? I cannot even consider just leaving Mama and my brothers in the middle of this challenge.*

§

I found the letter waiting back at my room at the end of the school day. *Lowery has no choice except to stay with his family until the situation improves.* Spring turned into summer, and then the fall of 1936 moved in. Day-to-day work at the homeplace and his job at the nearby pharmacy made it almost impossible to write with any regularity. To make matters worse, I had not been able to return to the university because of a lack of money once my first-year scholarship ended. I sent my answer as fast as I could write it down. "I plan to marry you, Lowery Baker. If I need to move to Mississippi, then so be it. I trust you to make the arrangements. Please allow me a little time to break the news to my family and spend some much-needed time with them."

§

As I kissed Father goodbye, I recalled the major changes to my life years back as the family rode away in a carriage from our ranch near Rio. I said goodbye to so much at that time. Now, here I am with equal measures of excitement and concern as I face the unknown once again. Lowery met me at the train station in Winona. We headed straight for the homeplace. The Baker family Bible holds the record: Anna Isabella Campbell married Lowery Jackson Baker at 8:30 p.m. on the night of July 27, 1937. Except for occasional visits to see my family, Lowery and I never returned to live in Arizona as we had once planned. We lived and raised our family in Mississippi.

Chapter 15

"Belinda, I am so sorry to be calling at this time."

"Sarah, what is wrong? It's 4:00 in the morning. Only something serious would get you up at this time of day. Tell me before I pass out from worry."

"I am very aware of the time. Listen, Belinda, I'm in a real hurry. You're right. I'm caught up in a bit of an emergency. I'd rather explain all the details in person at some point. Is there any chance Stephanie is still in town? I know they always come to your place for New Years. Any chance they are still there."

"No, she and Brian headed back to Asheville yesterday. Sarah, what is going on? What do you mean a bit of an emergency? Are you hurt?"

"Belinda, I've got to talk to Stephanie. She's the only person I can think of that might help under the circumstances. There's a baby involved. He is sick and needs to see a doctor immediately. Don't even ask why I can't just go to the local emergency room. Please, Belinda, just trust me on this. We've worked together too long. You know I would not ask if there were any other way. Remember, my doctor just retired, and Shelly, my PA, is visiting her parents in Florida. Instead of me wasting time to make the call, can you let her know we are on our way to Asheville.?"

"Of course, I will. But please tell me what is going on. You know Step will want more information."

"We have the mom and baby ready to load in the car. We need to get on our way."

"Sarah, who is "we"? Oh, never mind. I know you won't tell me over the phone. I'm coming over right now. As soon as I can get service, I will call Stephanie and give her your message with the promise to let her know more. I am going with you. You know, good and well, you better be prepared to spill the details. And don't even think about arguing with me."

"Belinda, you can't possibly go with us."

Colin, who had stepped back inside was listening to every word of my one-sided conversation, suddenly grabbed my elbow and said into the phone. "That may not be a bad idea. How quickly can you get here?"

Giving Colin a questioning look, I added. "Hurry, Belinda."

Just as I was about to hang up, I heard one last tirade of questioning. "Was that a man's voice?" Then before she had time to pursue that question any further, I heard her explanation to her husband. "Hon, I'm driving in to meet Sarah. We are heading to Asheville."

Scott's deep voice reply came quickly. "Why the hell you doing that?" I could only hope she told him to go back to sleep and forget anything he just heard.

§

The moment I got off the phone, Collin started in. "How long will it take Belinda to get here?"

"Twenty minutes, probably less. "

"You got everything you need together, right?" Glad we got my car from the bed and breakfast earlier." He shook his head and added, "I've never told so many lies in my life as I did to the owner. Sarah, I want to explain why I think it might be a good idea to have Belinda come along."

I rolled my eyes and commented. "Well, that would be appreciated. I question getting one more person caught up in this situation."

"Sarah, I can tell you with certainty the one person we do not need involved… my wife. I have not yet figured out what sort of explanation I will give Megan for my absence. She may have already called my parents and found out I have not been with them." He stopped talking. It was obvious he was deep in thought. She's already on a tear because I walked out and did not attend that damn party with her. She will only be more irritated when I show back up. *I don't know if I've ever seen her as angry when I didn't cave to her idea of a happy New Year celebration. I've always done whatever she wants. I'll never forget the shock on her face when I walked out the door, assuring her I would not attend another party that was guaranteed to end the same way they always did.*

"Sarah," he paused before finishing. "I think it's better if we have two cars in Asheville. I am scheduled to meet someone on campus this week with the research I am close to publishing. Also, I want to be at the hospital as much as possible. I do not think Megan is someone you want to know about our adventure in time travel, much less the Cherokee mother and child that we brought back with us. I can't imagine she would ever believe the truth. However, that would not stop her from gossiping about the far-fetched story as she attempts to explain my absence with her friends. Megan is not used to being told no. A line has been drawn in our sandbox, so to speak. Please, help me keep her out of this situation."

I did not have the time or energy to ask the questions building in my head. I nodded toward the bedroom door. "I need to check on Savannah and the baby."

Little William cried. I stepped into the bedroom and offered to take the baby. The exhausted mother looked at me in desperation. She tried to speak. But words never came. I saw the concern in the dark pools of her eyes. I simply took the child into my arms.

"Savannah, try not to worry. We are going somewhere to get some help. You have been through a great deal. Please, just rest while you can. I've got your baby."

Colin stood at the bedroom door. "Sarah, I want to gather up some blankets and pillows for the car." As I helped this man who, in many ways, was still a stranger to me, I once again noticed the care and thoughtfulness that he had about the situation we were caught up in. Reality pushed in on me. *The long-anticipated year 2000 has arrived. Yet here I stand looking at a young Cherokee woman from another century, lying on my bed. She's worn out from childbirth that occurred less than a day ago in the year 1900. No woman should have to endure what she has been through in the past hours. First, Colin carried her to the old store. What must she think about the strange occurrence that has now landed her in an even stranger world? A modern house, with all of its new noises coming from appliances she has never seen the likes of before.... How could I begin to explain, if she were back in her time, that Miss Sadie's house is right up the road from where my office home presently sits overlooking the bend in the river. All would have to wait until she was past her exhaustion, her shock, and, of course, the ordeal she was about to face as we attempted to get the baby the medical help that we suspect he needs.*

As I bounced the baby into quietness, Colin talked more. "Sarah, I trust you will explain to Belinda what is going on. What's the point of not telling her everything? Do you agree?"

Tired, worn, and worried, I nodded a yes.

"I'll be right behind you in the Land Rover. I have a bag phone. Any chance Belinda has one? It will help to be able to communicate the closer we get to Asheville. You know Belinda's daughter-in-law will want some explanation. I know I am the one that insisted we get the baby to a bigger city. I still think I am right on that. We would end up being transferred to a bigger hospital anyway. I'm sure that mind of yours is thinking ahead to the paperwork at the hospital. How can we explain to Savannah what to say or not say?"

I found it impossible to focus on all Colin's questions at once. "Belinda does have a phone and just confirmed she is bringing it. I need to give all my attention to the infant." I could feel his feverish body through the layer of blanket. *Come on, Belinda. We need to get to Asheville.* I soothed the baby until he gave over to sleep. *Perhaps I can now think for a few minutes, undisturbed about Savannah and what happened back at the store in her time.*

I suspected the whole ordeal, on top of childbirth, and the arrival in our time has rendered her speechless. *That may not be a bad thing. In fact, it solves many of the problems we might run into with doctors and the world of the hospital.* Although Colin and I had experienced the time travel phenomenon once before, when it started once again, we too were taken by surprise. I suspect I had convinced myself it would just not happen. There we stood. Still somewhat shaken from that ever-so-slight shift in the air, my eyes then adjusted quickly to our new surroundings. With the help of the lantern Colin held in his hand, I knew immediately we had somehow ended up in the springhouse on my property.

The little house that enclosed the double springheads, built at the very place we had first found Savannah when she was in labor, messed with my mind for a bit. The nagging details finally surfaced. Colin's and my second trip through time had us departing from the same location both times. Wonder why we have arrived back in our present at a yet different location? The area down near the depot had initially welcomed us to the past. My springhouse took us in as we returned from Savannah's time. As I took in the boxes built around the springheads, I was reminded that Colin and I recently drank from those sources of water in a time period before the boxes were built. It stunned me momentarily that this water still ran, now filling the wooden boxes that Macy had discovered that first spring we lived on the river property. My initial shock passed as I realized we were in close walking distance to my office. The thought of reconnecting to my time filled my brain.

§

Savannah remained almost silent. Extremely tired, grabbing short naps between bouts of little Williams's crying left her exhausted. Several times she looked at one of us as if she were about to ask a question. Her energy failed her time and time again. As I reached for the fretting baby again, I wanted to explain we would be leaving in a few minutes to get the baby to a doctor. The fact that we would be going in a car seemed to throw my brain into a state of confusion. *What can I possibly say that will make this person, who is new to our time, take in the concept of a fast-moving car? How do I begin to give her an idea of the sights she will soon be seeing?*

Colin followed me into the bedroom. He saw me comforting the baby. As he had so often done in the short time we were in each other's company, he came out with the very thought that seemed to be trapped in my head. "Savannah, we are leaving for the doctor. You will ride in a car. More than likely, you have never seen one. If you somehow saw a picture of the first car that came out in 1896, the one you will be riding in today is very different. Again, you will have to trust us. Sarah will not leave your side. It will take a while to get to the town where the doctor is located. Take the opportunity to sleep as much as you possibly can. Someday we will try to explain more to you." As he finished his thoughts, I heard Belinda's car pull up.

I dreaded the round of questions that my dear but bossy friend would certainly ask. Tired and still unable to truly process the depth of the event that had transpired over the hours leading up to our departure to Asheville, I knew this strong-willed woman would eventually pry every detail out of me. The trip we were about to take would not be relaxing at all. I could hear the front door opening. I looked at Colin, thinking briefly of all that we had shared in just a matter of hours. "Can you take the baby? Let me say something to Belinda before she takes in..." I hesitated and looked at the three people in front of me. I could not find any more words.

Within moments I faced my dear friend of many years. Her eyes locked with mine. Before she could say a word, Colin decided to once again force the conversation into full gear. Belinda took in his tall frame, then quickly cut her eyes back at me with a slight grin forming. I do not think I will ever forget her first words as she quickly diverted her eyes from the man who had casually walked into the office space from my bedroom to Sadie's lamp that made the journey through time and now set on the edge of the kitchen bar. "What's this? "Are you expecting the lights to go out?"

I decided quickly not to explain. Instead, I asked, "Did you reach Stephanie?"

"Yes, she's going to meet us at the clinic. She has lots of questions and wants to talk to you as soon as we can get on the road and have some decent service."

At this point, Belinda's lanky form paced back and forth across the office area. I recognized her nervous gesture of tossing her head of thick blond curls back and forth in a state of confusion. Her silence filled the room in the midst of the look she kept giving me. Again, Colin set us in motion. "Ladies, we have to get Savannah and the baby to a doctor."

With that comment, Colin and I left Belinda in her state of confusion and walked into the bedroom. When we came out in a few minutes, I held the baby. Colin carried Savannah. "Belinda, the mother, and child will ride with you and me in your car if that's okay. Colin will follow in his car."

I had earlier decided that Savannah had to change clothes. The calico dress that she wore from her time would be an instant giveaway that something was not quite right with the situation. The loose-fitting sweat pants and top I chose bought us some time with Belinda's questions that were sure to come. Little William spared us any further explanation as he began, once again, to cry in earnest.

§

Savannah held her baby very close as we nestled her into the back seat, made into somewhat of a makeshift bed, in hopes she could rest as we made our way to Asheville. Little William's nonstop crying temporarily squelched the conversation that was certain to surface. We passed the exit to Robbinsville before the baby dropped into a sound sleep. I saw Belinda try to glimpse the backseat. Then she started in a low voice. "Listen, Sarah, you have got to tell me what you think is going on with the baby. Why did we not just go to the emergency room? As soon as I know more, we need to get Stephanie on the phone once we are out of the gorge." Once again, she shook her head of blonde curls as if in response to the many answers she needed. Then added with a snicker. "Of course, I am suspecting there are several more details I need the scoop on also. Since I'm assuming someday you plan to wake up and come back to teaching, I'd hate not to be able to hire you because I don't have enough information!"

"Belinda, after I tell you all, you may hope I never return to the classroom. More than likely, you will think I've lost my mind."

I smiled. Her eyebrows raised as she added, "My dear friend, I came to that conclusion years back in our friendship."

"Savannah has never seen a car before today, much less ridden in one. Perhaps even more importantly, she just gave birth last evening." I could not help but notice that for once, Belinda did not say a word. "In other words, take it easy in the gorge. A bat out of hell does not begin to be an adequate description of your driving." I took a moment to look at Savannah in the back seat. Her eyes were closed.

"Much of what I am about to tell you has never been told to this incredible young woman asleep on your back seat. I hate to add more stress and concern to her life at the moment. First and foremost, her child is very sick. We cannot get the fever down. You can tell by his crying that something is wrong. He is barely nursing. Why waste time at the ER when more than likely, he would be sent on to more specialized pediatric care? Then it might also be wise for other reasons not to deal with this situation in the town of Hunterstown."

Belinda spoke in her authoritative principal voice. "Now, you certainly have more explaining to do."

"I just so hope Savannah is sound asleep."

Just as I was about to start the saga, the young mother spoke very softly. "You helped me at the springheads. Now you are helping my William." Those were the only words we would hear from this gentle person for several days. I did assume from that point on that Savannah had and would continue to listen intently to all that went on around her.

"Belinda, I need you to confirm the date. And, also, did any of the concerns play out with the Y2K situation?

I actually thought she might drive off the road. As she corrected the wheel and responded, I could easily sense the shock in her voice. "Sarah, it's January 4th. The New Year came in without incident except that I had a bit too much to drink at the New Year's Eve Party. I've been back at school for the past two days. Why would you not know the date and what is now common knowledge about Y2K to most of the world?"

I felt stunned by the date. I failed to take in that Belinda was no longer talking. My mind tried to make some sense of the still unexplainable time situation that Colin and I had experienced. *Was there some significance to the fact that once again, it took two days to make the trip through time? I wonder if Colin is figuring out some of these details from the radio as he drives?*

Belinda's voice brought me back to attention. "Sarah, keep talking. You've yet to really explain anything."

Meanwhile, I grasped at straws for some explanation that did not sound like lunacy. I went back into the history. Shared the two dreams, then I tiptoed into the discovery of the building just down from the property. The time travel piece that led us to Savannah in labor seemed to come out in broken bits and pieces as I still struggled to make sense of what had happened. I turned in my seat to look at this dear Cherokee woman that I described in my explanation. No doubt, she, like my friend Belinda, listened to every word.

I expected Belinda to react any minute. She certainly would declare my story to be ridiculous. Her condescending tone would be heard any minute, more than likely suggesting I had lost my mind. Instead, she kept her gaze straight ahead as if she dared not take her eyes off the road.

Silence filled the car. Finally, she turned her head, just briefly, and looked me square in the eyes. No mistaking the look of concern. Within a moment, her eyes locked with mine. She never said a word. Instead, she turned her gaze to the road ahead and remained silent. I knew by that one look she had given me that she believed every word. I also suspected she was as scared as I was at the moment.

Except for what turned into non-stop whimpers from little William, we drove in silence for several miles. Belinda broke the quiet as she softly said my name a couple of times. Then she added, "How..." but stopped after the one word. She then shook her head as if clearing out some unwanted clutter. "When..." Once again, she paused. With a little chuckle, she tried again. "Okay. Sarah, there's a very nice-looking man following right behind us, presumably going wherever you lead. This man is obviously involved in all that you have just told me. For once, it would be perfectly fine if you told me you met him through some online dating service. In fact, that would almost thrill me at the moment. Is there anything I need to know up-front about how you met this man?"

"Belinda, that's another story in itself. He showed up, out of the blue, one day at the office. I will tell you more some other time. I do think we better try that call to Stephanie since we are out of the gorge. The baby had stopped crying several minutes back. I reached back to place my hand on his little head. No question, the fever raged.

My attention turned back to Belinda, who mumbled under her breath, "A friend? Maybe…he just happened to join you on this unexplainable trip into the past?" Then a bit louder, "Sarah, why don't normal things happen in your life?" She had turned briefly to face me. Both eyebrows shot up with questioning as she spoke again. "Let's get Step on the phone."

"Let me run something by you. Colin and I have had very little time to process what we are caught up in. We did conclude pretty quickly 'our story' could quickly become the newest three-ring circus if word gets out of all that I have just told you. Should we tell Step all the details? It may make a difference with the baby's treatment. I get that we are putting your daughter-in-law in a position to never say a word as she somehow navigates this little fellow through the medical help he probably needs. What do you think?"

"Maybe we just tell her that mother and baby mysteriously showed up at your place. We explain that it took some time to even get her name from her and to hear her whisper "William" to her baby. Then if complications develop, we may have to tell her more. Can you encourage Savannah not to say too much?"

"Belinda, I don't think there is much to worry about in that department." As I turned again to check on the two in the backseat, I added. "No doubt she is traumatized by all that she has been through. But, yes," as I nodded at the young mother, her dark eyes locked on mine, "I am sure she understands she is not to say a word about how she got here."

With that answer hanging in the air, my friend reached for the clumsy phone. In seconds she stumbled through opening apologies for calling at such an hour. Stephanie had married Belinda's eldest son just a little over a year ago. She worked as a physician's assistant in the Asheville area. "Listen, Step, it's a strange situation. A very sick baby is involved. Sarah feels the little fellow needs more specialized medical care." She stopped talking for a moment. Stephanie must be asking questions. Then Belinda spoke again. "Well, of course, it's the Sarah you think it is. Here, why don't you talk to her? And, Step, trust me on this one, okay?"

"Step, I'm so sorry to disturb you." I explained that I had monitored the fever for some time. I could not get it down, then his incessant crying, I became concerned the child would need more than the Hunterstown Medical Center could offer. Then, to be very honest, this is a strange situation. I felt better about working with someone I knew personally."

Step kicked into her professional mode. "Tell me more about what has you so concerned about the baby. I want to make sure I get the right help lined up."

I shared every detail I could about the baby's symptoms, then asked, "Should I be concerned that the baby is no longer crying, not even a whimper?"

I could hear the intake of Step's breath before she responded. "Sarah, it sounds like an infection of some sort. I'm sure we can get to the root of the problem. You know you need to get here as soon as possible. Have you noticed any difficulty with the baby's breathing?" Once I assured her I had not, she added. "I'll meet you at the clinic. If anything new develops, please call because you may need to go straight to the hospital."

"I have one more concern. This young mother has no identification on her. Will that present a problem? What kind of red tape are we going to run into?"

"Sarah, we'll worry about those problems when we need to. Just get to Asheville quickly and safely. Remember, my mother-in-law is driving! I know a lot of people at the hospital. We will get this child the right medical attention. Now, it's your turn to trust me. Let me talk with Belinda. I want to make sure she knows where to come. Sarah, Belinda says frequently that she always drives the two of you because you can't follow directions for anything. This is no time to get lost."

As Belinda finished up with Step, I returned to the questions that bombarded my mind. *What could explain the loss of time when we traveled back and forth in time. When the question comes up as to when the baby was born, will my answer be accurate?*

I decided to tell Belinda the thought I struggled with at the moment. Again, I saw her shake her head of blonde curls. Before giving her any time for further questions, I said. "I need to give Colin a call and let him know what is going on. Just as I was about to reach for the big phone resting on the center console, it rang. Belinda answered. Then looking me once again directly in my eyes, she added. "It's Colin."

Before I thought about it, the words slipped out, somewhat under my breath. "That seems to happen a great deal." I reached for the phone. "Colin, I know you must be anxious to know what is going on."

"How is the baby doing? I cannot begin to imagine what Savannah must be thinking about her first car ride." I tried to bring him current. As soon as I shared that I had told Belinda the story of how Savannah and the baby entered our lives, he immediately asked. "Did she believe you?"

"Interestingly, Belinda did not question the truth of what I shared. She feels strongly that we tell Stephanie only what she needs to know to get the baby to the right medical help. We have decided to say that the mother and child just showed up at my place, and the mother seems to be in perhaps a state of shock. I have only confirmed she gave birth within the past 24 hours and the situation with the baby's fever and state of discomfort. You know we both agree the fewer people who know the details, the better."

Colin responded with questions. "How is the baby? What about Savannah? How is she handling the car ride?" Do you think she is taking in the conversation between you and Belinda?"

"No question, little William is feverish. Not much crying, just whimpers now and then. Savannah does not seem to be noticeably bothered by riding in a car. On that last question," I paused, feeling fairly certain, this stranger to our modern world, was taking in a great deal as she sat on the back seat of an automobile for the first time in her life. "I would say indeed yes to that last question." Taking in our location near Waynesville, I asked, "Are you coming to the clinic with us?

"I would like to. Then I'll see what unfolds for the baby before I decide what to do next?"

"Colin, I just found out the date from Belinda. It's January 4th. Yes, it took a couple of days to travel. How do you plan to explain that many days away from Asheville?"

"Sarah, I have been listening to the radio. Of course, I noted the same detail with the date. It won't be the first time I have stayed away from home for several days. She's used to me heading to my parents' house when I can't…." He hesitated. "When I need to get away. She typically never calls to find out if I have any plan of ever returning." Then he surprised me with the direction his conversation took. "I wish I could find the courage to take the step."

Silence passed between us. "Colin, I think I better make a call to Mississippi. There were a couple of calls from my family on the answering machine back at the office. I don't want to let too much time pass before I touch base with my kids. If my mom senses anything is off, she will pack the kids up and head to North Carolina in a heartbeat. Now, why don't I let you talk to Belinda. She will explain where we are going in Asheville."

My mind drifted briefly into deep thought about Colin. He had only once referred to his wife by name. Never used the word "wife" in the time I had known him. Pain filled any conversation he had about his marriage. *Is it possible I am so filled with anger over men that I have shut out the possibility that a man could be on the hurting end in a marriage gone bad?"*

"Before I hand the phone over, I need to know how you are doing. We both have been up and under stress for many hours nonstop. There's not a chance I could fall asleep riding with Belinda, but what about you?"

"I'm fine. My mind is on overload and has been the entire time I have been on the road. I know what I am about to say is really not a priority at the moment, but it's a problem I can't shake from my brain. Can we possibly hope to make time travel work on demand once again when Savannah and her baby need to go back? "

I could not take on the question at the moment. "Drive carefully, Colin. Here's Belinda."

The moment I handed over the phone, Savannah called out to me from the back seat. "Sarah!"

As I turned in my seat, I could see worry all over her face. She handed her baby toward me.

"Belinda, slow it down. I am crawling over the seat."

As soon as I got closer and took the baby in my arms, I could hear the struggle for breath. His little body reacted with the effort of each breath. *This is the concern Step had raised. To make matters worse, he is burning up with a fever.*

I heard Belinda explaining to Colin what was going on in the back seat. I interrupted. "We need to get Step on the phone. Now."

Once Belinda explained the current situation to her daughter-in-law, I knew from her silence, Step must be reacting. Then my dear friend assured her that she knew how to get to Mission as she added one last thought. "I get it. There's no time to waste."

As Belinda increased her speed noticeably, she explained further for my benefit. "Step will have a pediatrician and a respiratory team ready when we pull in. The urgency of the situation will cut down on the red tape." I saw her shake her head in the manner that she had done repeatedly as I told her the details of our saga. Then she added as she forced calm into her voice, "Step believes time is critical." She must have said something about how long it would take to get there. Belinda added. "I will cut that time down to ten minutes."

"Hand me the phone. I need to let Colin know the change in plans."

Moments after the update, I worked to give both mother and child my full attention. Savannah seemed to watch the increased traffic in a somewhat hypnotic manner. Addressing the obviously scared young mother, who seemed not much more than a girl at the moment, I said, "We will soon arrive at a large hospital where there are many doctors. Savannah, you've never seen anything like what you are about to take in. I can only imagine how strange everything will seem. It may even frighten you to some degree. There will be many people asking questions. Please, I need you to agree to stay silent. Let me do the talking. I need to tell the doctor that I do not know when little William was born. I know you get that is not the truth. I have my reasons. Savannah, I promise you this is the kind of help Miss Sadie hoped we could find for you. You will need to continue to trust Colin and me."

As she continued to stare out the car window, Savannah responded very quietly. "Just help my baby, so we can get back home to Charles."

As I held the struggling baby in one arm, I reached for her hand. There were no words for the moment. All would have sounded like empty promises.

§

The moment we pulled up at the ER, the baby's breathing became even more labored. Tears came down my cheek as I saw the medics coming toward the car. Savannah let out a wail as I handed her baby toward the hands of the emergency team. Even before they cleared the door, I could hear a trauma nurse give the order to intubate the baby. *No doubt Stephanie came through with the help she thought we might need. What would Miss Sadie say if she could see all that is unfolding?*

Colin moved close to my side of the car. Within moments, he opened the back door of the car and lifted Savannah out of the back seat. Catching up with his long strides as he neared the ER doors, I took in his words with the assistant following at his side. "This mother also needs attention. Although she has hardly said a word, we believe she gave birth only shortly before she showed up on my friend's property."

Belinda parked the car and eventually found me in the NIC waiting area. "One of the nurses recommended we wait here. Colin has taken Savannah to get some medical attention. Belinda, she had an easy birth in many ways. But on the other hand, she has been moved about a great deal, never mind the high-stress with her child. Now she is caught up in a world that must bury her deeper into the state of shock she has been operating in since we…" my words caught in my throat. All that had taken place remained inexplicable. *Time travel? Get real. That is only found in novels.*

Belinda thankfully pressed no further. She put her arm around me as I let my head fall on her shoulder. Stephanie walked through the waiting room door. The news was not good. The baby's lungs had failed. "Little William is presently on a respirator, and the prognosis is challenging. The doctors are concerned that his other organs could also fail. Sarah, I need you to come with me. Let's focus on Savannah's needs for a bit. I cannot get a word out of her. She only stares at the many machines in the room. Colin offered that you know nothing more than he does about this young mother. He also insisted that he stay with Savannah, who is at least off her feet and wrapped warmly in blankets. Colin made me promise I would bring you to the new mother as soon as we can get her settled a bit more. Sarah, I could not help but notice at the mention of your name, the flicker of awareness in her otherwise blank stare."

I took the opportunity to repeat our story to Stephanie. "The young mother and her child showed up at the door of the real estate office in the middle of the night. I figure Belinda already told you I have been living there for some time now. I suspect this is a case where neither mother nor child has seen a doctor. I do feel that someone helped her with the birth in some way."

"Sarah, I have already spoken to a doctor who should be coming in to examine her any minute now. We need to get blood work on her. After all, anything we know about her condition may be helpful with her son." We stepped into the area where Savannah and Colin waited. Colin's face reacted to what Stephanie next said. "I will be surprised if she does not get admitted. One of you will need to talk with the Admissions Office."

Colin immediately offered. "Why don't I take care of that, Sarah? I can at least tell the little bit we know about Savannah and the baby's situation."

I nodded in agreement, trying to conceal the worry that threatened to consume me. Soon someone from the lab staff would attempt to question Savannah. The best I could, I would try to steer the conversation in a safe direction.

I pushed Savannah's wheelchair as we followed a CNA to the lab area. As we entered, I placed a reassuring hand on the young mother's shoulder. Her body tensed. The sights, the sounds, the lab crew in the scrubs, all had to fill her with uncertainty. As it turned out, Savannah never said a word throughout the lab work. She did answer a couple of questions with a nod of her head. I was so relieved when one of the nurses filled the gap in this precarious lack of conversation on my part. "This poor girl is in shock. This is more than physical exhaustion, in my opinion. I would indeed like to know the real story behind this situation. "She seemed to mull that thought for a bit before continuing. "I think we need to stop the questions." After the lab work, the CNA returned to lead us to Admissions.

§

The morning stretched out with slowness. Trying to stay focused on the whispered thoughts that seemed to pop up between Colin and me, fatigue won out. Sleep wrapped its welcoming arms around me. The sound of Stephanie's voice woke me as the cramp in my neck reminded me of my efforts to find a comfortable position in the waiting room chair. "How are you folks holding up?" Not waiting for an answer, she continued. "The NIC team agrees that the next twenty-four hours are critical. The focus at present is to give full attention to all the vital organs that are presently in jeopardy. Every hour little William can hold on will increase his chances. But, please understand, it will be a long wait before the doctors have any solid confidence to share with you. Someone will come out occasionally to give you an update. With our help, on top of her obvious exhaustion, Savannah is deep in sleep. Colin and Sarah, I assume I will not talk you into taking a break from the hospital? It is easy to see you are both committed to seeing this situation through." She looked us both full in the face. We only nodded in agreement before she spoke, "Belinda, would you like to come with me for a bit? I have to head home and get ready for work. You could clean up and rest some. I know you all were up early."

"Belinda, you should go. Colin and I will be fine here. I can sleep anywhere. I would appreciate a toothbrush and any other toiletries you can think of. Step, I trust we can see Savannah when she wakes?

"Of course. Let me quickly talk to the nurses on duty." Looking at her mother-in-law, she added. "Take this time to make sure you know what all Sarah and Colin would like us to bring back to them."

Of course, as soon as Step was out of earshot, I started in. "Belinda, you know you simply cannot decide to tell Step any more of the story. Promise me, please, that you understand the problems that could arise if you do spill the beans?"

"Sarah, you have known me for a long time. When I give my word, I mean it. Your story is safe. Now do not think for one minute I do not have plans to get more of the story out of both of you once we are past this crisis. No question, there's a whole lot more I need to be told. Now is not the time."

Step spoke as she made her way back from the nurses' station. "I let them know you want to see Savannah as soon as she is awake. As much as I suspect you both need to get some rest, I also asked that they wake you if a doctor comes out with an update. Of course, you know you can call either Belinda or me if you need something."

§

Time stretched out endlessly between fretful sleep and worry for Savannah and her baby. One of us would wake to see the other twisted in the uncomfortable seats that served as the only places to lay our heads. The worry of how we could get our two charges back to the past was the last detail Colin and I talked about before I had no longer been able to hold open my tired eyes or mull another thought in my worn-out brain. I stood up, stretching as I ran my hands through my hair. *Now I need a cup of coffee.* At that moment, a soft voice broke my thought. "Mam, are you the folks who brought in the Martin infant?"

One of the nurses from the nearby station stood with the man dressed in surgical scrubs. The dread washed over me. Before he could speak further, I offered. "Please give me a moment to wake Colin. I know we both need to hear what you are about to tell us." As I gently shook him, Colin responded immediately.

"Yes," as he nodded at both of us. "I am one of the pediatricians working with the infant William Martin. It is my understanding that this newborn and his mother showed up at your property. I am not clear what made you head to Mission versus your local hospital, but I must say it was a wise decision. Although you are not officially family, you are perhaps all the young mother and her child have at present. The mother is still sleeping. I have also been advised she is more than likely in a state of shock. Under these circumstances, I would like to speak openly with the two of you."

I nodded as Colin answered. "Please do."

"The infant's condition remains serious. As you have been informed, fairly soon upon arrival, his lungs and kidneys failed. His heart is also showing a tremendous amount of stress. Unfortunately, in the past hour, his stomach has started bleeding, and his blood is now septic. The little fellow faces a serious battle to make it through the next few hours. We have him on I.V. antibiotics and dialysis. Of course, he cannot breathe without a respirator. I think it best if you plan to be with the mother when she starts to wake. Our team is doing everything we can for the child. Please know we are not giving up. After all, this mother and child found you two. You made your way to us. Let's give it some time. I encourage you to rest as you can. It is our hope we can somehow get this infant through the next several hours. If we can hit that milestone, please understand there is still a long, uphill battle. I need to get back to the NIC. We will keep you informed."

Before the doctor could get away, I asked. "Any sign that the mother is waking?"

"No. I was told to inform you that between her exhaustion and what we are administering, she will probably sleep for at least a couple more hours. Be assured, she is getting some much-needed fluids. This might be a good time for you two to get a bite of food, at least some coffee. When you head back this way, we will get you to her room."

Colin spoke before I could find my words. "Thanks for your help. Sarah, I could use some food and certainly some coffee. Let's take advantage of this time."

It all seemed so futile. All I could do was shake my head in desperation. A spigot opened. The words poured out in a torrent of emotion. "I just don't get it. What has this been about? Has this whole ordeal been nothing more than a fluke? I remember when we were there at the springheads, back in Savannah's time, when she was in labor. I was so certain we had been pulled into her world for a reason. I think that thought has kept me going. Now, I just can't make any sense of the whole ordeal. Why us? Why and how did we stumble through the inexplicable fold in time? If we've somehow managed to be in two different times and bring this child this far, I don't think I could handle the idea that little William may not make it. Why did we find his mother when we did? We could have so easily ended up in the home of someone who would have shot us and not had a second thought about it back in the early 1900s. Instead, we connected with a wise old woman. She accepted that we were from another time. Then on top of that had the insight to realize we might be able to help the baby. She knew his little life depended on something beyond her cures. Now, it has come down to this slim chance for little William to survive the next few hours. Colin, I just can't accept it. There's some reason this child's life has to be saved. I just know it. I swear, I just know it." Exhaustion and a faint hint of belief silenced my rant.

Colin wrapped his arm around my shoulder as we wandered down the hospital corridor. Once again, the tears came just as they had when we first stood on the cliff above the bend in the river in our travel back in time.

"Sarah, Sarah, I can't begin to answer all of your questions. I typically reach conclusions logically. Yet, I, too, can't get away from the seeming sense of inexplicable purpose behind all of that we have experienced. Is it possible that we have the ability, or say the choice, as humans to align with the purposes of the universe? On those rare occasions when we manage to walk in sync with that greater power, we stumble right into that which cannot be explained by logic. The doctor did not say to give up hope. He did want us to know the reality of what the baby is facing. I say we wait and hope. This little one would not be the first to defy all odds in the face of death."

Calmness surfaced. A sense of shelter moved over me as I allowed myself to accept the support of the strong arm that pulled me closer.

Then Colin spoke again. "Since we set foot in the building of your dreams…no, that's not right. More accurately, since I first stepped into your office sometime back, a spark of curiosity, a sense of wonder, flickered in me. Call it what you like; it is now the source of my hope. Without understanding the why's and the how's of what has happened or what may yet be, I am eternally grateful for choosing to walk into your world that day."

Colin's words settled deeply into my heart.

§

The early morning of January 5, 2000, pressed into our still fatigued brains. Colin and I both opted to stay overnight in the NIC Waiting Room. Sleep at best had been fitful. Once, around 2:00 p.m., I checked in with the night nurses. Our little man was hanging on. Savannah remained in a deep sleep interspersed with short periods of wakefulness. The nurses expressed concern that they could not get her to say a word. I breathed a sigh of relief.

Colin stirred in the chair next to mine. As I forced fingers through my matted hair, I asked with a bit of laughter to my voice, "Do I dare go look in a mirror, or would it be best to remain hopeful that I don't look as rough as I feel?"

"Why don't we each freshen up the best we can in those rest-rooms just down the hall. I am very appreciative of the care packets Belinda brought us earlier. Once we check in with the morning staff, I'd like to get some coffee, maybe a quick bite to eat. It's still early."

Savannah's little man had fought hard. Although still very weak and compromised, he had made it through the night. The nurse let us know that we needed to get a birth certificate estab-lished. Colin quickly suggested we should try to talk with Savannah regarding the needed information. He assured the nurse we would help as much as possible to facilitate the necessary communication with the still almost non-verbal mother. He added. "If anyone can get a word out of the mother, I think it will be Sarah."

As we made our way toward breakfast, a call came from Be-linda. After hearing that the infant was holding on, she decided to head to Hunterstown to pick up extra clothing and personal items that I requested. Her hopeful response encouraged me. "That little fellow is a fighter. Thus far, he is beating the odds of survival. I think you will be here in Asheville for some time."

"Oh! Belinda, I hope you are right. Thanks for thinking of my needs. Also, when you get to the office, please call me. I need you to grab a couple of files. I'll need to walk you through where to find them. I keep reminding myself of the need to stay on some real estate deals that are near closing. Again, I don't know what I would do without you."

As the coffee and food started to work in our tired bodies, Colin shared his thoughts. "Depending on what unfolds with both Savannah and the baby, I may try to head to my house." He looked to me for any reaction but continued right on. "I typically work most every day and into the night from my office on campus. I will have no problem being here as much as I am needed."

I nodded my head in agreement. Although we never talked further about the details of what he would or would not say to his wife, I was certain he would stick to his initial reaction to not share any details of the circumstances that tied the two of us together. My thoughts quickly turned back to the need for a birth certificate. *I, of course, know the baby's name and the names of both parents. I hope I can keep up the pretense, knowing nothing. She showed up on my doorsteps. Who knows the extent of the spillover questions that are sure to surface as hospital staff tries to start processing the birth certificate and contacting the father?* Colin and I made our plan. We would claim that with a great deal of effort, we got Savannah to at least give us the baby's name. *I think Savannah remains in a state of shock. So, wouldn't her stressed and stunned state explain that she communicated nothing more than the baby's name? I can only hope Savannah keeps all of her answers quietly tucked away from the hospital team.* We knew someone would push eventually to get a location of the father. They may even bring in someone who speaks Cherokee. When we asked Savannah how she would answer that question, her answer filled us with heaviness. "I do not know where Charles is anymore." By early afternoon William Jason Martin had a birth certificate. Blood work confirmed Group B Strep in Savannah.

§

Stephanie explained that this bacteria is quite common in adults, although this has only recently come to light in the medical field. While harmless to those who carry it, Group B Strep weakens or kills two of every 1,000 babies born in the United States. Colin and I clung to our amazement at Miss Sadie's sage wisdom. She knew there was no hope in her world, in her time. The fact that she accepted the possibility of other times still proved a great mystery.

The days rolled by slowly. Little William gradually grew stronger. I stayed at the hospital, waiting with Savannah. She longed to hold her baby. The medical world that kept her at a distance added to her distress. She always wanted me with her if she went beyond the confines of her hospital room. Without fail, when she reached her hand into the controlled incubator to lovingly touch her child, I always heard the whisper start in the soft, musical lilt of her native Cherokee. *Does she revert to her native tongue so no one understands, or does it come naturally as a source of comfort?* Often an attending nurse would hear her and try to get her to talk. The blank stare she offered in response soon brought the questions to an end.

Belinda's son Seth found a place for me to stay during the

brief times I felt I could leave Savannah on her own at the hospital. When I left to get some rest or focus on work, Colin faithfully came to the hospital to take my place. On semester break, he made the first two weeks at Mission a much easier task for me. Belinda drove over regularly when she could get away from school. A little over two more weeks would pass before Savannah and her child left with Belinda and me to head back to my place at the bend in the river. Colin stayed in Asheville. I knew his mind, like mine, was filled with one overriding question. *How and when will we get these two back to their time?"*

§

Savannah, little William, and I had now been back in Hunterstown for two days, having left Mission Memorial on January 25th. The baby was scheduled to go back for a check-up in another two weeks. At that moment, my hands held my first cup of coffee for the morning as I looked out the back window. Colin should come up my drive anytime now. He got an early start leaving Asheville. We both knew the conversation had to happen.

Lost in deep thought, I did not hear Savannah come up behind me. "Sarah," she said in an almost whisper. I turned to see her holding little William tightly in her arms as she continued. "I could hear the river crashing over the rocks when I first woke. I longed to be back with Charles and Miss Sadie. Will you walk with me today? Then she hesitated before adding, "down to the double springheads?"

Her question tugged at my heart. *She instinctively knows she needs to get back.* Realizing I had hesitated, I finally answered. "Savannah, I think it would do us all a world of good to take that walk. Colin will be here any moment. I know he will want to join us. I would like to show you around the property a bit if you are up to it. I hope this land has not changed so much that you fail to see some glimpse of your time." Again, I hit pause as more complicated thoughts worked their way to the surface.

"Savannah, you have already seen so much of the future…our tall buildings filled with people, machines that beep and light up, elevators, telephones, and, of course, cars. As we await check-ups with doctors, we will try to show you more. Do you understand, however, that all you take in may never be shared openly when you get back to

Charles? Once Colin gets here, we will all talk more about the hope of getting you back to your time and the responsibility that comes with having seen the future."

"Sarah, I have had much time to think about what it will be like to return to my Charles and Miss Sadie. We stay to ourselves most of the time. I can say anything to Miss Sadie. Charles stays quiet, but I know he takes in our thoughts. What has happened…" she stopped midstream. "Well, all will be safe with Charles and Miss Sadie. But I do have a question. What about my people, the Cherokee? I have only met the one Cherokee woman that the hospital brought in to try to talk with me. Are there many of us still around? Although most of the Cherokee left this land along the river, Charles' family, like mine, chose to stay and hide out in nearby caves. Are there other Cherokee here now in this time who are descendants of those who found a way to stay? You have mentioned several times that Miss Sadie told you something about the strong seven-generational bond between her family history and that of my people. All I know for sure is that one of my elders by the name of Maidena insisted that none of her Taylor family should ever leave the land along the river. They hid in caves and did whatever it took to survive. They refused to leave. The story that came down through the generations was this: Maidena always said she had business yet to finish at the springheads. Is my family still here?"

I stood stunned at the depth of Savannah's thinking. My mind filled with layers of questions as this insightful woman stood before me and shared her innermost thoughts. *Why haven't I taken time to know more about Native Americans who live in these parts? I have been as guilty as most not thinking in terms of the individual families, their stories, and challenges. In most cases, the Indian families that refused to be removed had somehow lived through the upheaval caused by the white man. These survivors or their descendants eventually surfaced again in the world that Colin and I returned to when we first met Savannah at the springheads.* Then my thoughts grabbed at Savannah's mention of unfinished business. Just as I started to ask what her great-grandmother might have meant, I heard the car pull in. "Savannah, that has to be Colin. We have a great deal to talk about today."

§

William slept peacefully through his long morning nap as the three of us sat in the office area and talked uninterrupted. I almost laughed out loud, thinking back on my decision to unplug the answering machine. The closed sign showed clearly through the window. *The real estate world will just survive without me today. These three people in front of me are all I need for the present.*

The more time Colin and I spent with Savannah during the long wait at the hospital, the more we were amazed at all the grace and ease she maintained in a world full of strange goings-on. I no longer thought of her as fragile. I knew Colin felt the same way. Within minutes of sitting on the couch and stretching his long legs out as he crossed one foot over the other, he plowed straight into what needed to be discussed. "Savannah, as you well know, we've got to talk about how to get you back to your time, to Charles, to Miss Sadie. It still shocks me somewhat to talk about the idea of traveling back and forth in time. Yet, you remain incredibly calm. You never showed any real shock about the fact that Sarah and I first came to you from another timeframe of history. Now, you and your infant son are here in the year 2000, and we must talk about getting you back to your husband. How do you keep your composure?"

When Colin paused, Savannah simply nodded her head. He picked right back up with his thoughts. "When Sarah and I first found you at the springheads, we were still very confused by the fact that we had traveled through time. Then Miss Sadie voiced her suspicions that we came from some other place…we had no real, foolproof plan at that moment as to how we might get the two of you to our world. Once again, we stumbled onto the magic formula that night at Mr. Billy's store back when Miss Sadie insisted we could not put things off. I think what I am struggling with is this. We still have not mastered how the travel through time actually happens. Do you take that in, Savannah?"

Again, only silence filled the room. Colin sat quietly, looking at little William sleeping soundly in his mother's arms, then picked back up with his talk. "From what Sarah has shared, you seem to have great confidence that we can get you back to your home in the early 1900s. Until we accidentally showed up in your time, the idea of such was nothing more than make-believe. Now that we have experienced it twice, we are still in the infant stages of understanding how or why it happens. I'm still fumbling with what I want to say. Here's the truth of it. Savannah, we cannot promise we know how to make it happen again."

The deep dark pools of her eyes looked at both of us. Finally, she spoke softly. "I do not struggle with the idea that you came to my time. Now my baby and I have come to yours. I also know that I want to go back to Charles. William will need his father. And I need Miss Sadie."

I could not begin to understand the ease and acceptance with which she explained her feelings. As we had learned to accept when having a conversation with Savannah, she never rushed into her next thoughts. Her pauses helped to stop the urgency that threatened most of our conversations. "My people think of time unfolding in a great circle. Many of us have heard voices and seen visions from different places within that never-ending circle. Much of your world seems out of kilter with mine. But I find nothing strange about the two of you showing up at the springheads when my little William was finding his way into the world. My ancestors often called on the strength of many generations to reveal help in the time of our greatest need. I long to go back to my time. The circle of time will open up. As I heard the river this morning, I could see myself stepping through that thin veil."

Colin and I sat silently now. In one brief moment, this young Cherokee mother had shown more insight than the two of us had gained throughout this journey. Admittedly, I felt nudges of communication, in some sense of the word, from the river, from the land itself. Then there were my two dreams. Lost in the deep thoughts of the moment, I imagined myself standing on the outermost edge of the cliff that looked down on the bend in the river. *What would happen if I let go of logic? Can I accept there is no explanation? Can I be open to the forces that work on this land and the mighty waters that lap at its shores?"*

Colin spoke at last. "Savannah, would you like to try getting back to your time as soon as William gets checked out by the doctor?

Without hesitation, the reply came. "Yes, I would like that very much."

I turned our thoughts back to something that resembled the start of a plan. "Colin, the way I see it, there are three common factors both times we have traveled. You and I were both involved. We de-

parted, so to speak, from the same location, Mr. Billy's store. And...."
I needed to collect my thoughts before speaking more. "Well, I think
your ring is somehow involved. Remember the heat that seems to
radiate from it? Is there any chance it is simply a matter of putting
the ring on Savannah? The right people, in the right place, with the
ring on, and time travel will happen again?"

"Sarah, you know my ring is something I value deeply. I
would give it to Savannah and her child if I knew the journey could
go without a hitch. What happens if, somehow, it's not a straight
shot this time? Remember that depot you saw in your dreams?
What if...well...what if we sent Savannah and William back to or
even ahead to some time that would be difficult for them to survive?
Sarah, I want to see this through myself. I suspect you will not even
think about being left behind. Tell me your thoughts, please."

*Was there any guarantee we could roll the dice time and time
again and have it work out our specific wishes? What if we made it back
to the past but found no way to return to the present? Could I live with
myself if I turned my back on my two kids? I longed to be a part of their
lives as much as Savannah yearned to connect to her family. Of course,
Colin had his own life and obligations.* "Oh, Colin, we take a great risk
no matter the course we take."

Savannah spoke with firmness. "William and I can try. We
will find our way."

My mind filled again with struggling thoughts. *God knows,
I wish I had this young woman's resolve and assurance. I have always
struggled to some degree to find my way. Truth be known, there would
be some comfort in simply starting over in another time. The circumstance
of Tim's death still surfaced at regular intervals. What could I have done
differently? What would it be like to spend more time with Colin?* The
thought of opening myself to a matter of the heart shut me right
down again. *I can risk time travel and adventure. Possible failure in yet
another relationship? Count me out.*

At last, I spoke. "I guess it only makes sense to let Savannah
try traveling with just the baby. Maybe the ring is not a factor? We
go to the old store, she and little William step in without the ring,
and let's see what happens. We will have to experiment with the process till we hit on the right mix, or is it all about the right moment?"

Colin asked, "Remind me of the appointments with the doctors?

"Stephanie arranged both for the same day, almost back-to-back. Everything is set for Wednesday, February 9th. We will not get back until late in the evening from Asheville. I would think it wise for all to be as rested as possible for whatever may happen. Let's try the time travel on Thursday the 10th."

"Sarah, that will give you and me some time to put the details of lives into order to some degree. I can take some time from work. I am more concerned about arousing suspicions. Of late, I know that my preoccupation has become more obvious."

"Colin, my kids are caught up in college life. I still can't get over how it worked out for me to connect with both of them as they came in from Mississippi before heading back to their second semesters. What would I have done without you and Belinda covering for me at the hospital? If I can close this Friday on the real estate deal I have been working on, then I should be in the clear financially for some time ahead. I'll figure out some way to keep my kids from suspecting anything unusual if they happen not to reach me by phone."

At that moment, William began crying from the next room. *Was I imagining it, or did Savannah appear almost relieved to have an excuse to leave the room? She has to pick up on the stress we are feeling.*

Alone in the room with Colin, his next words surprised me. "Sarah, I think I have a good awareness of your situation between what you have said and perhaps more, from what you have held back. It's easy to see your pain as it washed over you back in the earlier conversation. The pain of my personal life shows through even though I work to keep it tucked well out of sight for the most part. I suspect you are aware of all I am saying. Hurt has established residence in both of us." I noticed a slight smile forming. "Hey, we've traveled through time together twice now and are hoping to do so again. We may as well know each other's flaws and weaknesses. That knowledge may be needed at some point." I took in the weary look that crossed his piercing blue eyes as he quit talking. *Pain long carried does take its toll no matter how hard we work to bury it.*

I found my composure. "So, we agree? We will attempt to send Savannah and the baby back to their time on February 10th if all goes well with both of their appointments?"

"Sarah, a thought just hit me. What if you are not part of the factor of travel? After all, when you first stepped into the old store, nothing out of the ordinary happened. I know we just talked about this, but if it does not work for just Savannah and William, let me encourage you to let me try next without you."

What right did I have to ask Collin to take on this risk alone? After all, it was my dreams and the discovery of the old store that got him mixed up in all that unfolded in our lives. Then, if I allowed honesty, I wanted to make the trip. Just as I was mulling over this last thought, a mischievous smile filled Colin's face. "Again, I am getting to know you better and better. There is no way I will ever talk you down. Why should I? You and your dreams are fully to blame. I think we both know we are in this together."

Savannah returned from the bedroom with a smile on her face as she took in the infant in her arms. William proved to be a contented baby once he got the medical help he needed. I still marveled over the fact that this same child had cried almost nonstop for the first hours of his life, then had respiratory failure along with so many other major challenges to his other organs. Seeing the two of them, I remembered Savannah's request to walk to the springheads. "Colin, Savannah would like to walk to the spring house. I think it would be the perfect time to show her around the surrounding property in greater detail. Thus far, she has only ventured out back of the office. She does enjoy sitting on the cliff overlooking the river. It is a perfect winter day. Let's get our coats on and do some exploring. We need to show her more." When we came back from Asheville, I pointed out many landmarks and bits of history that I thought would interest Savannah. I quickly realized that in her time, she had never traveled far from my property along the two bends in the river.

Colin's responses stopped me in my tracks. "Sarah, I think we need to be careful. What if…" As his voice trailed off, I could see something bothered him. He then continued. "The situation we find ourselves in thus far seems haphazardly tied to a few coincidences that make about as much sense as my ring being the cause behind all the travels. I guess I fear we could be setting ourselves up for something we're not ready for."

"We did indeed arrive at the double springheads when we returned to our time with Savannah and the baby. I suppose travel could also be jump started in any of these locations."

"Exactly! You know as well as I do, we need to follow through with the doctor appointments. Plus, I think we could send Savannah back with some tools that may make their lives easier. Let's be careful as we venture out today. I bet there are no guarantees about anything when we are on or near this river property of yours."

Savannah once again offered a thought that seemed to have alluded the two of us. "From what you have shared, Colin, before the first travel through time, you wanted to see the old store of Sarah's dreams." She paused as she nodded in my direction. "I know you, Sarah, wanted to share that with Colin. Then, before the second travel through time, you two and Miss Sadie, were all in agreement. I am certain that deeply felt thoughts and desires can work in powerful ways."

Both Colin and I were left speechless with the depth of her thought. My mind filled with deep layers of thinking. *If I were being honest, I had longed for a way to leave behind all the pain and failure of my life. My heart had often tugged at the desire to start over somewhere, anywhere.* Not yet ready to speak, I rubbed my head and let out a slow breath.

Colin filled the gap of silence. "Savannah, you have made a good point. Sarah and I did not plan our first trip through time. We did not even think such was possible. But Sarah's dreams and her find of the old store sparked a curiosity in me. I would be lying if I did not confess that a strong part of me hoped something inexplicable would happen when the two of us walked into Mr. Billy's old, dilapidated store that evening." Then, he turned and looked me in the face. "Sarah, we may need to accept that *state of mind and desires of the heart* are possible factors."

Before I could stop myself, I flippantly added. "Well, my state of mind and my heart's desire is to get outside. I would hate to think that we'd miss the opportunity of a lifetime to walk this property with someone who has experienced it from a whole different point of view. Let's get out of this darn trailer that should never have insulted this beautiful land with its presence."

I took the baby as Savannah snuggled into a long wool coat and wrapped the warm scarf around her neck. I remember my first thought when I spotted the black, full-length coat in the store in Asheville. *That's a timeless design. Savannah will not stand out like a sore thumb back in her time. Something in me at that point must have believed we would get her back to her time.* She quickly reached out for little William once again. I grabbed my jacket.

Colin added, "Ladies and little William, I'd rather be guilty of being open to possibility than afraid to move outside this trailer. Let's go."

§

Discouragement played around the edges of my thoughts. *Will our third attempt be the charm or....* The first try on February 10th, from the old general store, involved Savannah, little William, and Colin's ring. We purposely chose the same time of day that had first worked for Colin and me. Nothing happened. Colin and I used the day after our failed attempt to take care of a few present-day, personal details that, for some reason, we had not planned for earlier. Our second attempt on the 11th included all four of us. Again, no slight shift in the environment, no movement that threw us off our feet. We walked back to the office trailer in silence that evening. I know my head was filled with one overriding question. *What are we overlooking? God knows the "want to" is there in abundance in all of us.*

A few days later, still bothered by our failure to will time travel into existence, I stood on the cliff overlooking the turbulent, swollen waters that made their way through the bend in the river below. Colin had gone back to Asheville while we both spent more time thinking about our failed efforts. The moon, not quite full, still played across the whitewaters. *The moon was full both times we traveled.* Even as my mind completed the thought, I berated myself for becoming one of those kooks who attributed everything to a full moon. *But what if it is a factor? I know the tides and the moon move in sync with one another. Is it possible this property, surrounded by waters that also run behind the old general store of my dreams combined with the gravitational force of a full moon, are behind the possibility of time travel? The heat given off by Colin's ring may simply be a reaction to a much greater force.*

Back in the office, I called Colin's office phone, hoping he may be there working late. I had to leave a voicemail. When he called early the next morning, he quickly pointed out all kinds of books that told strange tales throughout the history of unexplainable events linked to a full moon. Of course, as I had also done, he nailed the date of February 19, 2000, for the next full moon.

We marked off days on the calendar. In-depth plans unfolded

as we asked troubling questions. *What if we are not able to come back to our time?* That question alone forced creating two letters stored in safety deposit boxes, one to my mom with instructions to share with my two children, one to Colin's parents. The details explained what had transpired up to the point of writing the letters and what we were about to attempt. Belinda held the key in safekeeping. We also spent considerable time weighing out what we should take with us. *What would we wish we had in the way of survival tools? What essentials should we send for the long haul with Savannah? We insisted on the smallpox shot and a measle's vaccination for these two. Belinda had cleverly talked Stephanie into several extra rounds of antibiotics. What were we not thinking of?* Very last minute, we had the idea for Belinda to meet Colin at one of the overlooks on the road that turns off to Robbinsville. He would leave his car there in case something happened in the past that caused us not to get back to our present as we planned. We certainly would not want Colin's car sitting at my real estate office.

Our thoughts finally allowed us to ask the heavy thought of "what if?" Where would we have ended up if we had not traveled into the future, back to our present time, when we left Savannah's time? What if we ended up in some life not yet lived? Somehow it seemed less scary to think of traveling from the past to our present. To travel to an unknown future was a scary thought. In the days leading up to the next attempt at time travel, both Colin and I had our moments of panic. Should we officially tell someone about the time travel we had now experienced twice? I don't think it ever crossed our minds to call the local sheriff. But what about reaching out to MIT? After many discussions, we concluded: The fewer who know anything about our travels, the better.

§

We made our way to the dilapidated store once again late the afternoon of February 19th. For once, Colin and I were more focused on Savannah rather than the what-ifs of time travel. As the weeks went by, Savannah felt the strain of being away from Charles and her life. We also knew she picked up on the layers of plans and excuses that we created as we tried not to raise suspicions with people around us. We also recognized the burden of details we had placed at

Belinda's feet. She felt the tension as she got caught up in the much-needed deception with her daughter-in-law and her son but agreed that the less who knew, the better. Fortunately, she had a long, strong marriage to a wise man of few words who helped her shoulder the strain of what had quickly become a very interesting life for me. We suspected Savannah would not hold up as well as Belinda amid the related stress if she never made it back to her time. She was not wired for the modern world for the long haul. Her strong belief that she would get back to her time gave her hope.

We stopped just outside the door that hung off its hinges. I could no longer step near the old place without seeing Mr. Billy's store in Savannah's time. As details of that turn-of-the-century store filled my head, I knew Colin and I hesitated for other reasons. We both still had misgivings about our final call to both attempt the travel with Savannah. All the possible scenarios of what may or may not happen had convinced us that we might as well all be in this together. We wore backpacks filled with all sorts of essentials. Colin and I had finally concluded that we would never be able to live with ourselves if we let this dear woman and child step into the store without us. The thick growth of old dead vines still provided cover from the traffic that passed on the nearby road. I looked up briefly at the old green light that hung precariously from the nearby pole. My thoughts rolled back to the second dream when my dear school teacher friends and I had discovered the depot, perhaps the passageway to the time warp itself.

Colin pulled me out of my reverie. With one arm already securely around Savannah who held little William tight against her chest, he held out his hand. "Sarah, let's go."

Colin and I never made it to the inside of the store. Savannah held on to Colin's hand as she stepped up into the entrance. I saw the scene inside the store change before my eyes. I knew from the look on Colin's face that he, too, picked up on the slight shift that we were now experiencing for the third time. He turned from Savannah only for a moment. He leaned toward me, reaching for me. When I attempt to put into words all that unfolded next, it takes much longer to talk about it than the quick seconds it took for it all to unfold. Our fingers curled around each other's. Colin held on with all of his strength as he pulled me closer to him. For that brief moment, before our hands had found each other, a scared panic moved over me. Even though I knew he had reached me, I still felt the aftershock from the idea of Colin and Savannah being drawn into the mystery of what was unfolding without me. As if he understood my frightened feelings, he drew me tighter to his side. My eyes closed as I finally took a deep breath of relief and allowed myself to give way to the nearness and security of his body. Then we both took in that he was no longer holding on to Savannah and little William.

"No, no!" I wailed. We should have known not to get near this place without holding on to one another at all times. How could I have let this happen?"

"Sarah, I am the one that let go of Savannah."

"Yes, but I am the reason you let go."

We both took in the unspoken thought that filled the space where we now stood. In the next moment, we awkwardly started to put some distance between us. Colin spoke urgently, "I will not let go of your hand again." It took another few minutes to take in the details of where we were. Once again, the scene from my second dream appeared in front of me. I was in the same much-larger-from-the-inside-than-the-outside version of a very well-kept depot. The green light hung securely from an intact pole as it shed light on a long passageway. I saw people off at a distance. I did not see Savannah holding her baby. "Come on, Colin. Let's head down this way. We've got to find them."

As we neared a cluster of people who stood outside windows waiting for service or tickets, or who-knows-what, I explained to Colin that just like in my second dream, these people had no awareness of us. We roamed as far as we saw people. Savannah and the baby were nowhere to be found.

"Here, let's sit on this bench and think a minute. I am fairly certain that I saw the environment of the old store shift the moment you helped Savannah inside. I suppose it is possible that she may be back at home in her time as we sit here worried sick over what has happened."

"Yes, we can hope that is the case. Unfortunately, we don't know for sure. We had insisted on not letting her and the baby attempt to travel by themselves for the very reasons we are now worried about. Sarah, there is something else I need to point out. Once you put your arm through mine, as we sat down here, I used my hand you had been holding to pull my sleeve up and check my watch.

Honestly, I think, once again, that I somehow thought my watch would cease to function. Then my mind went back to our first journey into the past. All preconceived ideas about time quickly turned meaningless and as useless as this watch on my arm when it comes to the now versus the past or future."

Without ever breaking the hold of our hands, I stood and pulled at Colin. "Come on, follow me. There is one more detail of my second dream that I want to see if I can locate." As we moved back in the direction we had just come, I explained the mysterious door with the glass window that looked into a modern-day conference room. I could clearly see in my mind the telephone that sat on the table. *Maybe we can figure out something about how this time warp works.*

Chapter 16

School starts in just a few days for the 2000-2001 year. Roughly six months after time travel occurred from what I now refer to as Mr. Billy's store, my mind is often full of thoughts of that moment when Colin helped Savannah and little William into the dilapidated entrance. For some reason, it is easy for me to believe her Cherokee heritage guided her safely home in the circle of time. I try to imagine how much the baby has changed in half a year. Gratefulness for the opportunity to make this connection with the past fills my being. Sometimes in the still of the evening, I swear I hear Miss Sadie laughing. More often, I hear Colin calling Savannah's name one last time.

Thoughts of Colin always fill my head. At times it seems he is in my airspace. His touch has become one with a gentle breeze. I often wish for a different ending to our story. Never have I regretted his presence in my life. I do understand that he could no more stop himself from stepping out that conference room door than he could have helped reaching back for me that fateful afternoon of March 20 when he thought I might miss out on that third time travel. Colin had become very attached to Savannah and little William in the short time we knew them. He would have never forgiven himself if he had chosen to play it safe.

The connection between Colin and me was strong the day he first walked into the real estate office and had only grown with time. If I knew with certainty that he found Savannah and the baby in their world, I could accept never seeing him again. Of course, I don't know what happened back in the time warp. I can only speculate and hope. I do know that Colin typically made decisions from his moral compass. Most days, I find comfort in the strength and goodness of this man. This particular day turned full-blown toward despair with thoughts of Colin.

For the first month, after I made it back to the present, heartache filled my life more than not. I had been so determined to never let my heart care for someone again. As many say, "I have never been lucky in love." I concluded it was best not to consider the possibility again. I now see that when Colin reached out for me at the entrance of the old general store, I did more than fall into his arms. I fell fully for him. All the self-created barriers to my heart crumbled immediately. Ironically, it felt like time stood still during this *easy to romanticize moment and the time that followed.* Shortly after arriving back in my time, I called Colin's office at UNC-A. I hoped against hope that he had somehow beat me back and had gone to Asheville. His voicemail recording pierced my heart. *How am I supposed to go on without knowing where you are? When do I need to reach out to your parents?* I shared none of these thoughts over the phone. Instead, I left a cryptic message about the photography project he was working on. Before calling Colin, I reached out to Belinda as soon as I walked up to the office from the springhouse, where I had returned once again from the journey through time. I could not stop crying as I shared with my dear friend the details of what had taken place.

Belinda and I then decided to not deliver the security box key to Colin's parents yet. I knew he had been at his parents' house a couple of weeks before we traveled. I also learned he had made the long-to-come-to decision to separate from his wife. As we worked out the details of upcoming trip, Belinda thought it best if she met Colin at the entrance to Graham County, picked him up, and drove him here. I agreed we did not need his car sitting at the office in case our attempt to get Savannah and the baby back to their time presented complications of any sort.

Three weeks after returning from the time warp to present time, would make my second time to call his office phone. I faithfully watched the newspapers and the Asheville news for any official word of Colin. Worry moved in on me when I realized there was no longer a voicemail for Colin Stewart in the English Department at UNC-A. My first thought got all caught up in not being able to hear his voice again. Later the day of the three-week marker, the WLOS 6:00 news first showed the picture of Colin. Next, his vehicle which had been found and linked to him a couple of weeks earlier, filled my TV screen. Seeing his picture and hearing the missing-person language proved too heavy to handle. My emotions tumbled down to rock bottom.

Belinda called within 30 minutes of the newscast. "Sarah, I stayed late at school today. As I walked in my front door after a long day of work, the WLOS 6:00 news just about knocked me off my feet."

"Yes, I've heard it all. I figured you would call."

"Well, before you go any further. Guess who else watched that newscast?" She barely gave me time to wrap my brain around an answer before she hit me. "Stephanie, my daughter-in-law. You know for sure she remembers the connection with you, Colin, Savannah, and the baby, as do many of the medical staff at Mission. Sarah, this has turned serious. Let me grab a bite to eat; then I'll be over. We need a plan."

§

As soon as I opened the door, Belinda started in. "You better not be hiding that man!" I can only guess she was joking, for she moved right on to another thought. "We have to think, Sarah. You realize the law could involve you before too much more time?"

"Belinda, I am very aware of the possibility, or should I say probability? The truth is the truth. I don't have a clue where Colin is."

"But you were the last person to see him!"

"You met him over in Graham County and brought him here. What if you get pulled in for questioning?"

"Sarah, Colin and I commented to each other that not one car drove by nor was the store across the way yet open when he got into my vehicle. I am also fairly certain no one saw me drop him off here."

"Belinda, I do get all of that you are saying. The hard truth is this. I did not last see him in any location that can be investigated by law enforcement. Do you really think I need to tell a policeman that Colin and I were together in a time warp back in March? Yeah! That ought to impress the investigating officer. I wonder how long it would take them to have me placed in Broughton?"

"Sarah, I know. I know. Let's both calm down. Why don't you fix us a drink? Let's try to breathe a minute. I think we both know you will never be able to tell the truth. It's not like you killed the man. I know you will do anything in your time-manipulating power to get him back. Don't think I haven't noticed the way you mope around. This is hard for you. Fortunately, most people have always looked at your personal life, well, your relationships, as being trouble waiting to happen. With Tim's death…" She stopped quickly. I think she knew she had gone too far. "Sarah, I'm sorry. You know I love you with all my heart. I think you are hands-down, one of the best friends a person could have, but, my dear, your love life always rides in or out on a bumpy road. Then, to beat it all, when it finally seems like you find someone who intrigues you and is also a good man through and through, what happens? You lose him in a time warp? Now that is an exit for the record books if I have ever heard one."

Her tirade gave me time to get our drinks made. "Here, let's sit down and regroup. I think perhaps the first question is this? Should I contact Colin's parents? At least let them know I knew their son? Or do I sit tight and wait till someone reaches out to me?"

"In my opinion, there is a strong chance some Asheville investigator will eventually link Colin to at least knowing you. Telephone records will connect the two of you to each other. Of course, there is also the bed and breakfast here in town where he often stayed. That owner just may pick up on Colin's face all over the news. How much does she know about his connections to you? Maybe you should sit tight. Give the situation a bit more time."

"Thankfully, we told your daughter-in-law from the get-go that Colin was on the property shooting pictures when the mysterious Cherokee woman and her infant showed up without any explanation. For sure, we stick to that story. As far as the bed and breakfast owner, I haven't a clue what she knows about anything."

"Then I suppose the only tale that makes any sense is what you told Stephanie within a couple of days of getting back to the present. It was brilliant on your part to call her and ask if the young mother and her infant by any chance had shown back up in the Asheville area. Your explanation that you awoke one morning to find her gone was believable. After all, as you said, she often woke up early and walked the property with her baby."

"Admittedly, it is problematic that Colin has now officially gone missing. I suppose some may think that, somehow, he and Savannah have gone off together? Oh my, what a tangled web indeed." My thoughts went inward. *And, oh, how I hope that he did see Savannah when he barreled out of that conference room door. I could live with that. If Colin somehow found his way back to the past, back to the life and time of Savannah and her Charles, and, of course, Miss Sadie, it would be easier to accept that I may never see him again. In time maybe that peace will come. As of today, one question permeates the air that I breathe: Will*

Colin ever again make his way to the present?

Belinda stared at me. I suppose she could see I was lost in thought. "You have the key to his safety deposit box. We were wise at the time to have you make those arrangements for both of us. Now, if you go in and remove his letter to his parents and close out his box, no one knows. It is all in your name. I would, however, feel better if you got rid of that letter."

"Sarah, I agree with you. God, how I wish that man would show up."

"Me too, Belinda. Me too."

§

Change works its way in and out of my life, sometimes in quick, sweeping brush strokes, but, oftentimes, like a painful chisel working to reshape the hardest stone. Somehow the seasons keep changing. The winter of Colin's disappearance has somehow turned into the fall of 2000. More times than not, I find some reason to hope the chokehold debt left in the wake of Tim's death is at least letting up a bit. Upon returning from the time warp without Colin, I turned to the real estate work to make as much money as possible, with the intent of loosening another creditor's tight grasp. I also suspected that staying busy would help to pause the thoughts that consume me. Tim's suicide still hangs like a heavy cloud of darkness over me. Thoughts of what I could have done differently mingle with bouts of anger. All it takes to throw me into a total funk is one moment of remembering the excitement Tim and I had felt when we pulled away from Floyd Logan's house so many years back. *Why Tim? Why was it not enough to have family and home? What pulled you back to the drugs time and time again? Depression can be managed, you know. Why didn't I just make you get the help you needed to battle that nightmare?*

Weariness fills my days more than I wish. I work hard. My emotions ping and pong from what seems like a total failure in my history of marriage. Some days it's the relationship that had unfolded years back with the children's father. Young and foolish, Taylor and I ended our relationship not-as-young, still as foolish, with two amazing children added to the mix. I hoped at the time my marriage to Taylor ended that I had learned enough about bad decision-making to avoid the same mistake twice. Then, before I even got my bearings in my second marriage, life with Tim quickly filled right to the brim with more troubles than I ever imagined. Caught in a daily struggle to keep my head above the drowning point for years, I chose misery over another failed marriage. When I did finally move out of the house to the real estate office, I thought I had at last moved past worrying about what people would think about yet another rela- tionship gone bad. Deep down, the move felt positive, and I held on to that feeling like a much-needed life preserver. I accepted I could not change Tim. *Wouldn't it be enough just to take care of myself and the kids?* Then Tim's death rolled in like a tsunami. Not a day goes by that I do not ask the difficult question. *What could I have done differ- ently?*

Colin's absence leaves a different sort of aftertaste. My heart- ache does not spring from emptiness rather from the fullness that came, even if briefly. I longingly recall the time warp and the details of what took place. Many days I am tempted to do whatever it takes to get back to that conference room. So far, the possible risks have kept me from that dilapidated building just down the hill. *Colin, you filled me with such hope. From the moment you first walked into my office, my curiosity got the better of me. I can't recall a conversation with you that failed to build my confidence, as it also made me want to know you better. When we stumbled into our first time travel adventure amid the unknown, I recall the excitement and the thought of possibility. Now time separates us…will that be the one gate I cannot storm?*

Conversations with Belinda are the only outlet for my *Colin's gone missing* moments. An investigator from Asheville showed up unannounced at the office mid-morning in early October 2000, six months after the WLOS news had officially picked up the story of his abandoned vehicle found at the entrance to Graham County. Two details lead this detective to my door: My calls to Colin's UNC- A office along with a couple of medical staff from Mission reporting their interactions with this man in an unusual hospital admittance involving a young Cherokee mother and infant, and, of course, with me. Thankfully the messages I left on the office phone all related to the photography projects related to the river property. Of course, I repeated the story that Colin and I originally concocted about Sa- vannah mysteriously showing up on my property with her newborn infant at the same time Colin was on the property shooting pictures for his collection.

I had the strong sense that the investigator suspected there was much more to the story that he had not unearthed. But as he made his way to the door that day, he stated firmly to me. "Mam, until a body is found, many speculate this is the age-old story of a man unhappy in marriage who has met someone that he thinks he loves enough to disappear into another life."

§

The river property continues to work its power in me. Most days, I hear the sound of water rushing over the rocks before I let other thoughts push aside the sheer pleasure of waking up daily on this land. Nothing compares to allowing the rhythm of its life force to pull me into sync. Many days I conclude my walk by sitting in the springhouse. The cold water splashed on my face never fails to restore my energy and faith in life. Funny that I never worry about being sucked back in time from the location where Colin and I first came upon Savannah in the throes of labor. That concern only crops up when I find myself tempted to explore the old, dilapidated store.

Sheltered time spent in the springhouse keeps the emotional storms at bay. Perhaps I have convinced myself that Colin will return someday to the double springheads. Also, the many tall, massive oaks on the property have a way of reminding me of strength that comes from their deep roots. Curling my back against the rough bark of one of these giants and enjoying the shade of far-reaching limbs can work a spell peace over me. In the still of such moments, the awareness of my roots is often enough to move me forward. The many layers of "why" questions can still move in unexpectedly. *Why had my path crossed with Colin's only to so quickly be removed?* Somehow, I am learning to balance the worry with an acceptance of the now.

Stretched out on the green grass, I shift my position just enough to feel discomfort from the root that now jabs into my spine. At that moment, a thought pierces my consciousness. *There was a full moon last night.* The harvest moon, as I watched it ritualistically take possession of the night, opened a floodgate in me. Thoughts of Savannah, little William, and, of course, Colin filled the air. As if in response, a breeze blew up from the waters below. The limbs of the giant oak bent and swayed in a dance of sorts. My spirits lifted. I entered a moment of knowing: *Do not ever doubt. There was a reason. There was a purpose.*

I don't pretend to fully understand that reason. What I do know is this: In those *moments of knowing,* I am convinced that action taken with intention makes for strong possibilities. Colin had stepped out the conference room door with purpose. *If I could stretch my hand out and pierce the veil of time, what would I find?*

Chapter 17

The ancient dogwood on the river property is always the first to show the fullness of spring. With an overabundance of blooms, the umbrella-like limbs weigh downward toward the earth itself. 2005 may prove to be a record year for the revered tree. Macy's graduation from college will take place in another month. Curious about every subject, my daughter managed to turn a four-year process into six. By the time she came close to obtaining the history degree she finally committed to, her interests had turned elsewhere. The day she informed me of her commitment to join the Peace Corps, she suggested that she may go to grad school someday. Thoughts of becoming an anthropologist now hold some vague appeal to her. I can only hope that when she runs into her life's purpose, she will embrace it fully. Rooted in well-thought-out plans, Duncan, on the other hand, prepared to soon wrap up his third year of college.

The turn of the century and the five years that followed had surprisingly produced an unexpected but abiding contentment in me. I can offer no concrete explanation of the seismic shift that grounds me with time, but I do not question the increased inner strength that has emerged. Facing long-buried emotions proved one of the hardest ongoing tasks for me. Serious self-growth brought about through counseling, enabled me to acknowledge that the kids' dad and I both gave less than we should or could have to our marriage. How freeing to no longer need to blame Taylor for the whole mess of our relationship. Once I lay down that tired old burden, he seemed able to release me of his own pent-up blame. Although it was a long time in coming, Macy and Duncan's dad now has a relationship with his "almost" grown kids.

Confirmation of Tim's suicide forced me into more counseling. Plain and simple, I needed help coping with my husband's hard, irreversible decision that robbed his very life and then reached out from the grave and continued to take from so many of us in ways we are still trying to understand. My heart aches most for the twins. *How does one offer any explanation that comes close to making any sense? Why could he not have understood that... debts... were no real reason to end his life? A couple of good real estate deals and a commitment to rehab.... he could have put the burden behind him.*

Almost a year after he had found Tim dead on the floor at

the construction site, Rick Dawson, Tim's faithful employee, came across a letter... a short note...scrawled in the close-to illegible handwriting that we all recognized. As Rick recalled, he had left Tim alone, at the beginning of their workday, in the truck, as he stepped back in the shop to grab the nail gun. "Sarah, he must have left the note at that point. I'm fairly certain he was not back in my truck at any other time that morning, for I kept it locked on that particular job. The paper seemed purposefully hidden under some other paperwork in my cluttered glove compartment. I know I've shuffled that mess around looking for one thing or the other. Hard to believe I did not see the note before."

Letting go of "what could I have done" did not come easily. I do think I have become better at seeing warning signs of impending trouble in people who are hurting and in danger of self-harm. Learning practical steps to help someone in depression has moved me forward with my own emotions. I cannot fathom that I lived so long, not taking in the overwhelming numbers who suffer from this relentless mental struggle. Tim's use of drugs still does not sit well with me. I can logically understand the monkey of addiction on someone's back, but I still lack any real compassion with that subject. The drug culture, in my opinion, seems intent on finding someone else to suck into the addictive circle. In hindsight, I am now aware of the group that circled Tim, enabling each other to get high. Maybe more compassion for the addictive behaviors will come with time.

Loneliness does not plague me. In fact, I often choose solitude. My dear friend Belinda points out regularly. "You have turned very introspective on me. You seem to thrive in being alone." Maybe she is right. I am certainly aware of a reserve of strength that grows with time in contemplation. Peace takes over. Now there is indeed a meaning to my life that had teetered on desperation as I had continued on and on in the nightmare marriage with Tim.

This spring day captured my full attention. The show of flowers, the tiny burst of green leaves coming from the many trees on the property reminded me how long I had held this favorite season at a distance in my own life rather than facing another failed marriage. With one glance at the grand old dogwood, I wondered if it had bloomed as beautiful in its early years. Or like me, had it saved full bloom for its later? I smiled at the thought as I acknowledged that even the absence of Colin no longer buries me under its weight.

There is so much to treasure about knowing him. Many days I find it easy to feel his nearness. I sometimes walk the property in the thick morning fog, hoping against hope that he will step into view.

§

The three years leading up to 2005 were packed with change. Back in 2002, Belinda insisted I come back to my first love, education. An assistant principal's position combined with teaching two grades of high school World Literature and Writing came open. She called me immediately. No question about it, as the opening of that school year unfolded, an excitement came back to me that I had not felt for years. I embraced the return to a calling I should have never left. Even after a long school day, I carved out time for my evening walk. I often remember my first years of teaching and the time spent jogging around the small Mississippi community. Initially the world of real estate and I had been at odds, to say the least. Every aspect of that business, the wheeling and dealing, the hustle and bustle, all reminded me of Tim. At the same time, it was real estate money that enabled me to hold on to the river property and at least get a roof put on the old house. For that, I am eternally grateful.

The day the office trailer sold in June of 2003 put a smile on my face. Yes, it felt good to see its backside pulled out into the street from my driveway. *I can't wait to spend my first night in my tiny house.* Belinda first told me about her aunt's mint-condition Airstream over two months ago. Her Aunt Bettye and Uncle Joe had traveled the country together for years and had only recently purchased the sleek new camper a year earlier. After Joe's unexpected death, Belinda's aunt lost all desire to travel. I assured her I had some interest in glamping. However, what truly hooked me was the thought of living in the warmth of the silver shoebox, particularly in the cold winter. I pulled the little camper in between the old house and the small, two-room dwelling that I have treasured since Savannah helped me to connect some dots with her time. When I take in the details of this old structure with the front room and attached lean-to that sits close to the big house, I shudder to think Tim and I had come close to tearing it down on several occasions. Still, termites and time have done their damage. I have put it to good use as a potting shed, lovingly named Sadie's Place. *It will stand as long as it stands. That is all I can hope for.* Macy questioned the name. I explained that I suspected it was someone's home at some point in history. She accepted that I liked the name. Only Belinda and Colin know the story behind Sadie and this old, close to crumbling two-room house.

During the relatively brief stay Savannah experienced in my time, I learned much about the history of my treasured river property. To hear the tales, the lore mixed with the observations from this young Cherokee woman who lived on this very land a hundred years before, remains a treasured time for me. My connection to this magnificent place became stronger than ever. When Colin and I had traveled back in time, the river house had not been built in Savannah's and Miss Sadie's world. My research had already known that construction started in 1902. Colin and I had wondered if the house and its residents would touch Savannah's life in any significant way.

Savannah also told me much about the talk of a lumber mill that would soon be built on the property across from Mr. Billy's store. If she did make it back to her time, her head must be filled daily with perplexing thoughts of what she witnessed in the future. I always recall that her most consistent comment as we talked of the past and the present time was this singular question, "Where are all the trees?"

I smile as I think of her words. Here in the present, I live on one of the most wooded bits of acreage in Hunterstown. Will my children or grandchildren someday ask, "Where are all of the trees?" Sometimes, almost as a whisper of Savannah's voice, I hear the call and know my purpose. *Stand guard and sentinel over this sacred land where the elements of earth, water, and sky are in perfect harmony.*

Chapter 18

The school day continued to pull me longingly into poignant memories. It seemed the hours would never pass till 3:00. Now, back in the classroom for ten years, the sheer joy of teaching remains strong. I am the teacher who longs to have another thirty minutes just to make sure my students really understand some detail. I could not put my finger on exactly what was pushing me toward home this particular afternoon. Contentment washed over me as I turned down the long driveway. For so many years of my life with Tim, I hated going home. Anger and disruption had dominated homelife. The verbal tug-of-war that always erupted, furniture kicked with force, those times when I took the hit instead, all such memories were tucked away carefully, held at bay by good therapy, unexpected joy, and, of course, the magic of the river property itself.

Today I remembered the day, now so many years ago, when I first turned down the long driveway, thick with the green of summer growth. Now, fall colors fill my senses. *Indeed, this land has "got in my bones." By some mysterious grace, I found this place. Or did it find me?* I continued down the gravel expanse to my little Airstream haven, sandwiched between the big house and the small, two-room potting shed. Above its slightly sagging door, I spotted the sign I had recently repainted: *Sadie's Place.* A soft smile moved across my face as so many dear memories rushed in. *I am home, yes, I am home.*

Short of torrential rains and thunderstorms or a blizzard, I walk the property and surrounding area every day after work. Today, as I make my way through nooks and crannies of rock and thick growth along the trail, I think back on the way the land looked in winter when Colin and I first traveled back in time. Down toward the old lumber mill, I decide to cross the state road and walk along the adjoining street. Not really in the mood for the distraction of passing cars, I veer off to my left and follow the railroad tracks. Eventually, I loop back, heading toward home. The afternoon sun seems almost blinding. As I near the dilapidated old store, I swear for just a moment, I saw the land once again as it was in Savannah's time. Of course, my mind turned to memories of the dear people who had so mysteriously become a part of my life. *I can only imagine how they have changed. The baby, of course, would now be twelve years old. I suspect Miss Sadie is much more stooped. How I would love to see her dear face. Have Charles and Savannah had more children?* Then, the thought that often crept in made me stop briefly as I took in what had been Mr. Billy's place. *Colin, are you there with all of those precious people? If only I knew for sure.*

As I turn back down my driveway on foot, another thought from the past pulls at my brain. Savannah had many times mentioned her great grandmother's insistence that her family stay along the river. Her version of the story always concluded with the strong words of her ancestor. *Never leave this property, these springheads, and the life along the river.* Savannah shared that Miss Sadie's mother had been very close to Maidena Taylor, Savannah's great grandmother. In short, the Taylor's owed their lives to Sadie's family, who had managed to provide food and supplies when the Taylor's hid out in the caves rather than be taken west with so many of the Cherokee.

The story fascinated me the moment Savannah shared this glimpse of her family's story. I added quickly that I could certainly relate to falling in love with the river property myself. Of course, I will never forget Savannah's response. "It is true that the Cherokee feel strongly that double bends in the river and double springheads are sacred signs. She added, "Our people answered the call of the *Conaheeta* many years back when we first settled here. But I do think it is important that Miss Sadie always felt the loyalty to the land was more about my great grandmother Maidena falling in love with a white man who had promised he would one day return to the springheads where they first met."

At this point in reminiscing, I began to toy with a nagging worry that often crossed my mind when I had thoughts of Savannah and William. When Colin and I took the then "little William" back to Asheville for his checkup, he had received a clean bill of health. Savannah was treated for Group B Strep at the time and was told it was highly unlikely she would ever experience it twice if she should become pregnant again. Even with those two good reports, a sense of dread had overcome me as we drove away from all the modern medical facilities that day in the year 2000. I could not help but think of the many childhood diseases that sent children to early graves during the early 1900s.

I had once described Miss Sadie as a woman ahead of her time. Over the years, I concluded that my description was not accurate. I now conclude Miss Sadie was a woman for all times. No question, she had tricks up her sleeve that were only starting to be acknowledged by present-day nutritionists. I knew she would do everything in her power to keep Savannah and William healthy and strong. My heart remains convinced that mother and child made it back to the love and care of this dear, wise soul.

As I neared the Airstream, I remembered the flashing light of my answering machine that had caught my eye earlier as I tried to rush out the door for my walk. Few people had my number. More than likely, it was someone I actually wanted to talk to. *Maybe it's Mama. Of course, could be one of the kids calling. I'll check as soon as I get inside.*

I kicked off my sneakers the moment I entered. The flashing light once again got my attention. I hit the play button immediately. The voice I heard stopped me dead in my tracks. "Sarah, Sarah, are you there? Pick up, Sarah." The message ended abruptly. There was no question about it. *That is Colin's voice.*

I spent the next hour hitting the play button over and over again. The sheer joy of hearing him speak almost outweighed the pain of wanting to know more. *What happened to disrupt his message? God, what I would give to hear the rest of what he wanted to say. Does this mean he is out there somewhere in time? Could he have found a phone somewhere in the past? Or what if it means he is somewhere in the future? Or maybe he is in the present, but miles away?* Then my memory shifted to the mysterious telephone in the time-warp that had shocked Colin and me to our cores when it rang. Questions flooded my mind as I reached back in time for the detail of Colin's discarded *Nike* jacket and the woman's haunting voice that longed to connect with someone by the name of James. *Had Colin reached out to me in a similar fashion? Oh, how I wish I had been here to answer the phone. Would an instant phone connection have worked?*

Soon I gave over to the memory of my last time spent with Colin. I recalled the moment when I first suspected Colin and I were suspended in time. I could easily recall the feeling of my feet hitting the platform. When I looked around, I knew we were in the same place that my school teacher friends, Mark and Alice had stepped into with me when we walked through the doorway of the dilapidated general store of my second dream. Yes, it had to be the same location that had greeted me in my sleep state when I had peered through the crack in the front door of the old place with the green light fixture hanging precariously off a nearby pole. I recalled that in my dream, I had almost fallen off Mark's shoulders when it occurred to me that the building was much larger on the inside than it appeared on the outside. I then recall that in my dream, once we made it inside and past the shock that we were possibly in a time warp passage of some sort, we eventually all noticed, almost as an afterthought, a second, half-glass doorway. We stood outside of it as we took in all the details of a modern-day conference area, complete with a table, multiple chairs, and a credenza with a phone nearby. The carpet had been plush. Of course, that was when I first marveled at the *Nike* jacket lying on the floor.

If memory serves me correctly, I awoke from the dream just as I reached out for the doorknob. In the time warp with Colin, I knew without a doubt that I clung tightly to his hand as I led him forward. I wanted to find that conference room. We passed several busy ticket windows. Different people waited in line. My hawk-eye awareness of clothes caused me to recall a detail from the second dream.

"Colin, are you taking in that none of these people seem to be aware of us. That was the case in my dream. My teacher friend Mark had cautioned me in the dream not to reach out and touch anyone. There was also a woman in the navy polka-dot dress that drew Alice and me to the conclusion that we were in a 1930s timeframe in history. I don't see that dress anywhere. I do see some clothes that remind me of my grandparents back in the '60s. The fact that none of these people seem aware of us remains true."

I soon spotted up ahead the half-glass doorway. Again, a light was on inside. This time I stated my intention. "Colin, see that entrance up ahead on the left. I want to go in. I wanted to do so in my dream but awoke too soon." As we moved in close to the door, I hesitated before reaching for the brass doorknob. "It's just like I recall. Are you game? Do we go in?"

"Are you sure you want to do this?"

This time I did not hesitate. As we stepped inside, absolutely nothing happened. Colin did comment. "Obviously this room represents our time. Everything we are looking at is familiar to the world we know: The décor, the recessed ceiling lighting, the soft glow of a table lamp, of course, a telephone."

As he took in the details, some glimpse of a thought lodged

uncomfortably in my brain. Shaking my head slightly as if trying to dislodge the nagging thought that pulled at my memory the moment we walked into the conference room, I joined the conversation. "I think it's safe to say I've never experienced anything like what I am feeling at the moment. Here I am, standing in a place that I first dreamed about in the second of a sequel of night tales. As best as I can figure, we are in a time warp where I just walked through a doorway that had remained a mystery thanks to "waking up" from the dream state where I first laid eyes on this setting. Then to think that by some inexplicable means you and I have now traveled through time on three separate occasion. Then, here I am in the very location that had filled me with wonder in my second dream."

"Sarah, the *how* is certainly beyond my comprehension. On occasion, I feel like I might understand *why* you are caught up in all that is going on. Please understand how fortunate I feel to have walked into your office that first day. Shortly upon meeting you, I suspected you might be interesting. Little did I know the degree to which that thought was an understatement. I am here with you. But where is "here"? What is this room all about?"

As I stood near him and looked deep into his questioning blue eyes, my mind went right back to the moment he had held me in his arms shortly after he had turned back to reach my hand when we were hoping to travel with Savannah and the baby.

Colin read my mind. "Sarah, I know with certainty the longing I felt as I held you in my arms. I sensed the feeling was mutual. He then let his hands find their way around my waist. Desire took over. Becoming almost frantic in his attempt to get past my clothes, there was nothing gentle about the way our mouths sought each other as our passion surged. We reached and responded to the long-anticipated touch and the feel of skin to skin as we pulled at each other's clothing. I felt myself losing all ability to stay on my feet. I wrapped my arms around Colin's neck as his hand reached around me, supporting my leg as it worked to wrap around him. Within moments, he carried me fully with his forward motion. The chair we collided with tumbled sideways. We landed on the conference table.

§

I'll never forget the first moments when I woke in his arms.

Nestled in the curve of his body, I knew Colin still slept. The weight of his arm rested heavily on me. I tried not to stir. I hoped to drink in the moment. All of our lovemaking came rushing back on me. Every detail of how he possessed my body came back to life in me. I had given up on experiencing the possibilities of physical intimacy. During the years I existed in the nightmare of life with Tim, I often thought of a line from a song I had once heard. "There's no greater distance than two people so far apart in the same bed." When deceit and broken promises are the basis of a relationship, sex becomes the ultimate insult. As much as I had given up on physical pleasure, I knew I had absolutely lost the ability to trust a man, much less allow love in. As I lay in Colin's arms, I found my hope restored.

Smiling, I realized I could not quite remember how we made it from conference table to carpet. I could not resist turning toward Colin. He stirred slightly. A smile spread slowly across his face. I could feel his body pressing up against mine. Within a matter of moments, a gentle, slow kind of love song flowed between us. The union, forged first in friendship, then in passion, now grew as strong as the sheltering oaks on the property. Rhythmic movement carried us like the river to a spent place of sacred silence. I stirred first. My hand traced the outline of his face. Gentle kisses covered his eyelids one more time. His hand played gently up and down my spine. His head moved downward to the resting place of my breasts. He spoke softly from that place of shared bliss. "I'm sure glad you came across this room in your dreams."

§

I recovered my clothing. Colin stood in his tee shirt and jeans, almost as if he had no desire to get fully dressed. Our outer layers lay strewn across the carpet. Reminders of shared passion. I found myself wishing we could stay forever. Silence hung heavy in the air. I knew I was deep in thought. Colin reached to upright the toppled chair. As he sat down, he pulled me onto his lap. Almost in a whisper, he said. "Sarah, I know the reason behind your downcast face. I, too, wish this would never end." Then with a bit of a chuckle, he added. "Considering the possibility that we are still in a time warp, I suppose that is exactly the case."

"Oddly enough, for once, I don't seem to be worried in the least about what may or may not happen next. I have spent way too much time dwelling on my regret-filled past or longing way too much for a better future. I can hardly find the words to say what I'm feeling as we sit here reveling in the moment. I don't know that I have ever been so content in the "now.""

Colin broke the silence of our reverie. "I suspect we are not the first to make our way into the mystery of the conference room. For some reason, I am convinced it is not meant to be a place to stay forever."

His words seemed to herald in the ringing of the telephone. We were both startled. I could almost feel time chomping at its bits. I asked, "Do you think we should answer it?

"Sarah, how could anyone not answer a phone that just keeps on ringing in this setting? You saw this place first in your dream. Don't you think you have to find out more?"

Of course, he was right.

I jumped to my feet as I kicked at Colin's big, outer jacket that blocked the path to the phone. My hand shook. Just as I was about to lift the receiver, I noted the speakerphone feature. I rested both hands on the sleek wooden surface, I think to steady myself. Colin stood on my right, but faced in the opposite direction, looking out into the room toward the half glass doorway. After hitting the button, a female asked, almost pleading. "James, James? It's Meriam. Tell me it's you at last!"

My brain could not fathom the situation that prompted the desperate tone. Just as I was about to answer her, Colin lunged from my side and grabbed for his heavy coat as he bolted toward the doorway. I heard the woman's haunting plea for James one more time. Even before Colin cleared the opening, I heard him yell at the top of his voice as he rushed down the platform, "Savannah, Savannah, it's me, Colin. Wait up."

I ran toward the doorway. My foot caught on Colin's lighter jacket, the layer he had worn under his bigger coat. The dots connected at last. The image lying on the floor burned in my brain. My scream came from deep within as I recalled the black *Nike* on the conference room carpet in my second dream. "No, Colin. Don't..." The rest of the words never came.

The few steps to the doorway seemed an eternity. By now, I was running with the *Nike* pressed close to my body. I hoped to catch a glimpse of him. He must have seen Savannah and little William. I just had to reach them. Within a moment, I knew my feet were no longer on the wooden platform. I recalled how I had been in Colin's arms when we first traveled in this suspended state. Then certainty of my thought moved in with a heavy thud. The *Nike* jacket that my dear friends and I had seen in my second dream belonged, of course, to Colin. *I had not even met him at that point in my life. Yet...* Before I could explore my confusion deeper, I landed hard on the ground. The wind whipped my heavy curls across my face. It took only a moment to take in the sound of the water crashing over the rocks below. As my eyes adjusted to the moonlight, I knew I had come home. I looked across the way at the familiar night lights of Hunterstown.

§

I keep the old phone with its voicemail feature. I recorded the recording eventually just in case the phone should someday cease to function. I take some comfort in knowing he is out there somewhere. I treasure the fact that I can play and replay the sound of him calling my name. Of course, I wonder about so many details. *Did he ever connect with Savannah and the baby? Did they somehow make it to her time, back to Miss Sadie and Charles?* I admit that I often sit in the now-potting shed, what was Miss Sadie's home, to feel near to these people that I love so dearly and deeply. Many days I think I feel the connection. There have been moments when I swear, I feel a brush against my skin. *Is it possible Colin is sitting in this same space, separated by years and time but close enough to sense his presence?*

Belinda remains an anchor in my life. *What would I do if I did not have her as a sounding board, someone to listen to my endless wondering about how any of this tale could have happened?* My dear friend often reminds me. "Sarah, we both know it *all* happened." She always adds, "I suppose we will never know how." Belinda wept when she first heard the mysterious voicemail left by Colin. We both cling to the hope that, somehow, he is with Savannah.

When I spend too much time wondering about the missed voicemail and if Colin made his way back to the time warp with the express purpose to try to connect with me, I find myself buried in questions. I sink in despair. *Did he attempt to travel and only make it as far as the time warp? If so, did he ever get back to Savannah's time? Did he find Savannah and Miss Sadie in their world only to risk that security to try to get back to our time or at least connect with our time through a phone call? Is the conference room the only place a phone call can be made? Or is he somewhere in the future?* I eventually force myself to let go of the uncertainty of it all. I have become very good at living in the moment. The *now* is my solace. No good comes from endless longing to go back. The future will be what it will be.

Many years back, my dear friend Belinda told me I had turned very introspective on her. Now, I realize that, at last, my peace comes from contentment with my lot in life. My own skin is a good place to be. No time for wishing *this* or regretting *that*. Simply put, I hold the responsibility for my happiness or lack thereof. Self-awareness has become a magnet for many interesting people in my life. Although I hold dear everyone who fits into this category, I no longer forsake the truth that the real treasure lies within myself.

Chapter 19

It felt wonderful to have some downtime in my own home for the holidays. The lure of retirement had pulled at me briefly this past year. Yet somehow, I knew I wasn't done with education. Belinda graciously understood that I needed to take an extended Thanksgiving break this year. Mississippi had called me home three times already in 2011. I knew Mama needed to see me more than ever around their Thanksgiving table. No question, her heart still ached over the loss of Jake, her only brother. For that reason alone, I had returned to Mississippi in November for several weeks, returning just in time for Christmas in North Carolina.

Macy, her husband, and my two grandchildren, along with Duncan, had all gone with me to Uncle Jake's memorial service back in July. I also attended his wife's service just a month earlier. Bonnie's tragic death as she was shot in my uncle's arms, followed so quickly by the senseless death of my mother's brother, had torn at the hearts of all of our family. The pain of loss took its toll on both my mother and Aunt Mary Louise, my mother's sister.

The river property pulled me into its promise of some needed downtime which seemed the perfect plan for the holidays. The kids and grandkids coming in for our seasonal traditions always sits well with me. Macy not only went for that extra degree but married an archeologist as well. They travel with the two kids anywhere their careers take them. Duncan and I often laugh when some artifact or architectural remnant is included in the kids' Christmas stockings.

When Duncan pokes fun at Macy for what he calls her eccentric personality, she always retorts "Well, at least, Scott and I have provided some grandchildren, Duncan. When are you going to leave your law office early enough to get out and even meet someone?"

§

We held our first Christmas celebration in the hip-roofed river house back in 2006. At the time, the festivity was confined to the recently renovated kitchen area, inclusive of a large pantry and an add-on area bringing in the much-need laundry and bathroom space to the original design. Mainly because of a lack of money, I tackled the renovation in increments. The new roof literally saved the historic place from crumbling while it caused me to pause before pushing ahead to what promised to be a costly kitchen transformation. I refused to settle. Eventually, as the wood floors were restored to pristine beauty, with sections of the original beaded board walls incorporated into a mix of decorative tile against granite countertops, my heart soared.

I cannot count the times I was counseled to lower the fourteen-foot ceilings. Instead, I chose to pick up some moonlighting real estate work and put in the exposed copper ductwork that highlighted the massive copper hood above my black AGA stove. I had waited too long to restore this dear house to settle for anything less than my heart's dream. When I was not defending my insistence that the house be restored to the fine degree that had originally gone into its construction, I could be heard bemoaning the sad state of an educator's salary. *Why is it that our society does not value educators as much as doctors and NFL football players?*

On that first Christmas Eve night in the river house, when I eventually walked out the kitchen door onto the screen porch that I just knew I needed, I looked back. The Christmas lights twinkling along the outline of the porch and kitchen portion of the massive seven-bedroom home worked their magic on me. I could spot the lone star of the small Charlie Brown tree in its place of honor on the massive kitchen island. The kids had decided to rough it in the massive dining room with camping gear suited for the Arctic. As I made my way into the warmth of my loyal Airstream, the smile stayed on my face. As my head sunk into the softness of my pillow, my thoughts turned to Savannah and Miss Sadie. This night, as I did every night, I hoped Colin had made his way to these dear people who would love him like family. Admittedly, thoughts of him often lingered a bit longer, eventually mixing into my dreams.

§

As heartbreaking as 2011 had been for my family, the time would go down in history as the year when I did not have a house project of some sort scheduled. Of course, as I understood all too well, my treasured place required ongoing love and attention like all homes do. Belinda often joked. "Hey, my friend, just think. You can now start over on many of those recurring items on your list of house upkeep!" I could ignore that reality for at least a little while. The thought of no major renovations any time soon did bring a feeling of contentment as Christmas 2012 rolled around.

After one last trip to the grocery store, I pulled onto the long drive. Red-berried holly trees and evergreens added touches of green to the winter landscape. A hawk soared overhead across the winter-gray sky. The house welcomed me. I never second-guessed my insistence of maintaining the original, dark wood stain I had seen so many years back. The beautiful stonework of the massive chimneys and under-skirting mixed in beautiful contrast with the white trimmed windows and expansive L-shaped porch. The smoke gently escaping from at least two of the three chimneys reminded me of the warmth supported by the multi-HVAC system supported by a massive wood-burning system in the basement. Six large rockers and a four-seater swing, all in white, often made it difficult to get guests to come on inside. The Christmas season lent itself to the plaid blankets in the tartan colors of the Campbell clan that draped the back of every seat. All the garland came from the land itself. Plenty of red ribbon and Christmas lights completed the seasonal welcome.

Christmas Eve once again filled with last minute gift wrapping, although I promised every year not to let procrastination win out. Then, of course, there was the cooking for the Christmas morning brunch that unfolds the next day as the children squeal in glee and the so-called adults decide whose turn it is next to open a gift. Although nature has been my cathedral for many years, in the past two years, I do occasionally attend services at The Messiah. The current Carpenter Gothic sanctuary was completed in 1896. The church was then consecrated a mission and named the Church of the Messiah in 1902. The fact that this building existed when Colin and I had traveled back in time seems to provide me with a much-needed link to the past. The Episcopal rituals that unfold in this beautiful historical setting in our little town often are the soothing balm my soul needs. This year we planned to attend the Christmas Eve service as a close friend. Christmas night gives over to our family dinner.

This Christmas, Duncan surprised us all. He invited a female guest to the meet the a close friend. Macy concluded quickly that her brother must be serious. Duncan's special guest was driving in from Asheville, where she had spent Christmas Eve and morning. He expected her shortly before dinner. Macy loves to cook. My job is typically left to a special dessert or two and, of course, the home-made rolls. "Macy, my rolls are just about ready to go in the oven. I wish Duncan's friend would arrive."

"Mom, you may as well give over to calling the mysterious woman something other than just a friend."

Still grinning at my daughter's confidence in her ability to read her brother, I heard the car drive up. I could hear Duncan barreling down from upstairs and hollering toward the kitchen. "Mom, she's here. She's here."

Macy grinned as she rolled her eyes and added under her breath. "Don't say I didn't tell you so!"

We both headed toward the front door. As I entered the dining room, I smiled as I noticed Miss Sadie's lamp that Colin and I had brought back to our time from the past. For years I kept it hidden from the kids. This year I pulled the treasured item out and included it in the Christmas decorations. For some reason, I had decided that soon I would tell the kids about my time travel adventure. Surely, if I got Belinda to attest to my sanity, they would buy the story. The massive dining table could easily seat fourteen. The antique tin ceiling joined the evening light still showing through the banks of the wide, triple, floor-to-ceiling windows on each side of the room. "Macy, don't let me forget to light all the candles. This room was simply made for candlelight."

Duncan started the introductions the moment we stepped into the living room. "Alexis, this is my mother. Also, my sister Macy." About that time, Scott was corralling the kids from upstairs to join the excitement. "This is Macy's husband Scott, and their two munchkins, Elizabeth and Alexander. My family, this is Alexis Morgan."

I, of course, took in the details of this woman who obviously had my son's attention. Her dark eyes were framed by high cheekbones. Her black, sleek hair glistened in the firelight from the massive living room fireplace. There seemed to be something about her that I could not quite put my finger on. *Did she perhaps remind me of someone?*

Before I could spend any time with the thought, Duncan spoke. "Mom, the first time I met Alexis, I noticed the unusual silver ring she wore. See, the massive silver ring on her thumb." Alexis held out her hand. I remember thinking at the time that you would like to see it."

The moment she reached her hand toward me, my heart seemed to almost stop. In one glance, a flash of recognition moved across my brain. *That ring has to be the strange silver band that I had noticed on Colin when he first came to the real estate office so many years back.* As I took Alexis' hand into mine to examine the ring better, I could not seem to find any words to speak. *Surely there could not be another one with the fine details of Colin's family ring?* My mind filled with the memory of the heat that had radiated from the ring every time we had experienced time travel. I found my eyes darting from the ring to her face. Again, my heart raced as my mind sought a place to rest. At last, I knew the resemblance. She reminds me of Savannah. At that moment, I knew with certainty that Colin had indeed made it to the place in the past where he was with people he knew.

Somehow, I managed a response. "Alexis, your ring is exquisite. Just beautiful. You will have to tell me more about your ancestry. I am sure there is a story behind this ring." I pulled my eyes away from the silver ring that I knew so well. "I'm sorry, but I've got to get back to the kitchen. Sure hope my dinner rolls have not burned."

As soon as the words came out, I knew that Macy knew that I had not yet put the rolls in the oven. I heard her start to call my name. "Mom..." but her voice trailed off. She did, however, follow me into the kitchen as Duncan and Scott were busy convincing Alexis that my rolls were a long tradition that was worth sampling.

The kitchen door swung open behind me. Macy started in on me. I had just closed the oven door on the rolls. "What was that about? You know good, and well, you did not put those rolls in the oven before we walked out to meet Dunc's woman. I remember them sitting on the island. Plus, you looked for a moment as if you were about to pass out. What's going on?"

"Macy, I think I just got too hot cooking. Then Scott had the fire roaring in the big fireplace. Let me focus on getting Christmas dinner to the table. Don't worry. I'm just fine...just fine."

"Sure, Mom." Then with what seemed like a deliberate addition of sarcasm, she added. "Whatever! I saw what I saw!"

Using just a tad too much energy to push open the door, my head-strong daughter headed out to light the candles. *That daughter of mine. Macy has never moved away from a topic so quickly unless she plans to come back with a vengeance, later on, to get to the bottom of things. Maybe she will at least wait until Alexis has headed back to the AirBnB before she starts her inquisition. Surely, nothing can top the start to this year's Christmas Dinner?*

§

The dining room of the river house centered me with every detail, from the high ceiling, a beautiful chandelier dimmed to perfection, the original wood floors shining in their refinished state, to the view out into the living room where the wood fire made for a warm and welcoming occasion. I treasured it all. From my vantage point at the head of the table, I could easily take in the details of Alexis' features. How I wish it was a dinner when the table was packed with people. Then it might be easier not to get pulled into those dark eyes that reminded me so much of Savannah. Over and over, I forced my attention elsewhere. As soon as I could convince myself that no one would notice, particularly Macy, I stole a quick glimpse of Colin's ring. I liked the way Alexis wore it on her thumb. Every time the candlelight caused the silver to glisten, every quick glimpse at the details of one of the Celtic symbols so intricately etched, I also thought of Colin. *I can almost feel you next to me. Where are you? Have I lost you to time? It's been close to twelve years? I have aged. Would you recognize me? Of course, you have aged too. God, I hope you are not dead.* I paused midstream as my brain tried to reach for some idea that seemed just beyond my grasp. *Colin, you can't be dead; you can't be. But, where are you? Why did you give up your ring? How did it manage to get passed down through time to this beautiful young woman next to my son on this Christmas night?*

"Mom, you are staring into space. Hey, Mom." Macy's voice shook me out of my deep thoughts. "Earth to Mom. Come back to us."

"Macy, I was lost in thought. Just walking down memory lane a bit with the history of this house. Alexis, turn around, please. See that built-in china cabinet? The first time I walked into this dining room, now some thirty years ago, I fell in love with that piece. It had been painted over with layers of light green paint that had chipped away, giving it a bit of what we would now call a distressed style. At first sight, I envisioned it filled with beautiful dishes as it is tonight."

Then switching gears, I decided it was now or never. I may as well plow in with some questioning that might shake me to the core when I heard the answers. "So, Alexis. Tell me more about your family? From your beautiful features, your shiny black hair, the lovely boldness of your cheekbones, I assume you are Cherokee."

"Yes, I am Cherokee." *Even the way she answered the questions reminds me of Savannah... always her replies were as brief and succinct as possible.* Alexis seemed to hesitate, perhaps deciding if she should offer more.

I decided to push further in the direction I wanted the answers to come. "I would enjoy hearing about the history of your family if you are willing to share those details. Let's start with the story behind that beautiful ring. Was it a gift for a special occasion? Please, tell us more."

"My ...." Her voice seemed to break just slightly. "I received the ring at my grandmother's death. I remember sitting in her lap as a little girl, twirling the beautiful silver on her thumb. I think she knew I loved it." Again, I sensed hesitancy before she spoke.

"It is such an unusual ring. Did she tell you the story behind it? It looks as if it were designed with meaning."

"Sarah, I wish I knew more about the ring. My parents were both killed in an automobile accident when I was twelve. My grandmother took over my raising. I loved her beyond compare. Unfortunately, in my late teens and much of my twenties, I gave in to anger over the loss of both parents. At the time I could have begun to know my grandmother in a more mature way, I was too self-absorbed in asking, "Why me? I hate to admit it, but I spent years, even into my early thirties, avoiding family gatherings of any sort. Honestly, I think I was too embarrassed about my behavior to reach out to my dear grandmother who could have told me so much more about our family history. I knew I had no right to be angry with her. It was, after all, not her fault my parents both died in that awful accident."

"Oh, dear Alexis. I did not mean to open up such a personal part of your life. Trust me, we all have our regrets. Failed relationships, wasted years, whatever the case may be, we all have our secrets and regrets."

I saw a shy smile forming on Alexis' face. Then she spoke. "I almost waited too late, but I believe Grandmam at least knew who I was some of the time up to the end. She developed Alzheimer's.

When her son William tracked me down and told me I needed to come see her, I did."

I could feel my heart racing. *Alexis just referred to her Great Uncle William. It has to be the "little William" that Colin and I had brought to the present with his dear mother Savannah, the woman who very likely is Alexis' grandmother.* I could not seem to find any words at the moment. Instead, the thoughts stayed jumbled inside my brain. *How in the world had my son Duncan found this miracle? Does he have any clue who and what he has unearthed?*

Just as I was about to ask the question that now burned in me, Alexis spoke again. "A smile filled Grandmam's face the moment I walked into her room at the memory care center. William had warned me she might not know me. He had laughingly told me that at his age he darn well did not remember lots of names himself, but he certainly came nowhere near telling the wild and crazy tales his mother would likely fill my ears with at some point in our conversation. She did call me by name, calling me her dear Alexis. Unfortunately, just as forewarned, she moved right into a line of confusing questions that made no sense to me except for one detail. She wanted me to have her silver ring."

Duncan's voice brought me back to the present. "Alexis, I think you ought to tell Mom more. I believe she needs to know."

That comment sure got my attention. Duncan, a man of few words himself, rarely pushed anyone to say more. *Then furthermore, what reaction is my son expecting?*"

"Duncan wants me to tell you more about Grandmam's ramblings. The first time Duncan and I went out with each other, for some reason, I did something I never do. I spilled all my family history out on the table for him. There is something about what my grandmother had to say in her memory care years that he thinks… He thinks you ought to hear what she said repeatedly over her five years with advanced Alzheimer's."

I felt acceptance wash over me. *Whatever this beautiful Cherokee woman is about to share regarding her grandmother's dementia-babbling may be the beginning of the revelation of my long-treasured secrets. I know recently I have certainly thought more and more about telling Macy and Duncan all that happened. Little did I think such would happen around our Christmas dinner table with Savannah's granddaughter sitting beside my son.* I looked at Alexis and encouragingly nodded and spoke. "Please. Tell me what Duncan thinks I need to hear."

"Soon after my grandmother referred to me as her dear Alexis, she became agitated, insisting that I must have her ring. The ring had been removed from her hand upon her entry into the nursing home. Uncle William eventually got it from safekeeping at his home and gave it to me. It has not left my hand since. The subject of the ring came up repeatedly every time I visited her. She would say the same thing over and over. "The ring, get it to Sarah. He left it so she would know." This command never changed over the five years of visiting her in the memory care center. I made no progress in unearthing any person named Sarah in my grandmother's life. She insisted I needed to help her find Sarah. Sometimes she would tell me to look at the springheads. At other times she went on and on about needing to get the ring to this Colin person. Sometimes she attempted to explain that Sarah would know what to do. Many times, toward the end, she started calling me by the name of Sarah."

I bowed my head almost prayerfully as I placed both hands over my face. Silence filled the dining room.

Then I heard Alexis' soft lilting voice. "Before William died, I asked him more about Gram's ramblings. He said there was a woman named Sarah that helped with his birth. He had been told the story for years. He never remembered meeting Sarah. He only knew her by hearing the story of his birth. He did recall Mr. Colin, who wore the ring that I had lovingly twirled on my grandmother's thumb so many years back. As William recalled, this Colin person had literally carried my mother to Miss Sadie's house as she was in labor. He remembered him as a different sort of man, not like the white men he grew up around. This fellow lived with ole Miss Sadie for several years, then one day disappeared.

The way my uncle told it, this Colin fellow left Miss Sadie with the ring. There is one interesting detail that William shared. Sadie refused to wear the ring. Instead, she kept in an old jar in her house. She gave specific instructions to Savannah and eventually to William as he got older that the ring was not to be worn. Sadie assured them that if Mr. Colin should return, that the ring belonged to him. William recalls the day his mother decided it was time that she wore the ring. That happened shortly after Miss Sadie died. Uncle William said he could never get any story out of her that made much sense. He did recall that Miss Sadie and his mom apparently knew more than they were willing to share openly about the mysterious silver band. Uncle William was always quick to point out that old Miss Sadie, as he often called her, knew a great deal about many things that were somewhat strange and mysterious. Then there was the bond between Miss Sadie and Savannah. That is another story that I wish I knew more about. Sadie's grandmother had somehow been involved in saving my Great Grandmother Madiena Taylor's life when they were hiding out in caves after the Cherokee removal. Then Madiena's daughter, my mother, protected Sadie's daughter from some prominent white man in the community who was determined to have his way with her. The two families remained strong friends down through the generations. Uncle William could not say enough how his mother rambled on and on about Sarah and Colin saving his life until the day she died. The last day I saw Grandmam alive, she said very little. Once, however, I am certain, as she held my hand tightly, rubbing the silver ring much as I used to do when it was on her hand, she said, "Sarah."

I knew everyone around the table was waiting for me to respond. I heard Macy whisper to Scott. "Get those big blocks for Alexander. Let him play on the floor next to you. Thankfully, Elizabeth is sound asleep in my lap." Something about her words brought me back to the present.

"Alexis, your grandmother's name was Savannah, correct?

She nodded. Her dark eyes asking the question she had not yet said out loud. Again, silence hung heavily in the large dining room. "But, how, how is it possible?"

"Alexis." Then I stopped and looked back and forth at my two children. "Macy, Duncan. I have much to tell both of you, as well as Alexis. This is not a short story." I let out a forced breath. Looked around the table at everyone and added. "Scott, if you can take the baby, maybe Macy can get her dessert served up while the rest of us clear the table. Let's move into the living room. This will more than likely be a long night. For once, Macy was speechless. She did, however, wrap her arms around me in a hug before she headed to the kitchen.

§

I started the explanation with the two dreams. Then moved to the day Colin showed up at the real estate office for the first time. When I got to the first travel through time, of course, the questions fired rapidly. Disbelief and logic wrestled to throw a questioning blanket over these sacred memories but deferred time and time again to the fact that Alexis sat in our midst with the ring on her hand. I finished sharing the details of the risk we all took to travel to the present with Savannah and her little William. Alexis, who had moved very close to my Duncan on the big leather couch, worked her way out from his embracing arm and came to stand in front of me where I sat closest to the warmth of the fire. She slowly took the silver ring off her thumb, then reached for my hand. With a great deal of tenderness, she placed the heavy ring in the palm of my hand and closed my fingers around the treasure. The tears started gently as I slipped it on my thumb.

I came close to not revealing the intimacy that occurred in the time warp. Deep down, I knew the kids would read between the lines. Plus, the *Nike* jacket held such a pivotal place in all that I shared. Macy was the first to react. "Mom, so that's the old, black *Nike* you insist on wearing around the house the moment it gets cold? That explains why you always point me to another sweater or jacket when I need to add a layer. You went ballistic the first time I asked to borrow it."

"Macy, now you know."

The hardest questions were about Colin. More than once. "Mom, where do you think he is now?" At one point, I suggested we all take a break. "There's something I want to get for you to hear. Plus, I would like to change into my pajamas. Don't dare let me go in that kitchen where I know I will be tempted to start the clean-up recovery process from Christmas dinner. I may as well tell it all before this night is over. All those dirty dishes will still be there in the light of day."

When we sat back down, I held the phone in my hand that could still be plugged into an old wall outlet. Every time I heard Colin's voice, the shiver still ran down my spine. My family and Alexis were close to being in shock." I could only speculate, of course, that Colin had attempted to come to the present. He had made it back to the time warp in the modern-day office where there was a phone. He obviously decided to leave his ring behind as proof he had made it to Sadie's place. What happened from there? Well, we could only guess. Is he somewhere back in the past? Perhaps the future? Of course, there was no way to know.

Alexis asked the most telling question. "Sarah, what does your gut tell you about Colin? Do you think he is still out there?"

"Alexis, I felt like I could almost reach out and touch him tonight at the dinner table. That may be wishful thinking on my part or a very good intuition. Time may yet bring him back."

Of course, everyone loved knowing the connection to Sadie's Place. Perhaps most impressive was the absolute agreement on one very important point. No one beyond these walls, of course, except for my dear friend Belinda and her trusted husband, would ever know the time-travel adventures that seemed to be connected to the springheads and nearby remains of Mr. Billy's store. Not one of us was interested in the circus of curiosity that would unleash on our river property if word ever got out. Duncan did shake his head in wonder about the fact that Belinda had managed not to tell her son and Stephanie.

"Son, I suspect the whole time-travel adventure is just too far beyond logic for Belinda to bring Seth and Stephanie in on the details. After all, her children do threaten on a regular basis to have her committed. This could be the situation that pushes that button." We all needed that laughable moment. A smile spread across my face as I heard Duncan continuing the talk about my entertaining friend of many years as he headed out the front door with Alexis.

§

Two o'clock in the early morning of December 26, 2012, before heading upstairs to my bedroom, I stoked the fire in the living room, then double-checked night lights throughout the downstairs in case someone went roaming. I made it to the first landing of the stairway. The big window, surrounded by a border of cobalt blue stained glass, allowed the light of the night sky to filter into the house. I recalled how much I admired the window placement the first day I walked into the river house. I have no clue what made me think, at that moment, of the pile of mail that I had crammed into the drawer of the entry table at least two consecutive days before Christmas. *I may as well head back down to get it, for there is no way my filled-to-the-max brain will allow me to sleep just yet. Probably a mixture of junk and Christmas cards certain to put me to sleep eventually.*

By the time I made it to my bedroom, I had convinced myself that a soaking bath in front of the fire, which Scott had assured me would burn for the night, was just what my tired body and high-alert mind needed. The big clawfoot tub, part of the original house fixtures, called my name as I placed the mail on my night table next to the bed. As soon as I sunk into the warm bath, my eye noticed the strange horn that I had insisted on hanging above the bathroom fireplace mantel. *I wonder if Alexis remembers any stories about why someone went to great lengths to hide an animal horn away in a most remote spot of the attic. Was it kept out of easy reach much like Colin's ring?* Nothing like a candlelight bath and memories of Colin to bring on relaxation even with so many questions whirling in my mind. I fell asleep in the tub. The big clock on the mantle showed it was now close to 3:30 in the morning. No wonder my skin looked like a prune in the now cold water.

With somewhat of a second wind, as I made it back to the bedroom, I decided to at least sort through the heap of mail. I brought the trash can over as I sat on the edge of the bed. About halfway through what had indeed been mostly junk, I spotted the addressed-by-hand, somewhat tattered-looking envelope. *Sarah Baker Bryant. Not just everyone calls me by my full name. No return address. Postmarked in some New Mexico town I had never heard of before. Wonder who this is from?*

As I carefully tore into the letter, I looked at the signature first. My initial thought; *this has to be an old letter that somehow got lost in the mail. How else can it possibly be that I am sitting here holding in my hand a letter from my Uncle Jake? After all, I attended his memorial service back in July of last year.* I could not speed-read fast enough. *Oh, my. Do I head to Mississippi immediately? No, no, I need to get Mama and Aunt Beth Ann to come here. I guess I should wait for the promised phone call from Uncle Jake that I am to expect sometime within the next week. How do I begin to tell them their brother is still alive?*

Uncle Jake, you always said Mama and Daddy had raised me in a way that assured I would march to the beat of a different drummer. Of course, as I got older, I concluded you did not have much room to talk. Now, for some reason, you have decided I am the family member that needs to break this news to your sisters. I swear, if either my mom or my aunt has a heart attack, you need to know I will never forgive you. And why have you decided on me for this other request to hide you in these mountains? Sure, there were the Cherokee, then the Hatfield and McCoy sorts who found ways to hide in these remote Blue Ridge Mountains, so I suppose it could happen. And yet another alias in this tribe of mine? Why can't I be part of a normal family?

I was about to conclude this had to be about the strangest news I could think of. Instead, I smiled and laughed out loud. *No, by far, not the strangest news! Colin, I am certain you would agree with me on that point.*

Author's Acknowledgements...

The death of my brother, Arnold Dyre, forced me back into the world of novels. A draft version of Springheads sat in a dust-covered box until I published Dark Spot, co-authored with my brother following his death in 2017. Now I cannot quieten the stories that must be told.

Others who must be thankfully acknowledged include my family who love and put up with me with very few questions asked; Karen Brinke, friend, colleague and encourager of my many ideas and projects; other encouragers: Mary Ricketson, Dana Bolyard. Mildred Lee and so many dear faces from Quitman County High School and the small Delta town of Belen; Paige Brinke, PA, for her medical knowledge. Photographers: Analeash Hopper, author picture and cover inspiration photos; Matthew Crawford, cover design. Artist: Pam Strawn, who captured the magic of the sense of place through her paint brush. The many people who have read Dark Spot and begged for more. In general, I am thankful and blessed to be surrounded by so many who have never clipped the wings of my imagination, people who instill and encourage the spirit of "I can" as I write my story on my terms.

A special thanks to Patty Thompson and her dedicated team of editors and publishers at Redhawk Publications.

About the Author...

A native Mississippian, born in the backwoods near Kilmichael, *Mary Jo Dyre* eventually finds home in the Appalachian Mountains of North Carolina. Roots and legacy remain the drivers in her life-long dedication to education and her writing. Her heartstrings tug toward rural and underserved fueled by a sense of possibility in all mankind.

Learn more about the author here: www.maryjodyre.com